SON OF A GUN

SON OF A GUN

Melvin J. Bagley &
Marty Ann Halverson

Tate Publishing & Enterprises

Son of a Gun
Copyright © 2011 by Melvin J. Bagley & Marty Ann Halverson. All rights reserved.

No part of this publication may be reproduced, stored in a retrieval system or transmitted in any way by any means, electronic, mechanical, photocopy, recording or otherwise without the prior permission of the author except as provided by USA copyright law.

The opinions expressed by the author are not necessarily those of Tate Publishing, LLC.

Published by Tate Publishing & Enterprises, LLC
127 E. Trade Center Terrace | Mustang, Oklahoma 73064 USA
1.888.361.9473 | www.tatepublishing.com

Tate Publishing is committed to excellence in the publishing industry. The company reflects the philosophy established by the founders, based on Psalm 68:11,
"The Lord gave the word and great was the company of those who published it."

Book design copyright © 2011 by Tate Publishing, LLC. All rights reserved.
Cover design by Kenna Davis
Interior design by Lindsay B. Behrens

Published in the United States of America
ISBN: 978-1-61346-033-7
Fiction / Westerns
11.07.25

To my children and their children.

ACKNOWLEDGMENTS

I owe deep gratitude to those who have listened to my stories over many years: Hawley, Adelila, Alan, Gerald, Jeanne, Marie, Barbara, Nancy, Mari, Hawley, Bobbi, May, Parris, Jessica, Andrew, Hayley, Athena, Hannah, Jeri, Theodore, Calli, Aristotle, Jaylin, Gabriel, and Roxanne.

PREFACE

On New Year's Day, 2010, my uncle, Melvin J. Bagley, turned eighty-six and prepared to get new knees. Instead he got a staph infection and ended up in the hospital for a month. Uncle Mel has poor eyesight, but he can see stories inside his head. He entertained himself and everyone else with tales of the Wild West, based on some of his own experiences and characters he remembered from childhood.

On March 5, 2010, he called me in Salt Lake City from Henderson, Nevada. "Martha Ann," he said. "I've got a story in my mind. Do you think you could turn it into a book?"

Five days later, I received a digital recorder with his story locked inside, and in another five days, I read it for the first time. A true western, complete with gunfights, saloons, and fallen women, it was set in Texas sometime after the Civil War. Jack, Indian Joe, Ruby, Sam, Leo, JJ, MJ, and of course, Big Red, came to life in my mind. It took some effort to get familiar with the setting and time period, but when I began to write dialogue, the characters introduced me to new characters and told me the rest of the story in their own words. The plot thickened. I found it wasn't just a western story; it was timeless.

Six months to the day, September 15, 2010, I sent Uncle Mel his manuscript. It was an incredible experience to put his story into words, and I'm grateful for the opportunity. Everyone who knows him would agree that he's a *Son of a Gun*!

—Marty Ann Halverson

1

Ruby had always planned to tell her son the truth about his father and the truth about herself. But as the years went by, it was easier to let him think he knew the truth. Besides, she'd never actually lied to him, although the lie was there every time she said his name.

March 1887, Greenville, Texas

JJ saw the men in the window's reflection before he heard their words. About to say, "Howdy," he caught the drift of a conversation that would change his life.

"Saw Leo Barlow in town. You hear his wife Ruby is starting a Sunday school?" The younger man guffawed as he hefted a sack of feed onto his wagon.

"Can't see her as no Sunday School teacher," the older one said. "Sam's upstairs girl? His Jewel? Jesse had the goods about that kid of hers, almost claimed him hisself! I've always wondered who's his daddy. Lucky cuss. I got a look-see at Ruby one time at Sam's saloon. O-o-oh my!"

"She's a respectable business woman nowadays. Maybe we can pay her a visit sometime, and—you know—do business." The ranchers rode off, still sniggering to each other.

JJ recognized Swede Dobson and Len Grove. "Pa, are they talkin' about Mama? Did you hear them?" His youthful voice cracked from high to low. "Aren't you going to say something—set them straight?"

Leo Barlow didn't look away from the store window, staring in at glossy black boots with two-inch heels, digging his own into the soft dirt. He didn't meet the dare in his son's eyes, the same blue eyes as Ruby's, although his hair was blond instead of red and not as curly as his mother's. JJ was thirteen, already taller than his older brother, MJ. *He must have inherited his lanky, slender build from his father,* Leo thought. He couldn't be sure—he never met the man.

"Pa, didn't you hear..."

"Quit dawdling, Jage!" His father barked at him harsher than Trespass ever had. The tone was unfamiliar—you'd never guess this man sang lullabies to his cows if you'd heard him just then.

"Get the buckboard, son," Leo said, his voice gentler, now under control. "And you better water those horses." Leo stopped to stretch his stiff right knee. It bothered him more after sitting in the wagon all day, and he tried walking it out, leaving JJ in front of Holt's feed store.

It was typical of Pa to ignore gossip, thought JJ. Pa stepped around contention as nimbly as he did cow-pies. But why wouldn't he defend his own wife's honor? It reminded the boy of a time he trailed a fox to a nest of Texas bobwhites. The hen let out a shrill whistle to scare off the fox and heroically spread her feathers to protect her young. The male skedaddled into the brush. Disgusted, JJ let the fox go and took "daddy quail" home for dinner. Mama had agreed the coward deserved roasting.

Necessaries were chosen, corn, dried beans and bacon, and Leo topped off his purchase with a bolt of calico for Ruby. Holt's new man loaded the goods onto the wagon, and Leo felt the pale blue eyes studying him carefully, noting in particular, it seemed, the absence of a gun. Leo endured the scrutiny without resentment; he had become used to the way people dismissed as insignificant any man who was not weighed down with a firearm.

Greenville was a good fifty miles southeast of Barlow Ranch, and a fully loaded wagon under the Texas sun made it a long, three-day round trip. That was okay with JJ. While Pa bought supplies, he browsed in Brunner's Mercantile, looking at wallpaper, stationery, potions and tools. Then they made their regular stop at Quincy's drug and cigar store to get cigars for Turk. An indefinable scent hit JJ when they walked through the door, a combination of sweet tobacco, cloves and cedar, a dark musky odor that tickled the back of his throat.

They were quiet on the ride through town. *If Josey were here,* thought JJ, *he and Pa would be talking about books.* Pa was obsessed with anything to do with letters—why else would he insist his two sons both be called by their initials? It was embarrassing.

Preacher O'Brien had once announced to the whole school that the Barlow boys were there mainly to teach the other kids their alphabet—just repeat their names. His older brother was named after Uncle Josey, as well as Grandpa Manchester Josiah Barlow, and called MJ to avoid confusion. It hardly seemed a problem, since both his namesakes were dead. JJ had taken to calling him Josey, although Pa claimed the name might conjure up his uncle's ghost.

"What does JJ stand for?" the boy asked for the thousandth time in his life. The conversation he'd overheard in town had reminded him of his perplexing beginnings. "I hate not having a real name."

Leo gave his stock answer. "Your grandpappy was called Jeremy." He had caught the hesitation in JJ's voice. "Son," he said with promise, "you'll make your real name for yourself."

Mama's old iron bed, where JJ would sleep that night, was tucked in the back room of Grandma Dawson's, the house with the coffins out back. Grandpa had built furniture, but coffins were needed more often, and with his lumber and expertise, he'd doubled as Greenville's undertaker. Grandma's neighbor, Nate Brannigan, did all that now.

After looking to the horses, Pa read the *Fort Worth Republic*, followed by the new *Texas Star*. Grandma busied JJ with chores, and she told him old-time tales of Cherokee raids, floods, and droughts. She liked having someone around for listening and complaining purposes.

"The mice were running crazy last night," Grandma told JJ as they walked toward the house from the clothesline. Orange spilled from a gold horizon and painted the fields copper. "They raced along the logs next to my bed, scampering all over the planks playing hide-and-seek. Frightened the life out of me with their squeals. You'll hear them tonight, I reckon."

"I'll get rid of them for you, Grandma," said JJ. He pulled a Colt.44 out of his waistband.

"Laws, JJ! You're a mite young to carry a gun, especially in your drawers," his grandma said. "Aren't you afraid of what you might shoot off?"

"I'm good with a pistol, Grandma! The holster slips down, so I developed my own way of carrying it." JJ tucked the .44 back in, then drew it out like lightning with his left hand, his laugh sudden and happy. "Pa's not much for me shooting, but Mama thinks I can handle it." He said it with pride. "Watch." He shoved his thick, blond hair off his forehead so he could see better and focused.

A crow was circling above the cornfield, and JJ brought it down as easily as if he'd just pointed his finger. "I think I was born with a good aiming eye," he told his grandma as he ran for the bird. "But, I didn't get it from Pa. He's gun shy."

"Your pa aims true. Don't be fooled," Grandma said. But JJ was already scrambling in the brush for his unfortunate target.

"Olive, there's talk about Ruby," Leo told his mother-in-law that night as she cleared off the table.

"Now, Leo, there's been talk about Ruby since before you knew her. I don't listen anymore. Some folks would rather discuss a scandal than a success." Olive looked fondly at the handsome man who'd rescued her daughter. "Let it go."

"Can't this time. I'm going to town to see what prattle folks are passing around. Tell JJ I've gone over to Shack's to price lumber. I'll do that, too." The old Kentucky drawl was almost gone, but it came through when he teased. "Don't let that boy shoot at any of your mice. He'd tear up your floor boards protecting you!"

His smile didn't quite reach his eyes, and Olive knew his bygone worries were rising in his stomach. Before he put on his well-worn Stetson, she noticed his dark, blond hair was grayed on the sides and thinned on the top. The sun-browned face pinched into a frown, and he pulled on a shaggy red woolen vest, buttoning it against the March wind. Leo never wore a gun, and he left the ancient shotgun in the buckboard when he saddled Rascal, his white-legged sorrel.

The Bull Horn Saloon was hopping that night when Leo pushed through the doors.

"You're puttin' on some belly, Leo," said Sullivan from behind the long bar. Leo patted his soft, flat gut and sat down on a stool. He didn't come to drink or gamble, although he'd been known to do both. His were usually social calls.

"That's what happens when you hire a dough-puncher, Sully," Leo answered. "Turk's cooking is growing on me. Course, you already noticed that!" Leo looked around. "You seen Swede Dobson or Len Grove tonight?"

"Swede's over with the boys in the corner. Len doesn't come in too regular anymore, now he's a husband again. Swede's got a new sidekick, name of Woody, that bulky fella, with the wandering eye."

"I know him. Replaced Erly, one of Sam Lester's boys," said Leo.

Sully said, "Take this over there for me." He handed Leo a bottle of whiskey and jerked his head at a large drawing of a grizzly bear, the only decoration in the room. Railroad workers, cowhands, and ranchers surrounded the table where Dobson was dealing.

"You in, Barlow?" Swede refilled his glass with a nod of thanks at Sullivan before flicking the cards to the players. "Didn't know you were in Greenville," he lied. Greasy gray strands of hair separated across his knobby skull. The man wet his pulpy lips and glanced around at the others. "The lovely Ruby with you?" he asked, a sarcastic smirk in the lines around his mouth. "Or Jewel, as she was sometimes called?"

Leo's words were as cold and biting as a northern wind. "Ruby has too much class to be in a stall of mules, except to muck it out. She's my wife, and you'll speak of her with respect or not at all." The muscles in his neck clenched, and he breathed hard. Leo Barlow was not afraid of the man, but he disliked trouble and would ride around it when he could. Tonight, he might have to plow down the middle.

"Plenty of men polished that jewel, Woody," Dobson said. The words were offhand and careless, aimed at the man sitting next to him but bouncing around the table.

A deep wrath flared in Leo's stare. With cool calculation, he moved swiftly and swung his right fist into Swede's meaty face. The rancher was surprisingly powerful, and his victim screamed as flesh and bone were savaged under the blow. Swede's head was driven far over to the opposite shoulder, and his face twisted in shock, hatred, and humiliation at being mauled and beaten barehanded in front of many of his neighbors.

The impact shuddered back through Leo and when he shook his hand, red droplets of blood flew off. Swede already had a handkerchief to his bleeding nose. Leo felt no pleasure. A beating, he knew soberly, would not change Swede Dobson; in fact, the man might try to kill him for this. He could certainly find partners for that endeavor.

Swede slapped his palms on the table and thrust upright, his mouth bloodied and frenzied. Scrambling to his feet, he pulled out his pistol. Leo glimpsed Sully pulling him back. One of the ranchers protested, "The blamed mule-head ain't even got a gun, Swede. Leave him be."

A bullet spattered near Leo's boot, and Swede's malicious voice boomed through the bar, "I might chip off a toe, or worsen that knee, use you for target practice. Guess a Quaker sissy don't know much about that."

"No, Swede, I don't. I don't shoot at rats or skunks just to practice. But when a murderous animal stalks my family, I get down my gun. And then, I shoot to kill."

Sullivan shoved his solid girth from behind the bar and came up next to Leo. His long, black moustache drooped, and his bushy eyebrows were knit together in concern. "You and me been friends a long time, Leo. I don't want nothing happening to you in my bar."

"Nothing's fixing to happen." Leo's hazel eyes gleamed like wet slate, framed in dark circles. "Swede here just asked after my wife, and I gave him an update." He rolled his shoulders a couple of times and said, "Pour him another drink, Sully. He's looking peaked."

A splinter pierced JJ's palm as he slid onto the blue seat next to Leo the following morning. The protruding piece was easy to pull out, but a sliver tore off and stuck deep in the wedge of flesh under his thumb. "Don't pick at it, boy," said Leo. "Your mama will lift it out with a needle when we get back to the ranch tomorrow."

JJ kept digging. Suddenly, the horses pulled back at a thrashing in a thicket off the road. "Whoa, boys," Leo said.

"There's something in the bushes, Pa," said JJ. He stood up in the buckboard and craned his neck. A wild hog, tangled in the underbrush, rooted and squealed in vexation.

"We'll leave her be. She'll get out of there all right." Leo shook Rascal's reins.

"Tarnation, Pa! She'd look fine dangling from the hook in the smokehouse, though." He knew Leo didn't like to kill animals in the summer, when the fruit and vegetables were fresh, but it seemed crazy to leave a hog in early springtime. "Why don't we take her?"

"Think it through, son. Our wagon's already full; we got a long way to go. We'd waste most of that meat. Plus she's a sow with teats—babies to feed. I don't kill just to kill."

"You always been this way? Even when you was young?" JJ asked, gnawing at the splinter. It was unusual to have this much conversation on the long ride.

"My ma named Daddy's gun the Last Resort. Quakers don't take to killing much. Guess I just kept the habit."

"You ever killed a man?" JJ asked.

"No, and I don't want you to, either."

JJ studied his hand like a gypsy. "Yeah, but sometimes you gotta make 'em think you could."

The crackling of the fire that night gave off the perfume of years, and it smelled good. Leo wandered down to the bank of the stream in the darkness and bathed in the cold water of the creek. JJ had already taken an unexpected bath when they'd been trying to catch their dinner.

A decent-sized spotted bass had latched on and as JJ reeled him in, a thirty-pound flathead leaped up to grab it. Suddenly, the pole lurched, and the boy toppled into the stream while Leo pulled the fish in. "Nice catch!" he said.

"Thanks, Pa." JJ climbed out, shook himself like a dog, and emptied his hat.

"I was talking to the catfish," said Pa, with a smile.

Now, as JJ watched the flames strike pitch, flare up, and change color, leaves rustled, and the heads of the horses came up, startled. Firelight reflected from their flanks.

"Pa? That you?" The wind scurried the fire, spooking the boy. "Pa?" Leo sat down on a log, rubbing his hair dry. "Oh ... Pa," JJ said with relief. Then he asked, "Hey, Pa? Do you believe in haunts?"

"Hearing some, are you?" Leo chuckled. After a pause, he went on, "Yeah, Jage, I do." He stirred the ashes and carefully placed a chunk of log where it would catch some sparks. "I'm not afraid of them, though. Somehow, I like thinking ghosts watch out for their kin."

Placing his boots next to his saddle, Leo said, "Your Uncle Josey's wife used to say she could push a plow harder after he died. Thought he was behind her shoving."

"Was she the Indian?"

"Her name was Nataki—she was Kickapoo."

"Why did she leave the ranch?"

"Your grandpa and grandma had died of the measles a few years earlier, and with my brother sick, the ranch suffered. Nataki cared for Josey through his cancer. Afterwards, she thought the ranch would die, too, with just me working it, so she went back to her tribe. An Indian woman alone wouldn't have much of a life."

"Where was MJ's mama then? Didn't she help out?"

"It was before her time." Abruptly, Leo was through talking. "Go to sleep, Jage. We're leaving at sunrise."

Lying there later in the smoke of the dying fire, JJ watched the moon come up and listened to the wind. It seemed to be talking to the ghosts. The horses snorted and cocked their ears. There was more swishing in the bushes.

"Pa!" JJ whispered. "You hear that?"

"I hear it," said Leo, sitting up.

Three horses pulled up next to their makeshift corral. Leo calmly stood up and put on his hat. "Evening, gentlemen," he said, "your boss Sam got you looking for somebody?" he asked the intruders.

A Mexican was in the lead. He was liquored up, wearing a red Indian blanket over a loose, sweat-stained denim shirt. A black sombrero hung around his thick neck. He ignored Leo's hand and spat. "Lookin' for you, Mees-ter Barlow." He hocked, spit again, and reined in his jittery mount. "We don't think you're safe."

Leo glanced at JJ with a look that said, *Sit there and be quiet.* "I'm mighty obliged, Bolte," he said with exaggerated good nature. "And why are you worried about my safety? With you boys hovering around, I've always felt well looked after." He'd stepped into his boots, and his stance was rock solid, dignified. He almost seemed friendly, but JJ recognized the tightness in his neck.

A man with gouty knuckles lifted his gray hat and wiped watery eyes with a blue bandanna. "Just watching out for Sam Lester's interests," he said. "Your wife set out long ago to destroy him." Leo saw it was Woody, Swede's friend from the saloon.

"Woody's right, Meester Barlow," the Mexican said. "You're inviting misery, poaching Sam's clientele. You're being watched."

"We've been watched for twelve years. You boys are like cockroaches," Leo said.

Woody sucked at the tobacco juice dripping from the sides of his mouth. "Sam don't like your pretensions, Barlow. You better be expecting him, because sometime when you turn around, he'll be there."

"I highly doubt that," Leo said through the tense jaw. "Lester's a coward and wouldn't stand behind a jackrabbit. I assume you were the boys playing with fire out on my ranch last fall? At Sam's request? You should be ashamed, impersonating hired guns for that bully. Makes me feel sorry for you, crawling in the dirt like pissants around his filthy feet."

"I'd w-watch m-my b-back..." Haze, a slim, squirrelly-looking fellow, spoke with a stutter. His pockmarked face was grimy with dust and sweat, and it glistened in the darkness. "R-right, B-Bolte?" he said to the man in the red.

Bolte pulled a Winchester from a buckskin scabbard and pointed it at Leo. JJ thought about the Colt .44 tucked in his own boot a few yards away, but Leo glanced hard at him, warning the boy to keep still.

"Look, Bolte," Leo said, apparently unfazed. "I'm a peaceable man, trying to get by. We've kept ourselves to ourselves, out of Sam's way. He keeps his feud going all by himself. I'm surprised he'd look for pretend battles, seeing as how he ran away during a real one." Leo's tone was one of disgust. He turned his back on Bolte's rifle and snapped, "Get out of my camp."

"You're not rid of us," Bolte said angrily. He shot the rifle into the air, and Rascal reared back with the other two horses and whinnied. "Woody," he growled, "you and Haze scatter those animals."

As the men rode off, JJ grabbed for the gun, but Leo caught his arm. "Leave it, JJ."

"They threatened us, Pa! Why didn't you stand up for us? Or for Mama back in town? It seems to me that peaceable is another word for yellow." JJ kicked the dirt and glared at Leo over the dead fire with disgust and disappointment.

"How's that splinter?" Leo asked unexpectedly.

"What?" sputtered JJ. "What's that got to do with anything?"

"It got under your skin. Leave it alone, and it'll likely work it's way out without too much trouble. Pick at it, and it'll swell up with poison—cause you more pain."

The horses had followed the smoke and wandered back to camp, hearing Leo's voice. He tethered them to a tree while JJ's dark mood festered, and then he continued, "When something gets under my skin, I let it work itself out. That way, I avoid the poison."

The buckboard bumped over the ruts leading up to the house. Leo had been content to ride silently all day, while JJ stewed like a sour cherry. Startled by a sudden noise, the horses reared when the front door banged open, and MJ burst out. It was still strange to see him without Trespass tagging along behind.

"Jage!" Handing his younger brother a warm biscuit, he pushed his spectacles back on his nose and said, "Ma said we could shoot to kill!" JJ whooped. Stuffing the bread in his mouth, he checked the gun tucked in his waistband, and the two brothers sprinted toward the woods, JJ's vexation with Leo forgotten.

"Shoot to kill" was code for a private contest the boys had invented years before. Leo had given them fishing poles when they could barely lift them off the ground. Although MJ was content to sit with his line drifting down the stream, fishing could never hold JJ's attention.

For him, it was Ruby's pistol—a Colt.44 with a dark blue barrel and wooden grip. JJ spun the cylinder and aimed at birds, holding it with both hands. "When can I shoot it?" he'd whined to his parents.

"You can hardly lift it," Leo had told him. He laughed when JJ tried to fasten on the holster and it fell down around his feet. "When you're older," he said.

For his seventh birthday, Leo whittled him a wooden gun. "You practice handling this for a year or so, and you can use a real one when you've earned my trust." But it wasn't enough for the boy.

JJ begged his father to let him shoot, but Leo was adamant: guns were not for sport; they were for food. "We're not wasting ammunition so you can cause a commotion and chase off the fish. When you're older, I'll teach you, but there'll be no showoff shooting. Barlows don't waste bullets or life. You find a turkey fat enough for dinner, and then you can shoot to kill."

Ruby was nervous at how the boy was obsessed with the .44. "Leo, you've got to teach him to use it, or I'm afraid he'll shoot one of us." When the lessons began, MJ was only mildly interested, but JJ took right to it, cocking the hammer, spinning the cylinder, and practicing his aim.

With the gun tucked in his waist, he practiced drawing it with his left hand. "You're doing it backwards," said Leo. But it was a natural move, and JJ stuck with it. "Aim it a little high to allow for the timing," his father told him the first time he held it loaded. "Watch for a rabbit, and then shoot to kill."

Before he was twelve, JJ was fast and accurate, past asking for permission to take the gun. Leo was disapproving of Ruby's lenience but unwilling to fight her on it, and eventually, the pistol seemed to be JJ's property. MJ still preferred a fishing pole, so on days when Turk was sick of bacon fat flavoring the turnips, Ma sent the boys out to get them some fresh meat.

"I can hook a trout faster than you can shoot a squirrel," was MJ's initial wager a few years earlier.

Nowadays, the bet was laid with the rallying cry JJ heard from his brother as the dust flew underfoot. "C'mon you son of a gun! Shoot to kill!"

2

1865–1872, Bosque County Texas

"Shoot to kill" was a phrase used by JJ's real father long before the boy was born—long before he was the proverbial twinkle in his daddy's eye. Truth be told, Jack Smith's eyes didn't twinkle—they blazed like burning coals on the fiery Texas plains. His soul had been seared years ago at the end of the War Between the States, when he'd watched a cabin burn with his mother and little brother trapped inside. He'd been only seventeen, but that fire still smoldered deep in his eyes, ready to ignite with the smallest spark.

Back then, his hatred wasn't focused on the Rebs or the Yanks or even the Indians who had torched the house. Jack had been consumed with resentment for the man who had abandoned them to peril. Knowing full well he wasn't trusted by the Indians he'd vowed to protect, Cyrus Smith had deserted his family, to save his own life. Now Jack saw his father's face imposed on anyone who showed cowardice.

At twenty-four, with strong shoulders and a straight back, Jack looked like the man he remembered riding away every week from their farm in Oklahoma. "Watch out for Indians!" Cyrus Smith would yell as he waved to his younger son, Henry, sitting on Jack's shoulders. It was a joke, since they lived just outside Fort Gibson, where Smith was the government agent to the Cherokees. The only neighbors they had were Indians.

He remembered one particular day vividly, a year before the fire. Sarey Smith sat weeping silently, like she did every time her husband left them alone. Jack tickled four-year-old Henry as he set him down and chased him toward the corral. Aware that she was listening, he had teased, "C'mon Hank! Mama's gonna feed us cold bacon again if we don't get her a rabbit for supper."

"Can I shoot it this time?"

"Sure thing. I'll load the gun, and you can pull the trigger. Shoot to kill, as Papa says. You'll be a crackerjack shot by the time he comes home." Jack called back to his mother, "We'll check on Autumn. She ought to be foaling any time."

Inside the house, Sarey threw off her woes and made her voice cheerful. "That mare needs trusty watching, Jack. And Hank, you had better shoot me a nice, fat rabbit! The bacon got sent off with Papa, and you can't let us starve."

She'd watched as the boys went toward the barn. Jack carried responsibility well, she thought, much better, even, than his father. Her son was lean and hard and tough to the bone. Unfair as it was, she relied on him as her protector, and so did Henry.

The foal looked to be less than an hour old. She had a slick dark hide and long legs stretched out in front. Her head came up kind of shaky when the boys entered the stall, her ears already working back and forth to find the sound.

Autumn was weak from the birth, panting, shivering, lying in a pool of blood and not responding to the nickering and nosing around of her baby. Jack saw she was in trouble.

"The baby's getting up!" said Henry. The foal made a sudden scramble, but her legs wouldn't work right and just when she got her belly off the ground, one of her front legs quivered and buckled at the elbow.

Autumn should be nudging her by now, Jack thought. But the mare was breathing heavily, shuddering from the loss of blood, oblivious to the foal.

His throat heaved as he saw the suffering horse. This felt too ponderous a burden, but he swallowed the nausea that rose, letting his duty settle on him as he had done since he was twelve.

"Go tell Mama she's foaled, Hank. But stay inside for a bit."

Jack got what he needed, then knelt down and found the sensitive bump between Autumn's ears and rubbed it gently. He could see the wild fear in her eyes, and he whispered, "I'll take care of your baby, girl. She's as beautiful as you are."

Gradually, the horse's heart began to slow to Jack's soothing sounds; the panting subsided. Jack kept murmuring. "We'll call her Big Red." He put his cheek on her neck and continued to whisper, "Don't be afraid now, girl. You've done a good job. There now..." Her flanks had stopped shaking, and she looked at her friend with trusting eyes. Choking back tears, Jack released her from pain with a shot carefully placed at the base of her left ear.

Thirteen months passed—it was May 1865 when Sarey watched Jack lead the yearling around the yard. Her coat had become a brilliant chestnut, almost red in the right sunlight. Her mane and tail were white and, against the blue sky, she made a pretty picture. Already agile and alert, Big Red stomped a rattler that looked poised to strike.

Snakes, wolves, bears—Sarey wasn't afraid of them. But she lived in fear of the people under her husband's jurisdiction. The Cherokees were panicky about the government interference he represented and had threatened to retaliate. Cyrus kept himself scarce, telling his family that they were safer when he was gone. He was wrong. Flaming arrows shot threw the windows of their house that day and proved the hatred the Indians felt for their suppressors.

Jack had lived a lonely man's life since that horrible day seven years before, after losing illusion and direction. He'd left Indian country for Texas and learned to fight and to use a gun, to drive a bargain that was tight and cruel, and to despise weakness. He saw the strong survive and the weak fail, and he determined to be not only strong but the strongest.

Back then, he'd had no trace of the dark shadow that haunted his jaw even after a close shave or the deep baritone that charmed women and intimidated men. Now his handsome face had the imprint of death, worn and sad deep down under it's leathery tan. At twenty-four, his dark gray eyes already looked old.

"Come on, Big Red," he murmured, although she responded to his movements as if she was part of him. The magnificent red mare blew out through her thin-veined nostrils, stomped a trim foot, and whickered demandingly. She was tough, more intelligent than a trained dog, and as sensitive as a woman. She adored the tall man with the soft voice and gentle, steady hands.

"Where'd you blow in from?" asked a wrangler as he swung open a large gate just outside Sam's Town. Expertly, he herded Jack's remuda of mustangs into the corral. "Beautiful animals," he said, slapping the rump of a flea-bitten gray. "You ride for Gollahers?"

Jack didn't like questions, even those he could answer honestly, and barely nodded a greeting. After making sure the horses were contained, he tipped his Stetson toward a colt with large white patches on his black body. "That pinto over there is hot-blooded. Don't sneak up on him," Jack warned. "I'll be at the Fat Chance."

Big Red loped over and talked to Jack with small grunting nickers. Jack scratched her under the jaw, spoke to her softly, and swung onto her back. The cowboy and his horse had been a team since she'd first tossed her pure white mane and gazed up at him as a foal. Her blue eyes were unusual in a horse without face markings, but Big Red was unique in many ways. The striking filly was the only female Jack had ever been faithful to.

In this last hour of glassy light, saddle horses lined the long rail of the Fat Chance Saloon. Jack tied Big Red next to the water trough, where she stood out like a copper penny, her bright coat frosted with dust. Inside the slatted swing doors, he found the usual late afternoon din of talk and a yeasty haze of tobacco smoke, laced with the richer mixed odors of whiskey, beer, leather, and sweat.

The spacious, log-walled saloon was a rendezvous for forty miles in any direction. Cowmen and merchants, traders, lawmen, prospectors, and ranchers—sooner or later, everyone moving about these parts stopped in Sam's Town.

In this vicinity, one man ruled supreme. He never went out unattended, and he issued orders and bestowed favors like a king. If there were those who chose to dispute his authority, he crushed them without hesitation. With some, the pressure of his disfavor was enough. With others, he simply offered them a price, and their choice was simple: give in or be forced out. Sam Lester owned the saloon, the exclusive Empire Hotel, the Bosque Boarding Hotel, and had an influence on all the businessmen in Sam's Town, including the sheriff. He held court at a private table in the Fat Chance Saloon.

Jack used the place to his profit, never drinking much and always listening carefully. "Smitty!" One of the local boys hailed his arrival in a too-friendly voice.

"It's Smith," Jack snapped back, his left hand hovering over the pistol he wore tucked in the waistband of his pants.

He'd been here before, and his drinking preference was known. The barkeeper slapped a bourbon bottle, glass, and water before him without asking. Jack, moodily turning the empty whiskey glass in lax fingers, glanced indifferently at him. As usual, three of Sam's boys were hovering about. Haze, the pockmarked kid with a stutter, rocked back on a chair near the door, his eyes sharper than his tongue. He'd once shot a soldier who'd cut off Sam's thumb and thereby earned a place of honor at his boss's table. His youthful looks and slow manner of speaking belied his influence on the tyrant.

"Mr. Lester likes the look of your horses," said another man in a derby. He was a big man, broad of shoulder, with soft-packed muscle that bounced as he pulled out the stool next to Jack. "Without a lot of hoopla, they could get 'rustled' like. You could pick up a little something extra, still deliver a herd, explain the unfortunate loss, and collect your salary from two directions."

The bartender slid a glass across the mahogany to the man. "Your beer, Snake," he said.

Jack rolled a cigarette and sipped from his glass for the first time. The drink was sour and bitter. He spit it out on the floor. "Last time I visited Sam's Town, I had a packhorse borrowed—'rustled like.' Your fine sheriff and the dubious Mr. Lester were both certain none of the upstanding citizens of Sam's Town had a hand in it." Jack censured Snake with brusque annoyance. "Looks like you and your skinny friend over there have too friendly an arrangement with the law." He gestured toward the stutterer, who was listening closely.

Haze stiffened. He wore a frock coat that might conceal all sorts of things. "T-talk like that can g-get you k-killed, mister." He held his forearm in a way that suggested to Jack that he had a knife up his sleeve. "You sh-shouldn't go around insulting p-people." Tobacco thickened his lip. He glared across the room at Jack, eyes narrowing until they were slits of evil.

"I expect to find a replacement for my misplaced packhorse with my remuda tonight, plus an extra mount for the inconvenience," Jack told Haze. "I'm not of a mood for taunting by a little runt Confederate runaway like yourself." He dropped his cigarette in Snake's beer and said, "You boys don't want to rile me."

"I'm plumb scared," Snake mocked.

"And I'm tired of your guff. Shut up."

Snake shoved himself out from the bar. "Take a look at that table to your right. Erly over there has a gun pointed at you, Smith, and all I have to do is nod for him to pull the trigger." He indicated an unshaven man, sickly looking in spite of his girth.

"You see my left hand?" Jack asked quietly.

"What?" asked Snake. He looked at the bar. Jack's right hand was wrapped around his drink, but his left was nowhere to be seen.

"I've had a Colt .45 lined up on your belly pretty much from the moment you sat down," Jack went on. "My thumb's over the hammer, and that's all that's holding it back. You can have your anemic friend shoot me, but you'll get a bullet in the gut at the same time. I've got a hunch there's not a doctor around here that could pull a man through with a wound like that. You'd be a long, slow, hard time dying, too."

Snake's lips writhed with hate. "You..." he snorted, "you...get out."

"Have Erly put his gun on the table first, and then he can stand up and move away from it."

Snake hesitated, and for a second, Jack thought the man was going to call his bluff—although it wasn't a bluff at all. Jack was prepared to shoot his way out of here if necessary. Then Snake made a curt gesture to Erly and told him, "Put your gun on the table and get out."

"But, Boss..." the whiskered man started to protest.

"Just do it!"

Erly laid a heavy revolver with a notched grip on the table next to his glass and glared at Jack as he moved toward the doorway.

Jack got to his feet, keeping his Peacemaker in his hand. The men drinking sensed that something was going on, and at the sight of Erly's gun and now Jack's, they knew it. Most of them headed for the door, eager to get out of the line of fire if gunplay broke out.

"You're going to replace my packhorse," Jack told Haze. Their eyes dueled for a second; then Haze muttered a curse and stood up. "I don't like you," Jack said. "Somebody ought to stand up to what you're doing out here. But I'll be gettin' my mustangs over to Gollahers." He dunked Erly's gun in his beer. "If you and your boys take care of your end by tomorrow morning, I won't bother you. But if I don't have my full herd plus the two you owe me, I'll be coming back for you, Snake."

"You always act so high-handed with folks, Smitty?"

"Only yellow-bellies. And you'll call me Smith."

Muttering under his breath, Haze turned toward the door. Jack followed closely behind him, gun still drawn. As they stepped out onto the plank sidewalk, Jack glanced in both directions. A Mexican, sweating in a red Indian blanket, stood nearby. Alongside, a shapely black hussy was being led by a greasy man, with milky blue eyes set close to his narrow, pointed nose. Small, pursed lips were drab in a sallow, scarred face; lanky, yellow hair hung over his collar at the back, and there was a sour-whiskey reek Jack could smell from ten feet away. His hands looked soft and damp, the left missing its thumb.

"We both got a problem with our thumbs, Sam," Jack told the town's kingpin. "Yours is a dead giveaway, and mine could be. If anyone comes up behind me, my thumb's going to slip off this hammer." Jack mounted Big Red, unflustered. "At this range, the slug will blow your spine clean in two, Mr. Lester."

Sitting astride the satiny red mare, Jack Smith was conspicuous when he rode out of town. Big Red had a distinctive gait that caught attention first, but then it was Jack that kept it. He stood six feet five inches, but he was so perfectly made, so beautifully muscled, that he appeared no taller than the average man.

His hair, black as a crow's wing and barbered to keep it out of his eyes and off his neck, gave him the look of an Indian with some white blood, an impression strengthened by his dark-tanned skin and piercing gray eyes. A reluctance to talk and his superb horsemanship did nothing to weaken the impression of part Apache ancestry. It was the soft wave in his hair that spoke of proud English mountainfolk. He could trace his lineage as far back as Plymouth Rock, although he did nothing to dispel a rumor that he was "three-eighths Kioway," which followed him around Texas.

Through the wilting stifle of a September heat wave, Jack drove his herd, plus the two new packhorses, the last forty-five mile stretch between Sam's Town and Gollaher Ranch.

"Anybody caught picking lice and throwing them on the floor without killing them first is charged ten cents for each offense." He heard the familiar threat as he unloaded his gear in the breezeway. Gollaher cowboys lived in a bunkhouse attached to a combination kitchen and mess hall by an open, roofed passageway. Saddles, bridles, and ropes hung from pegs. Old timers had spruced up their quarters with a coat of whitewash on the walls and a real wood floor. Buffalo robes and wolf skins softened the bunks, and there was even a crude rock fireplace.

Cowpunchers on the small Texas ranch admired Jack, even while they feared him. Drifting like tumbleweeds after the War, the broncobusters had blown onto the Gollaher Ranch for board and room and just enough to spend at the saloon in town.

"Who threw this louse down without killing him first?" Smith asked as he stepped over a filthy man wearing a linen vest that fairly jumped with the vermin. Jack pulled his gun from his waistband in mock horror, and answered himself. "Why, it's the gallant Indian Joe," he said, sarcasm dripping from his mouth like tobacco juice.

Indian Joe had nicknamed himself. He was a conglomeration of races, but he claimed a Comanche father he didn't actually have. "I inherited his sadistic streak," the man bragged. Jack knew the cruelty came from a seething, bitter, lonely place inside Indian Joe. He recognized the void.

"That infested bully shouldn't be allowed in the paddock with the horses," Jack told Frank Gollaher early the next day. "He's more of an animal than any of them."

To Indian Joe, breaking a horse was often literal. Instead of taming it to be a disciplined worker, Indian Joe's harsh treatment was known to break a horse's spirit, emboldening its wild nature. A ragged scar on his arm, visible as he shoved a bit between the giant, yellow teeth of a raisin colored colt, was a vivid token of such ruthlessness. The colt reared, and Indian Joe swore, jerking its head by pulling on the forelock, switching him with a braided grass quirt.

The man was strong but no match for the three-year-old horse and when Indian Joe was soundly kicked in the shin, Frank seemed pleased. Bucking for all he was worth, the colt was doing his best to keep his autonomy. Jack reached into his pocket for a bag of Bull Durham and settled down to roll a cigarette. He'd never heard a horse bellow quite like this one did. The commotion grew when Indian Joe uncoiled his long rope and the horse heard the loop whiz past him at the speed of a bullet. It coiled around both front legs like a snake. Terror blazed in his eyes, and he squealed as he was snared.

"You'll learn to behave!" Indian Joe wrestled with the snorty horse, which nipped and bit until Frank yelled for him to loosen the rope. Breaking horses was the Gollaher business, and the United States government paid them for well-trained mounts only. They lost money on the broncs that went outlaw.

Even without boots, Frank Gollaher was a head taller than his brother, Luke. A week's growth of dark beard stubble softened the sharp planes of his weather-browned face, giving him a rough look at odds with his toffee brown eyes.

"Let the horse keep his pride, Cowboy!" Frank snapped the words like an order. Indian Joe relinquished his hold on the hackamore, with a snarl at his boss. "You'll turn that horse into a brute," said Frank. "He'll be no good to us then."

Jack followed Frank from the corral toward the mess hall. A haze of dust hung over the raw broncs and the men working with them.

"How many horses you broke for us, Smith?" asked Frank. "Somewhere around eighty? You ever produced an outlaw?"

"If one turns outlaw once in a while, I figure it's their natural instinct to be that way. I can handle and ride them all just the same," Jack said. "Rough ones been jarring my teeth loose since I was twelve, but I'd rather have a kicky bronc that's feeling good than some gentle old plug that's leg weary."

There was a softness that came to his face whenever he talked about horses. Jack had been with Gollahers near two years; he'd worked for other outfits before that, training the animals. He liked just being with a corral full of them, handling them and feeling their hides. The satisfaction he got out of seeing some four-year-old colt learn the things he taught meant more to him than the wages he drew for the work. There were times he'd be breaking some brainy gelding and watch the horse pick up fast on the moves. For all his sharpness, he could get misty eyed when he had to give one of them up. Jack was sensitive that way.

"He's a horse whisperer," Indian Joe said behind his back. The rumor spread, but the hands didn't let Jack know they were talking about him. There was something spooky about Jack's knack with wild horses. Frank and Luke Gollaher counted on him, though, and the United States Army bought their horses by the herd.

Luke Gollaher seated himself at the end of the long table, made the good morning noise that was expected of him, and gulped a mug of coffee. The cook, a small, round, brown man with ropy, black hair and a Spanish accent, immediately set a well-filled plate of beans and eggs in front of him. Luke watched his men and listened and kept his silence, as was his custom. He was not one of them, and everyone in the kitchen knew it; they tolerated him and they took his pay, but they had reservations about rich men.

A hard-bitten bunch of ranch hands, there was no doubt that some lived up to their menacing appearance. Luke had witnessed savage fights between them and even fired men for shootings, fair and unfair.

He was a stringy man of medium height, whose black hair was interspersed with gray, giving a pepper-and-salt effect, not only to his hair, but to his eyebrows and thick mustache as well. He kept the books and, as far as the men were concerned, had nothing to do with the daily operation of the ranch. Breakfast was usually the only time they saw him.

Now he pushed his chair back slightly and leaned back to roll a cigarette. It was a recognized signal, and those who had not yet finished increased the pace of their eating.

"Indian Joe!" bellowed Frank as he entered the kitchen. He shoved a hat off the breakfast table and kicked it outside in the mud by the pump. "Keep your filthy sombrero away from my food." He spat as his spurs clinked against the floorboards.

Frank stood next to his older brother as he gave the daily briefing. "Smith brought in some new horses last night. They'll be the first order of business," he said. "There's a painted colt as fierce and unmanageable a horse as I've ever seen. I'll give twenty-five bucks to the cowboy who can ride him first." As a whoop went up from the table, Frank consulted his watch. "Nine a.m. at the corral." The informal meeting was over, and the men dispersed.

Jack followed Luke from the kitchen into a rough room given over to the business of the ranch. The scarred, old desk in the corner held the accounts. A heavy, round table held a lamp that needed cleaning; there were a few large chairs, a rack of rifles of assorted makes and calibers, and a threadbare Indian rug on the floor. Books were stacked in dusty piles beyond the fireplace.

"Sam Lester wanted to pilfer a few horses," Jack told Luke.

"Not the first time," Luke replied.

"Might be the last time," Jack said. "They even made amends; I brought back a couple of extra packhorses."

Luke looked up in surprise. "Never knowed that to happen. You better avoid Sam's boys for a spell. They don't take nicely to being embarrassed." He dug around in the safe. "Payday's tomorrow, and there'll be a bonus for getting those horses back."

Jack turned to leave the room.

"I'm not much for advice, kid," said the older man. "You've got a quick draw and a temper to match. They'll get you in trouble. But I've never seen a man with more horse sense. Blend that into the brew, and you'll make a fine name for yourself."

Without looking back at Luke, Jack nodded at his words and headed in the direction of the corral.

The contest had turned into a tournament of sorts. Knives had been thrown at a target to determine who would ride first, and Indian Joe was the clear winner. Displaying the quickness Luke had talked about, Jack pulled his big .45, twirled it on his finger, and hit the bull's-eye from fifty yards. Indian Joe and Jack were now opponents.

Bets were placed, and the cowboys hung on the fence or sat on their haunches in the dirt, enjoying a break from the routine. Jack saw Frank herding the other horses out of the corral, leaving the black and white pinto alone. He squatted down in the grama weed and prepared to watch Indian Joe at work.

Men talk of the skill between the angler and the trout, but the skill of a hundred-and-eighty pound cowboy holding eleven hundred pounds of ferocious, wild horseflesh is a battle worth watching. This horse was savage, untamed as any animal could be, and Indian Joe had the same qualities. Staring the horse down with fierce eyes, he roped him, hobbled him, and swiftly got a saddle strapped on. In one practiced movement, he untied the rope and vaulted into the leather seat.

The horse's head went down, a howl came out of him, and a leap made the saddle twist like it was on a pivot. Steel muscles shot out of the dirt and carried the man and horse up in mid-air, where they seemed to shake before coming down. Saddle string was popping like a whiplash, leather was squeaking; the fence shook as the hard hitting hoofs of the horse hit the earth; dirt was stirred into a dark cloud. The horse was scared, mad, and desperate. All the action, strength, and endurance that was in him was brought out against the cowboy. Not a hair on his hide was lying idle through the performance; every muscle tightened and loosened in a way to shake the weight from his back.

Indian Joe cussed mightily and jerked the colt's neck backward. He was still to one side and well up in the saddle, his right hand high up in the air, but the side winding resulted in a few more ground-shaking jumps.

"Take that, you monster!" He whipped the horse mercilessly, but the colt proved too much for the man to handle. Indian Joe landed in a pile of steaming manure, to guffaws and kudos from the men.

The horse's eyes fired as he snorted; sweat dripped from his slick hide; after a minute, he stopped bucking and looked at his audience. Frank had a couple of hands remove the saddle and nodded at Jack to take his turn.

Jack could still see fear in the colt's eyes, but mixed in with that fear was a lot of nerve that showed fight. He knew the horse would struggle and make himself hard to handle, and he'd have been disappointed not to have seen those signs in the horse. He figured the wilder the spirit, the bigger and more worthwhile the win would be.

Calmly, Jack held out his empty hand and walked toward the animal. Looking him right in the eye, murmuring sweet nothings, Smith seduced the horse as easily as he did a woman. His hand touched the horse's ear and then his forehead. Pretty soon, a hackamore was slipped over his head, a rawhide bosal around his nose, and then a rope around his neck. All the while, Jack was making low sounds that kept the horse still. "Come on, son," he breathed, "we're going to have us a time."

He hefted up the saddle, and the horse went wild-eyed at the sight of it. "Don't you like the smell of saddle leather, son?" Jack asked softly, still rubbing its forehead, persuading a hint of trust. He mounted with hushed whispers and petted the mane while he clamped his knees tight for the ride.

Jack felt the muscles go to work, even through the saddle. Every part of the horse that his legs touched seemed as hard as steel, full of fast working bumps that came and went, twisting the saddle under him. Sometimes, the horse was headed one way and the saddle another, and he wasn't always sure of the whereabouts of the colt's head in this zigzag pattern.

Without warning, the horse jack-knifed and brought out wicked swivels, jerks, and recoils. He bucked in a circle, crooked, high, and hard-hitting. Every time his hooves hit the ground, he was a whole length from where he'd started up.

Jack was still straight up and on top when the horse's hard jumps finally dwindled down to crow hops and then a stop. The horse needed wind mighty bad, and as his nostrils opened wide, taking in the necessary air, he felt a hand rubbing along his neck. Wild eyed, ears cocked back at the cowboy that was still there, he stood and heard him talk.

"You done a mighty fine job, son," said Jack. "I'd have been disappointed not to have found that kind of spirit in a horse like you." He dismounted and took a mocking bow.

Indian Joe swore and muttered. "That filthy son of a gun. I softened the colt up before he even got close." He spit in the dirt as Frank handed Jack the $25 prize.

The Paluxy Saloon in Burleson was rambunctious by the time Jack got there.

"Bring that prize money to our table, Smith," shouted a cowboy as he dealt a round. "We've got a glass and a chair." Indian Joe was sitting at the bar, well into a second bottle. He saw Jack and kicked over the stool next to him, as he knocked his own to the floor.

"You cheat," he snarled, getting up. His greasy, black hair fell across his eyes, and his sweat-streaked neck bulged. "You swine." Flailing his arms, he lurched toward Jack. "That money is mine." Indian Joe's black eyes were unfocused as he pulled his gun and swung it in the air. Even he seemed surprised when it went off. "You owe me twenty-five dollars," he growled, and shot again. A bowie knife appeared in his other hand, and he held it, ready to throw.

Jack's clothes were powdered with a fine dust that sifted out of the creases in his shirt as he quickly moved his rugged upper body to the side. He never wore a holster. The pistol leapt into his left hand, and, fast and deadly as a snake's tongue, his gun spit its poison. Indian Joe fell dead across a table, scattering poker chips and cards onto the wooden floor, the knife still clutched between his fingers.

"That crazy Indian," someone said to the room. "He's been begging to be shot since he got here." Then, to Jack, "You couldn't of done nothin' else, kid."

"Jeb, get the sheriff," the barkeeper yelled to his son. "And bring in some sawdust to clean up this mess."

Jack poured a whiskey down his throat. He'd never killed a man before, but he didn't feel any remorse. The world was better off with one less coward. There was a certain satisfaction in knowing he was capable of such a deed. He wiped his six-shooter and stuffed it back in his waistband, just as Larabie Morgan swung through the doors with Jeb. The boardwalk was already crowding up. Burleson, following the custom of all small towns, would turn out when there was anything unusual going on, and a killing was good entertainment.

"Look, Larabie," said the barkeeper as the sheriff elbowed his way through the crowd, gun drawn. "It was self-defense. I saw it."

"I don't give a hoot what caused it. You, kid, need to cut and ride," Morgan said, pointing at Jack. "There'll be folks'll want to string you up for this. I don't know who will miss this lowlife, but I'm not interested in hosting gunfights, hangings, or funerals."

Jeb had pried loose the knife and was ready to pocket it when the sheriff held out his hand. "Nice Bowie." He looked at Jack. "I'm glad you're a quick draw. A knife is a plumb ungentlemanly weapon, and it sure leaves a messy-looking corpse."

"I'll be gone by morning," Jack told Morgan.

3

September 1872, Greenville, Texas

Greenville was a two-day ride south through sage and Indian paintbrush. Jack reversed his bandanna, pulled it above his nose to cut the trail dust, and settled down to the long day's grind. The coolness of night had gone completely from the desert, and sunlight began to bite his skin.

After collecting his wages from Luke Gollaher, he'd strapped his possibles sack and bedroll on Big Red and set off before dawn. At noon, he threw off for an hour, eating cold bacon and bread by the wet seep of a spring.

"Red, what would Mama think of us now?" Jack found the horse a good listener, especially when they were far from civilization. She seemed to bounce back the responses he was hoping for.

"She'd have me hell-bound for killing a man. I've done most of God's sins, Red. Heck, after Indian Joe, I've probably done them all. But here I sit, as fresh and fit as a boy could be. No devils with little pitchforks after me, far as I can tell. Maybe Mama was wrong about God caring about all that." Heat crowded around him, and the soil glittered between its patches of rock and dried bunchgrass. "Or maybe God just don't care much about me."

To the west, the desert looked smoky with dark, dry clouds; to the east, the near-by buttes were baked, barren, and arid. Twice, riders appeared in the far distance, stirring up vague spirals of dust. In the middle of the afternoon, a band of antelope scudded down a sterile draw and crossed the trail with the speed of gusty wind, racing into the desert. Four piled cattle skulls marked the turning to Greenville. At dusk of that long day, Jack came to a shallow crossing of the Brazos that lay half hidden in the junipers and set up camp.

After a supper of bacon and canned tomatoes, he leaned back to smoke away the last of the day's light. The stars were shining out of a black sky, and the night wind turned quite cold. Wilderness winds and coyotes were calling out of the near hills. Jack's thoughts ran freely and odd and a little sad.

Embraced by the dark, he told Big Red, "Sometimes a man's pressed by his mortal questions, girl." It wasn't often that Jack thought of his mother, but he remembered her telling him that large, fragrant, white flowers bloomed on the triangle cactus at night, closing up by morning. Years on the desert, and he'd never seen the sight, but he knew he was like that; the stars and moon brought out a tender side in him that disappeared when the hot sun beat down.

"You miss your mama, Red?" he asked the horse. "She was a pretty one, just like mine was." The mare only laid down full on the ground every other day and then for just a little while, but tonight, Jack had his head propped on her belly. "You think they're together up there, ridin' with Hank amongst them heavenly clouds?" Big Red snorted, and Jack caressed her muzzle.

"Don't think I could ever love anybody like I did that boy. He put such stock in me...shoot..." he muttered as he stirred the fire. "I'm getting maudlin, Red."

Loneliness touched his nerves and got in his bones. "Here I'm talking to a horse!" He took off his boots and stuck them on two sticks to dry out. "Tomorrow, I'm looking for a different kind of ponytail," he told his only friend.

Jack made good use of the next day's travel time. Every movement in the purple squaw-weed gave him a target. When a lizard scurried among the black-eyed Susans, he pulled his .45 and sent it flying. At midmorning, he ate some beans then set the empty can on a tree stump and knocked it off with one bullet. Later, when a diamondback slithered in the scrub brush, Jack's left hand yanked the pistol and pulled the trigger. Six shots divided the snake into pre-cut chunks for lunch.

His fast draw seemed to be inborn, but he made the most of it by practicing. He couldn't remember a time he wasn't shooting rabbits or squirrels, blue jays or black crows. It got so he even let them play his game. If a bird wasn't flying, he kicked up some leaves to scare it off the branch and into the air before he brought it down. He shot without hesitation, with the intent to kill. Aiming his dark blue Colt was akin to pointing a forefinger.

"First off in town, we need us some bullets," Jack told Big Red. "Then one of us is taking a bath." Farms and ranches were getting closer together, promising civilization within the hour.

Greenville was a T-shaped town, the cross-member of the T being Front Street, along the old stage road. Main Street was aligned as it had been from the first, with stores, a post office, bank, and saloon. Jesse's Livery was on the corner across from the church and cemetery.

Jack guided Big Red easily with his knees, past a wagon loaded with produce. Driving it was a girl, small and slender, jolting on the buckboard seat under a man's large, domed-straw sombrero. Dust covered her blue calico skirt and denim jacket, masking her small face with a grayish film. She'd perspired, and he saw her swipe a jaunty dirt smear across her mouth.

"Watch where you're going!" she yelled as she cut in front of Big Red. Stopping without warning, she turned into a small alley leading to the back of a restaurant next to the Bull Horn Saloon. Jack watched her maneuver the buckboard skillfully between the buildings, and his stomach growled seeing bushel baskets piled with fresh peaches, squash, and corn.

The afternoon sun threw long shadows on the street, turning its deep dust to silver. It was a harsh light, unkind to the gray, weathered storefronts, a tangle of corrals, homes, and sheds that rose up in front of Jack. He tethered Big Red in front of a place called Turnaround, where the sign promised cowboys, "We'll make a new man of you."

An hour later, his new, white shirt crisp against his skin, Jack walked out into the evening and paused on the edge of the plank walk. A hot bath had soaked the stiffness out of him; in his nose was the pleasant reek of bay rum from his shave. He watched the traffic of the street, heard the cheerful talk shouted from boardwalk to boardwalk, and eyed the restless ponies racked in front of the businesses. A housewife, a sack of sugar under her arm, left Brunner's Mercantile, gathered her skirts, and ran past him in her hurry home to a late supper.

It was all homely, all familiar. He fashioned a cigarette and struck a match on his flat heavy belt buckle before he walked Big Red down the street to stable her for the night.

"Decent grub over there at the Blue Belle?" he asked the young owner of Jesse's Livery as he unsaddled the horse.

"Better'n the pork and beans I'm eating, and the company's a might prettier." Jesse's randy snicker showed a rotten tooth in front. His eyes had a sunken, permanently squinting look, and his stained overalls were too loose and too short on his gangling frame.

"She's stuck up as a skunk's tail but worth a look. Plus, there's dancing at the saloon next door, and a bunch of the boys play Faro every night. Greenville has its diversions. The hotel's full, though. For an extra fifty cents, I'll let you have the hay right next to your animal."

The aroma of roast beef and hot biscuits met Jack when he pushed open the door. "Welcome to the Blue Belle." An auburn-haired girl smiled, her eyes repeating the color of the blue gingham tablecloths. She indicated a table by the window and poured him a cup of coffee. Pulling his gun from the waistband of his trousers, he set it carefully on the chair next to him, but he kept his Stetson on.

"So are you Blue Belle?" Jack asked, openly admiring her soft curves.

Adjusting her bodice, she retorted, "Belle's the cow out back. I'm Ruby. And you can quit staring. I've known men like you, and I'm not interested." Her voice was kept low, but she had no shyness about her.

Jack tipped back in his chair, and ogled her. "You've known men like me? What are you... about fifteen? Too young to be so sour on love." He reached out and grabbed her around the waist. "Some schoolboy pull your ponytail too hard?"

"Laws! I'm eighteen, and I can rope a calf and break a colt better than most boys. I support a household and work a farm, so don't toy with me, mister." She refilled his coffee cup and twisted away from his grasp. "I'll get your roast beef now, if you'll kindly let me go."

"You're the girl with the wild buckboard! You do know your way with a horse, I'll give you that." Remembering the grimy face, he looked her over. "You clean up well."

"So do you," Ruby said, recognizing him. "I thought you were just a pile of whiskers and dust on that red mare."

"You'll have to meet her, tell her you're sorry for almost running her down."

"You tell her for me. I don't talk horse," she said with a flippant laugh.

"Big Red understands human. She doesn't just have beauty, she has brains, like all the fillies I take a fancy to." His gray eyes were soft as pussy willows as he looked at her over his coffee. "Course, red hair is the main requirement," he said as she walked off.

He watched her sway and turn as she moved about the room, saw the slight changes of her face and the small expressions coming and going. Ruby kept at her work, but she knew he was watching her.

Glancing over at Jack when she went through to the kitchen, she saw how black curls hugged his neck under a brown hat decorated with tiny silver studs. Through the stiff, store-bought shirt, she could see powerful shoulders lift the muscles of his back.

"I know him," Turk said as she set down the tray. "I've cooked at his campfire and slept on his blanket. Don't be taken in, sweetheart."

"What do you mean, you know him? Really, Turk?" asked Ruby.

"Not this one personally, but I know cowboys like him. I've been at some of the roughest camps in the territories and seen some rough men, men like that bounder. Every one of them was a bad man and had a gun in his hand when he fell. This one's no different."

Mashing potatoes with one hand, Turk stirred the large pot of beef gravy with the other. "They were rough, unschooled drifters, all of 'em," he went on. "Some of them were wanted by the law back home; others never had a home or knew a law or cared about either."

"Turk, you sound like my father. In fact, I wish you'd marry my mother. You could both worry yourselves silly about me, and I wouldn't have to worry about neither of you anymore." Ruby took the tray and set it on her curving hip. "I just may lasso myself one of them cowboys," she said, with a tease. "None of them is going to mind if I climb on behind and hitch a ride out of Greenville."

Turk was used to her saucy talk, and smitten by it. "I'm sixty years old, young lady," he told her. "You better not sass your elders."

"If you were just ten years younger, Turk, I might fall in love with you." She sashayed out and whistled him a kiss.

"We're out of pie for the moment," Ruby told Jack, clearing away his plate. "Turk'll have a fresh peach ready about eight o'clock. You can come back for it then. I'll hold your tab, but we close at ten."

"Will you still be here? I'll treat you to a slice, if you'll save some for me."

"I'm taking the buckboard back when it quiets down. Turk won't make me come back in 'til tomorrow." Disappointment tinged her words, but she covered it with cheek. "Turk'll save you a slice, and he's good company."

"I was hoping to eat my peaches with a real peach," Jack said, tucking his gun back in the front of his trousers.

Ruby wrinkled her nose and made a face at his words. "You are a real sugar-mouth; a little too sweet for my taste. Give me tartness anytime," she said. Jack saluted her with his cigarette and walked out smiling. When he turned away, she smiled back in spite of herself.

From the box tucked behind the cooking utensils, Turk took a cigar and walked to the front of his restaurant. He stepped outside to light it, inhaled its tip to a glow, and clenched it in his teeth. All the while, his face was bland, but he studied the cowboy walking toward the Bull Horn Saloon. He didn't have much reason to hate Jack Smith yet. All he'd done so far was crowd Ruby. Maybe Jack would win his road stake tonight and be gone by tomorrow. Turk hoped he was an excellent gambler.

A honky-tonk piano banged and the blunt teeth of Jack's spurs jingled against tiny bells as he walked along the boardwalk to an open doorway. He paused at the door's edge.

Sound rolled out from the front part of the saloon, the sound of men's voices cheerfully arguing, the scrape of boots and spurs and chair legs, the dry clatter of poker chips. A little current of air pulled the smoke outside, although it was still visible above the tables. The Bull Horn had a long paneled bar of polished mahogany, where Jack dropped his coins and ordered a bourbon. "You don't put any coffin varnish in that stuff, do you?" he asked a barkeeper the other drinkers called Sullivan.

Pine-board walls were undecorated, except for a pen-and-ink drawing of two horsemen trying to hold a grizzly with their ropes. Lamplight threw a yellow shine directly against Jack's face, and he braced himself to the shock of the whiskey by pushing his shoulders forward and leaning on the bar.

Discordant music added to the din—seventy-five cents to the piano man, and the cowboys could take their pick of dancing girls and waltz for fifteen minutes at a time. The girls then two-stepped them back to the bar for another drink, taking a commission on every shot they sold.

"You in for a hand, Sully?" a dealer asked the barkeep.

"Not as long as there are thirsty customers. But you got a live body here." Sullivan thumbed Jack. "Not afraid you'll lose your money to hicks, are you, kid?"

A sizable man with a long, black mustache, Jack wondered if he kept an eye peeled for rubes. His new bright, white shirt and smooth cheeks might brand him as a dandy.

"I'd be right proud to play with you boys," said Jack. They sized each other up and got down to business.

"You ain't no easterner," observed a player named Swede after a few hands. "Where'd you blow in from?"

"Here and there," said Jack. "I was up at Gollahers for a while training horses. Now I'm heading to the Rockies. Denver, first, then the Tetons maybe."

The mention of Gollahers perked up Sullivan. "You the one who shot the Indian?" he asked.

Poker chips rattled between fingers, and the others didn't look up. Finally, Swede said, "Sully speaks afore he thinks sometimes."

Nobody spoke until Jack finally said, "Yes, Mr. Sullivan. That was me. 'Twern't without proper provocation, though." Pushing back from the table, he laid down his cards. "I didn't figure I was coming to a judgment. By the way, I got three men here." He laid the kings on the green felt, pocketed some silver dollars, and walked toward the dance floor.

Feeling relaxed and playful at the same time, Jack wandered back to the Blue Belle for his pie just after ten o'clock. Oil lamps on tall poles glowed in the street, illuminating store windows; the starry night softened the harsh reality of the town, and the shabby buildings took on a kind of dignity.

Ruby was counting money at one of the tables. "It's about time you came back. I can't balance my totals until you pay me." He dropped a dollar on the counter while she cut a slice of pie. "I thought you'd run out on me. I'd get docked for your bill, and I wouldn't even know your name."

"It's Jack Smith, and I'm not in a rush," Jack told her. "In fact, I'm planning to walk you home." She placed a fork by his right hand and noticed he picked it up with his left.

"You're wasting your time with me, but I'm too tired to argue," Ruby said, massaging her lower back. "I've been on my feet all day, and I'm not a pushover for some lusty dude, looking for a bright spot in a dull town."

"Why are you waitin' for me, then? I gave you time to make your getaway. Seems like you're the one looking for a bright spot in a dull town." Jack swiped a piece of peach off his lip with his tongue. "If Greenville ain't sparkly enough for you, why don't you leave?"

He pushed back his plate. "You got a mean daddy makin' you stay here?"

"Nothing like that. My daddy's dead, but I take care of my ma. She's had a rough go and isn't quite ready to be on her own yet." Paperwork done, Ruby shoveled the coins into a mason jar kept locked in a safe on the wall.

"Besides, she needs everything we have. But in a few years, when I have a bit of a stake, I'm starting a cattle ranch of my own. I've seen what happens when you depend too much on someone else. You'll hear of me again, Jack Smith."

"You'll want a cowman to drive all those herds. That's my specialty. I love pretty heifers."

"I can see that. But you seem like the 'love 'em and leave 'em' variety," Ruby retorted, taking a gray shawl off the hat rack by the door.

She put out the lights and locked up behind herself after she ushered him out the door. "I'm going this way," she said, turning toward the corner.

"So am I," said Jack, turning to follow her. "If you fancy horses, you need to meet Big Red. Your hair's the same color as hers." He twisted a lock from Ruby's ponytail. "She's just down at Jesse's here. You'll never see a prettier mare."

"Not a lot of imagination to her name," Ruby taunted.

"There was, considering she wasn't red when I named her."

As they strolled down the dusty street, Jack kneaded the sore place on her back. It felt good, and Ruby didn't mind so much, leaning against his shoulder for balance. In the darkness, Jack felt comfortable talking.

"We had a horse called Autumn Red. I had to put her down just after she foaled. Near broke my heart. Even though she looked black to begin with, I called the foal Big Red after her mama, and she grew into her name. I kind of feel like I'm her pa."

Ruby encouraged his confidence, taking his arm and kicking the dirt up before he went on.

"She's a little suspicious of strangers—skittish and nippy. But she's got a hair trigger with me, knows where we're going as soon as I think it." Jack bragged like a doting parent, and Ruby noticed how mushy he got singing the praises of his horse.

"Three years ago, I took her down a steep canyon. She sideslipped and hurt a ligament. It took months of poultices and root baths to get it healed, and even now, she has an uneven gait, but she's just as fast." Jack paused. "That horse is my whole family now." He knew he'd been rambling. "Sorry. Guess I'm gushing. Been missing another human to talk to these past days."

Ruby undid her hair and wrapped the ribbon around her wrist, weaving her fingers through the tresses to let the air cool her head. "Where's the rest of your family?" she asked.

"Dead," he said, without explanation. "At least my mother and brother are. I lit out young and don't know where my father is."

"Was he the 'love 'em and leave 'em' variety?" It was the wrong thing to say, and Ruby knew it instantly. She busied herself with her hair, tying it back up in its ponytail and falling a step behind Jack as they approached the livery.

Big Red and a short-legged black mare were the only horses in the corral. Jesse was outside oiling a saddle when they entered. He lifted an eyebrow as Jack pushed back the stable door, and the red filly tossed her head in greeting. Tucking himself in the shadows, Jesse settled in to observe.

"Hello, girl!" Ruby said softly, making her way confidently to rub Big Red's nose. "She's lovely," she said to Jack. Big Red was calm as the young woman stroked her mane, nuzzling her like an old friend.

"See the eye on her?" Jack came up behind Ruby. "It's real kind. And the slope on the shoulder and the muscle inside the hip? That's where she gets all her power from—inside. She's got a good heart.

There's a lot of cow in her, too. We've herded wild cattle many a time, and she's instinctive about it. I'm just along for the ride."

Ruby pulled a sugar cube from her pocket.

"That's not good for her," said Jack, watching the horse sniff and snort at the white lump and finally nibble at it a bit.

"She's not a sugar-mouth?" teased Ruby. "Horses will do anything for me because of my 'take-home pay.' Turk doesn't know he's sweetening up the town's horse population instead of their coffee mugs."

"So your way with horses is to spoil them with sweets?" asked Jack.

"That's my way," she teased. "It works with kids, animals, and even men." She popped a cube into her own mouth and sucked it for a second before she gave it to Big Red. "I bet she'd let me get right on." Ruby grabbed her mane and tried to hoist herself up.

"Usually, strangers make her skittish," Jack said, but the horse was serene as he took Ruby by the waist and lifted her on, sidesaddle.

The girl threw her leg over and leaned down, burying her face in the coarse, snowy white mane. "Laws, I could love you, Big Red," she said, getting a muffled nicker in response. Jack looked dumbfounded. Looking down, she told him, "You don't have to be jealous. Fillies love each other different than they love their cowboy. You'll have her heart and soul forever, while I'll be just a sugary memory."

She slid off the horse into Jack's arms. Standing so close, she could hear his quick breathing and she stood on her toes to kiss him lightly. Ruby was not inexperienced with the men around town, but she was not experienced, either. When Jack eagerly kissed her back, she was surprised at his fierceness. She submitted without making a protest.

He felt the sweet warmth of her lips, smelled her hair, and then stepped away from her. He was surprised at the strange reluctance he felt. For one moment, the truth was naked in his eyes, a kind of bewilderment. Ruby saw it and knew: he missed being loved.

When he spoke, he said with more harshness than he had intended, "You'll go now unless you want more of that."

Ruby said, "I don't want to go yet."

Jack's eyes held hers for a few seconds, and then he turned away. He sat down, arms folded on his knees, not sure if he wanted to spoil a girl with so much innocent trust in her eyes.

"I'm not the kind of man you'll be takin' home to meet Mama. I just need you to understand that."

"I don't know what you've been before, Jack, and I don't care." Ruby lifted off his hat and ran her fingers through his wavy, black hair, massaging his temples. Then he watched her take his bedroll off the rail and spread it over the straw, wrapping some extra in her shawl to make a pillow. Kneeling down in front of him, she put her soft hands on his face, closing his eyes with her fingertips as she pushed him back on the blanket. "I'm in your hands now," she whispered.

4

Afterwards, Ruby pulled the hay out of her stockings and wrapped her shawl around her chilled shoulders. Jack was turned away from her, snoring, and she stood up and touched her lips. Did it show? Would anyone be able to tell she was different? It had only taken a few minutes, but her life had changed.

It was an hour later than normal when she crept into the house, hoping her mother wouldn't hear.

"Ruby?" Olive Dawson called. "Where have you been?"

"Sorry, Ma. Turk kept me late to help with the baking," she told her mother.

"Well, you've got straw in your hair," her mother said.

It wasn't lost on Olive that her daughter attracted men like a magnet, but she was usually adept at holding them back, and her mother was relieved. Ruby hardly understood the obligations of womanhood, had never known what it was to love a man, or suffer because of him. That would come soon enough, Olive knew, and was glad for the wisdom her own husband had shown in raising this girl.

Jeremy had treated Ruby more like a son than a daughter, and in her young womanhood, she was capable and strong. Her generosities were magnificent; her angers were rages, her manner as simple and direct as her father's had been. Men adored her until they realized her spirit. Then they were sometimes intimidated.

Olive had wondered when Ruby would wake up to her allure, and it looked like it may have happened tonight. The mother's faded blue eyes had a hue of sadness, and she felt old and anxious.

The door to the back bedroom closed off further discussion with her mother. Through the black specks in the cracked mirror, Ruby examined herself, brushing out bits of chaff as she wove a fat braid. In the dim light, she noticed red marks on her neck and chest. She'd have to wear her high-necked brown dress tomorrow, she thought, even while she caught the tobacco-y scent of Jack's breath in her hair.

"I'm a fallen woman," she whispered to her reflection. "And I like it."

Warnings about sin and lust were exposed as lies to her newly awakened heart. Ruby had been warned in church that men took degenerate pleasure from good women. Good women participated only reluctantly, with husbands, and only in the begetting process. God and her father stood together in Ruby's mind, looking enraged and condemning.

Jeremy Dawson used to fret that his daughter's beauty would one day break his heart, but cholera had taken him before Ruby got the chance. "If he knew about Jack Smith, it'd kill him all over again," she told the mirror. "And then he'd kill me." She twirled in mild euphoria. "But I'm already in heaven."

By dawn, Ruby had her new life planned. She packed apples, beef jerky, a loaf of Olive's sourdough, and a tin of oysters in a satchel, along with the red flannel quilt from her bed, and left the house in the direction of Jesse's Livery. The September morning was crisp and alive, a reflection of her mood.

"Jack?" Ruby heard a horse stomping in the stable and stepped around a heap of threadbare saddle blankets. "Jack! I'm here," she called again, louder. Big Red wasn't in the stall where she'd been the night before, and there was no evidence of the blue bedroll Ruby had spread out for their comfort.

Jesse, roused by the creaking gate, spoke into the dark. "There ain't nobody in there. Who you lookin' for?"

"Jack Smith," said Ruby. "He may have left early to come for me. I'm going with him." Her words sounded condescending, and Jesse enjoyed the moment before he put her in her place.

"Sorry, Miss Ruby. Smith saddled his mare and left right after you did last night. Asked for his money back, even. Said he had no reason to stay, that his horse balked at being tethered. He'd got what he wanted... you know... food and all."

Jesse's smugness hit Ruby like a blast of muggy air, leaving her breathless. He went on, "But I could highly recommend you to the boys at the Bull Horn. Looked like that cowboy broke you in real good." His smirk showed the rotten tooth as he slapped the black horse's rump and shuffled back to his bunk.

Sourness rose in the back of Ruby's throat and she gagged, then wretched. The stall felt suddenly airless, claustrophobic. She pulled the tight ribbon off her wrist and unconsciously tied up her hair, exposing the love bites that were as ugly as the empty words that went with them.

I was a diversion, no more to him than that slice of pie. The thought felt like a kick behind the knees, and she knelt down abruptly on the patch of earth where Big Red had witnessed what Ruby thought was love.

What a foolhardy innocent I was... seduced by a horse, she berated herself. Well, I'm not innocent any more, and all of Greenville will know it by noon, thanks to Jesse. Bitterness churned in her chest. *I'll be stuck here, nursing Ma back from the cholera and the widowhood, waiting tables for Turk while folks whisper sordid tattles about me.*

The enormity of it all pressed down on her shoulders, and they began to shake under the weight. Tears burned her eyes, and a sob erupted from deep inside. Jack had represented a flicker of hope Ruby didn't even know she had, and her flood of tears extinguished any sparks that were left.

It's unfair. God's unfair with all His rules and judgments. Outraged at the guilt she felt, she thrashed at the straw, and her knees gave way. *Jack... stupid Jack...* she groaned into her hands as she rocked on her elbows. *I was such a fool...*

Jesse was standing at the doorway. A knowing fantasy played in his filthy mind when Ruby lifted back on her knees in the dirt, defeated, and saw him. "Quit your evil thinking," she said, wiping her face with the back of a hand. "You wanting to pile on my agony?"

"I'd be glad to help you outta' this here situation, Miss Ruby. You know what they'll all be saying 'round town if this should get out. But I could stand by you, like." Jesse showed the decayed tooth as his tongue caught a dab of saliva off his lower lip. "Stop by here a couple of nights a week and romp in that there hay with me, and I won't tell a soul what you really are."

"Living with these animals has affected you, Jesse. You're like the muck you stand in all day." Ruby gathered up her pride along with her travel satchel. "I'm not near brokenhearted enough to be blackmailed by a dratted peeping Tom."

"Don't be turning away from me, missy," Jesse sputtered after her, chagrined by the rejection. "You ain't gonna get no better offers around here. You have made your bed, and it's sullied." Ugly, red blotches came out on his angry face. "You're no better than a whore," he spat. The gate grated as she slammed it closed behind her.

"Late again," chided Turk absently. The kitchen of the Blue Belle was humid for November, and Ruby tied her mane of red hair up off her neck. "We're making a stew," he said. "Blue Belle contributed her all," he chuckled. Chunking the beef, he pointed to a set of brains on the counter. "I need you to get those ready and clean the marrow gut." With a wicked smile, he added, "Louisiana hot sauce is the special ingredient."

Ruby saw half a beef heart next to a pound of liver. Her stomach turned. "Are you using the whole cow?" she asked.

"No hide, no hooves. No eyeballs." Turk looked up from his chopping and said, "You look white as a sheet. Sit down afore you fall in my pot!"

"It's so hot in here," Ruby said, lowering herself onto a stool. "And the smell of your stew is making me puke."

"The sauce'll spice up the aroma," muttered Turk. "Look here, young lady. You can't come in here late every morning to gripe about my food and expect to keep working for me."

Now that he'd started his grumble, he couldn't stop himself. "I lost a few pious customers when those rumors were going around about you last month, and I kept you on in spite of it. Don't you go insulting my cooking, too."

Tears started in Ruby's eyes. "Ah, Turk. Ma's got me all riled up. I think she's punishing me for getting her talked about. She whimpers all the time about Daddy being gone, and she's still too weak to help out."

"Your color's back, girl. Work while you chatter," Turk said, embarrassed by her emotion. He handed her a knife.

"The animals wouldn't get fed if I didn't do it," Ruby went on. "All the chairs and tables Daddy put together last winter are just sitting in the workshop collecting dust, lumber chips scattered over the floor like chicken feed. Ma expects me to deal with the selling, the delivering, and the bookkeeping, just like Daddy did—"

"Turn the fire down," Turk interrupted. "You don't boil stew."

"Then I come in here and work for you every day. It's got me so tired. And Ma just sits and coughs, staring out the window."

"You got that staring-out-the-window disease, too, I've noticed." Turk tossed the beef in a bowl of flour and dropped the pieces in the hot fat before broaching his real subject.

"I heard something about your cowboy the other night," he told Ruby. The prominent Adam's apple bobbed when Turk swallowed. "He was working with the Gollaher brothers a while back and killed an Indian over a bet. You were lucky he left town. Now they say he's joined up with some posse, hired out his skill with a gun."

The mention of Jack gave Ruby another wave of nausea. "He wasn't all that bad," she told Turk. "He just set off my longings for more than a boring life in a boring town."

"More longings than that, I reckon." Turk had never questioned her about the rumors spread around Greenville. Jesse was a known liar and gossip, and his tales were eaten up by a town starved for excitement. Nobody had turned away when he told and retold what he had witnessed in the livery that night.

Remembering her hope of leaving with Jack, Ruby felt trapped. Her dress suddenly seemed too tight for her pounding heart, and she heard Turk say from a great distance, "Ruby! You're running sweat like swamp rain." Her insides were swimming, and she didn't feel the floor when it came up and smashed her in the face.

A minute or two later, Turk had her sitting up with a cool rag on her forehead. His smile was gentle. "I could get downright provoked with you, sweetheart, dropping my brains and landing right on top of them." Brushing back damp red curls, he said tenderly, "The only time I had a woman faint over my cooking was when my wife was going to have a baby."

Turk knows more about life than anybody, Ruby thought. He had a pleasant, almost homely face, with deep, brown eyes, and he was always soft spoken. He was unutterably and deeply in love with

Ruby, and she knew it again that morning. She even teased him about it after she got her humor back.

"Much as a kid needs a father, I'm glad you're not married to that outlaw," Turk said. "You'll get a husband if you want one. You could choose from an army."

"I'd marry you if you weren't such an old coot," she told him.

There was a dry zest in his keen smile. "I already had me a wife," he said. "Pretty as you, but her eyes weren't so clear. They held the sadness of lost babies and lost dreams, and then I lost her. Not so much lost her as let her get found by a man who didn't have as much baggage." He pressed fists into his back to limber the cramped muscles, not used to the weight of a falling woman. "Wives can get heavy when you need to be light on your feet."

"Well, Jack Smith will be lighter on his feet than I'm going to be." She looked down at her trim figure, wondering about the changes coming in the next few months. "I thought I could keep this secret. Go somewhere maybe, pretend I was a widow. I'm scared to tell Ma."

"Not much is lost on your ma. I reckon she knew before you did. Tell her sooner than later; get that part off your mind. She'll cry, you'll cry, there'll be some 'I told you so'n,' but she'll give you grit through all this. Might even bring her out of her doldrums, being a grandma and all. Do it today. Now."

"So, you can handle the stew? I'll come back tonight and serve it, I promise." He waved her off, and she hugged his narrow shoulders. "Sorry I spoiled your brains," she said.

"Go on, git," he told her, roughly. "Just tell her plain out. She's yer kin."

Turk was right. There were tears and words they'd both regret but in the end, Ruby felt better, and her ma became as protective as a mother bear in the next weeks. The soup she made to soothe her daughter's stomach strengthened her, as well. Whether it was the making of it or the broth itself, healing came after long months of affliction.

"I can't stand the way they look at me, Ma. Mrs. Dobson actually crossed the street when she saw me coming, scuttling her children away from the fallen woman."

Mud fell off her shoes as she kicked them off by the door. Her coat was wet from the winter rain. Ruby came home from the Blue Belle more tormented every day. "I thought Jesse was the head scandalmonger, but the churchgoing hypocrites have him beat to hell."

"No use cursing about it, girl," Olive chided automatically.

"I'm not cursing. Hell's a place, and they all think I'll be the only one in it." Her voice twisted with sarcasm. "I can't wait to welcome them." Buttons popped with relief, and Ruby dropped her skirt on the bedroom floor. "And to top it all, I'm fat; not delicate or blooming, just plumb fat."

Ruby's room at the back of the house was scantily furnished with an ancient iron bed, a cane-seated rocker, a lamp, a washbowl, and a pitcher. The winter sun glinted through pin-cracks in the weathered clapboards outside, and indigo shadows glittered in the corners. "There's nothing feminine about my 'condition'." Her wail was accompanied by squeaking bedsprings as she threw herself on top of the quilt. "And I'll be having a baby right here in my own bed." She rolled over with a dramatic whimper.

"Laws! I birthed you on a mattress of feedbags sewn together. Your daddy told me he'd stuffed them with 'Texas feathers,' but it weren't nothing but hay." Olive unfolded the Mother Hubbard Ruby wore around the house. "There wasn't another woman within twenty miles, but we managed just fine. Neither of us had ever seen a child born before, and the miracle of it took away the pain."

"Oh, Ma, you say that now because you're old and you can't remember." Ruby slid the loose dress over her head. "I've heard the cows bawl when they're laboring. Jack's horse even bled to death—he had to shoot her."

At the mention of Jack, Olive looked away. It put Ruby in even more of a misery. She moaned. "Lots of women die! I could die! No midwife or doctor wants to bring a bastard into the world. And don't you protest the word. That's what the Methodist biddies are calling this baby." Ruby's eyes welled up. "It's true, Ma. My baby won't have a name."

Carrying a basket of fresh laundry to the line out back, Olive took a detour to the old lightning-struck oak and stopped, peering along the slope to the spot where they'd buried her husband not even a year ago.

"I wish I knew what to do, Jeremy," she said in a hushed voice. "She done a sin, and now she's reaping the consequence—simple as that. But she's brave and responsible; she'll handle it. Seems like self-righteous folks are beating her down with shovels, though."

The slant of the morning sun caught the glisten of a tear on her cheek. "I sure miss you, old man. All I do is fret. Can't think straight without you calming my fears."

Listening for his thoughts on the matter, she dawdled a few minutes before she picked up the wicker basket and went back to work. "Nothing gets done around here by just thinking it," she said to herself.

Olive arrived in town the next day about noon, like she had in the times before her sickness: horses in a fast run, her old, topless wagon flanked by a swirl of street dung. The buckboard made a dust-roiling stop outside Holt's Dry Goods. A rifle scabbard was strapped to the whip socket, a canteen lashed to one side of the seat, and a rolled yellow slicker tied on the other side. She left Jeremy's old straw sombrero on the seat, and as her slight frame agilely descended, the buggy tilted, and she jumped to the ground.

Alice Holt, a thin woman of pallid elegance, tightened her lips as Olive stomped into her store. "Mercy, Olive, you're seeming fit. Can I help you find what you're looking for?" she asked.

"I'm looking for a muzzle, ma'am. One that is strong enough to keep the tongue of an old mare from flapping in the wind. Your tongue, Mrs. Holt."

Olive's bosom rose quickly as she took a breath. "Christianity is mighty hard to find in this town, especially when the Ladies of the Methodist Ministry are casting stones at all the sinners but themselves."

The door squeaked open, and Grace Dobson walked through with a smile that froze when she saw Olive's fiery red face. "And you, Mrs. Dobson, ought to look a little closer to home for adultery. It's not just under my roof." Olive's eyes blazed. "I'll not be using your Christian names until you live up to them." She caught the door and slammed it shut on the stunned women.

Olive gathered the reins and her temper. The escape of her harsh words had left her feeling deflated and small, and the reality of Ruby's condition crept back up her spine to tighten her shoulders. Veins pinched in her forehead, and she put the sombrero on to shield her eyes from onlookers, as well as the bright winter sunshine. Glad she didn't have to face Jeremy after her public outburst, she still wished she could see the understanding in his eyes and feel the comfort of his own worries about their daughter. Tears tingled. She missed a husband's friendship, knowing Ruby would, too, as she faced motherhood alone.

5

May 1873

Ruby maneuvered her belly around the wooden counter, avoiding the broom Turk was sweeping back and forth. "I can't stay in Greenville, Turk. I'm an embarrassment to Ma. Folks cross the street so they don't have to talk to me and then cross it again so they can talk about me." Wiping down the stove was the last of the kitchen chores.

"Once the baby comes, they'll have a bit more tolerance," Turk told her. "I've seen it happen. Right now, you're a fallen woman in their eyes, but afterwards, you'll be a novice in need of advice. Those old women will fall all over you in a matronly welcome, full of critique and opinions."

"After the way they've catcalled and gossiped? They're all hypocrites and frauds. I need to start over, make a life for us, find some man who's as kindhearted as you to step in as this baby's daddy." Her blue eyes twinkled. "But I want him younger and with more hair." Ruby untied her apron and flicked it at Turk, dusting his newly swept floor with a billow of flour.

"You find someone better'n me—someone who's made a good name for hisself," he told her.

"So, what's your real name, Turk?" Ruby said.

"Ain't you ever heard of courtesy, girl?" Turk asked, surprised.

"Laws, I was raised on courtesy! When I was a girl and a stranger showed up at our ranch, Ma always offered food. And my daddy gave him tobacco. In fact, he tacked a note to the door when we was gone that said, 'Help yourself to grub—please feed the chickens.'"

Turk smiled. "What if they was on the dodge from the law?"

"Most of 'em probably was, but my folks allowed them their privacy. After one cowboy had finished his dinner, I asked him what his name was. 'Jones is the name,' he said. As soon as he rode off, Ma laid into me for being so ill-mannered as to ask any man his name."

"So why you askin' me, if you know it's an impoliteness?"

"Because you're not a stranger—you're a friend."

The old man looked at Ruby fondly. "It's 'cause you're a friend that I'll keep it to 'Turk.' Don't want you influenced by my past."

"You think I'd judge? After all the mud I'm draggin' through? Come on, how'd you turn into a cook? Just tell me that." She got out a cigar and handed it to him. "Let's set outside a bit," she said, knowing he couldn't resist a smoke and an audience at the same time.

"Seein' as how you're producing the grandchild I'll never have, I'll trust you with my history." He carried the stool outside for Ruby and sprawled himself on a deteriorating rocker that squawked when he sat. "From the time I was fifteen, I was cow punching. Came up from the south and joined an outfit. But you can only be a cowboy for so long before your bones betray you," Turk rubbed his back unconsciously.

"Something breaks or the arthritis sets in, and you can't handle those thickheaded, panic-prone beeves any more." He rocked back and puffed the cigar. "Then a man finds another career. Like cookin' 'em."

Turk had been a top hand until his knees stopped bending backwards with every dip of the horse. He took over in the chuck wagon, where he was respected as a know-it-all and a considerable talker. He held that it did a man no good to be more brilliant than others unless he let them know about it, more or less endlessly.

"I ran foul of a bad man in some Abilene gambling house back when I was punchin.' And the bad man, who had a record of having killed someone somewhere, attempted to take some sort of liberty with one of my bets. When I politely requested the bad man keep his hands off, the bad man became very angry and made some rude remarks. I walked out."

"Don't you take it all!" Ruby said. "Is this a lesson on forgiveness?"

"You ain't heard the rest of the story. This same man hooked up with our outfit a couple a years later, and I recognized him right off. He didn't take no account of me, being bearded now, and a mere cook. He was a bit of a braggart, telling the boys how dangerous and feared he was."

Turk chewed on the wet stump of his cigar, remembering.

"Did any of the other cowboys know about Abilene?" Ruby asked.

"Yeh, they did. But cowboys are a private lot. They don't share news that's not theirs to share.

"Well, the bad man went on irritating the hands, and one night, a couple of weeks into the ride, he beat up on a boy who helped me with the chuck wagon. This particular boy was a mite slow, didn't catch on quick, and was a bit too friendly in a child-like way. He smiled too much, eager to please. The cowboys liked him and put up with his gregarious manner. But he got in the rascal's hair, and he beat the kid—boy lost an eye.

"There was talk of stringing this devil up or shooting him on the spot—he was a bad man, a killer. But cowboys are merely folks, just plain, everyday, bowlegged humans, not wanting trouble. They decided to let things ride till we got to town.

"Next morning, there was a little ruckus, and somebody found him dead in his blanket. No bullet, no noose, no nothing, but dead as could be."

Turk stopped talking, cracked his knuckles, and stood up. He looked back at the dark sky as if he had finished his story.

"Well, tell me the end!" said Ruby. "What happened?"

"I poisoned him," said Turk, burying the cigar stump with his toe. "That's why I changed my name." He chuckled silently and went back inside the Blue Belle.

Summer in Texas came early that year. Ruby was planting gooseberry bushes along the side of the house when a rider stopped out front and dismounted. "Name's Nate Brannigan. Mind if I have a drink of water?" he asked.

She nodded her permission and he guided his horse to the trough and pump. Sudsing his hands with the bar of homemade soap tied to the spigot, he doused his face in the large washbowl and cooled his head using a pitcher on an adjacent wooden stand. Ruby retrieved a batch of buttermilk biscuits from the house.

"Mighty nice of you, ma'am," he said, helping himself. "Your husband build that furniture?" he asked, indicating the chairs and tables stacked on the old buckboard used for display.

"My daddy did. You needing something to furnish a house?"

"No, just admiring the craftsmanship. I'm a carpenter myself. Right now, I'm looking for any kind of work. I'd be glad to do odd jobs, such as house painting, or fixups around the farm. Hoping to bring my wife out here when I get a place."

"You make coffins by any chance? They're always needed. That was my daddy's sideline, and it turned him into an undertaker. 'Make folks comfortable whether here or there,' he used to say."

Nate smiled easily. "This a friendly community? Been wintering at Sam's Town, but I didn't like the atmosphere. Kinda tight. Lots of work there, if you don't mind the folks running things, but no place for a family. Greenville any better?"

"Guess it depends on your perspective," Ruby said.

Olive poked her head out of the workshop. Her hair was grayer than usual, pushed up in a big comb, but her eyes sparkled with the old energy that had been missing since her husband died. "Does Turk cook rats?" she asked Ruby. "If so, he could keep the Blue Belle going for years on what I've found in here."

"Don't give him ideas, Ma. He'd douse 'em with hot sauce and pass 'em off in some kind of stew."

Brushing off sawdust, Olive shook out her apron and said, "I don't know what we'll do with that mess, Ruby. There're fixings for movables piled to the rafters, some of it damp and rotten. If the roof weren't leaking so bad, I'd set fire to it and cremate the remains. Oh, how we need a man."

Noticing the stranger for the first time, she looked at Ruby.

"Ma, this here's Nate Brannigan. Seems you two have a lot to talk about."

That evening was beautiful. Ruby and her mother sat on the porch in rockers her father had made and watched the moon sail across the prairie. Wind stirred the cottonwoods and willows down by the river.

"I miss the smell of tobacco," Olive mused. "Wonder if Nate Brannigan smokes." Jeremy had smoked a pipe. Every night, he'd knocked the dottle loose on the porch rail to indicate bedtime. The memory settled in on both women, and they rocked with nostalgia scenting the air with pipe smoke.

"I'm going away after the baby comes," Ruby announced quietly. "I been mostly worried about you being alone with all the work, but Brannigan seems anxious to help out. His wife'll give you company." She leaned back and lost herself in the bright sky. "I can't stay here, Ma; you know I can't."

Olive wasn't surprised, but the words saddened her.

"Maybe things will change for you after," she told her daughter. "Folks are always scandalized by a single girl in the family way but less so by a mother with a child."

"That's what Turk says, but I need a new start. Will you look after the baby until I get a job and a place to stay? I'll send for you then."

"Oh, Ruby, I can't leave the ranch. This is where my memories are, where your daddy's buried. It's where my life is."

"Not mine, Ma. I'll make good, though. I will."

She told Turk the next day, with a little more explanation. "Swede Dobson looks at me like I'm one of your chocolate cakes." Imagining his full lips made her think of a dog salivating over a hunk of meat. "He knows more details about that night than I do," Ruby said. "So does Len Grove. Jesse's made me out as a harlot—he'd like to ride me out on a rail, mainly because a baby might make me seem respectable. Then his tittle-tattle will be harder for the saloon boys to swallow."

"Where will you go?" Turk asked her.

"I heard there's jobs in Sam's Town, and the stage goes there. Ma said she'd take care of the baby for me, until I settle in."

"Sam Lester is a thug, runs everything over there and takes a cut. Steer clear of him."

"I'm getting used to steering clear of people. You and Ma are the only people in Greenville who speak to me with a drop of kindness. For the baby's sake, I'm trying to keep hatred from filling me up to the brim. Sam's Town can't be worse than here." Taking control of the tightness in her voice, Ruby went on. "Do you have any more of that poison? I'd like to invite a few of the townsfolk to tea before I leave."

The girl had sass, and Turk admired that. "Sweetheart, you couldn't kill a soul," he told her.

"I could kill more than one if I had enough reason," she answered without hesitation. "Some days I could kill Jesse, but then I remember he's just telling the truth on me. I'm not some innocent victim. I made a choice, and now I've got to answer for my own calamity."

The Bull Horn Saloon was jumping when Turk came out of the Blue Belle that night. Wrapped around the doorway, cowboys jawed about the upcoming cattle drives, reliving stampedes, and Indian attacks. Talk turned to the triumphant parades through towns on the Chisholm Trail, where knifings and brawls were a nightly occurrence.

"Wichita has the finest palace of pleasure I've ever seen," one puncher boasted. "Gilded chandeliers, gold spittoons, and the women are expensive articles. In broad daylight, they glide through the streets, carrying fancy derringers slung to their waists."

"They spread their diseases too generously for me," another man said. "I'd rather meet up with a fresh farmer's daughter who'll show me a good time in the loft."

Turk recognized Jesse's voice, crowing his own exploits to the crowd of strangers. "The hay in my stable was good enough for one red-haired bundle of fire. She's got the bluest eyes you've ever seen, and she couldn't wait to have at me."

The boy's eyesight was so poor, he didn't see Turk elbowing his way through the men as he regaled them with his exploits. "Then she pushed me back on the hay and said, 'I'm in your hands now.'" The gaping black hole in his mouth showed, and he went on, "Her legs were…"

Turk was six feet from Jesse now, and he lunged. He slashed savagely at Jesse's face and missed but followed through with his elbow and caught Jesse in the mouth. The younger man staggered backwards, and then Turk drove a smashing blow into his face that knocked him sprawling on his back.

He leaped on him and landed on his chest with his knees, driving the wind from him in one coughing grunt. Turk grabbed the straps of his overalls, twisted them in his hands and came off Jesse, dragging him to his feet.

When Jesse's knees took the weight, Turk hit him again in the face. He hit him with a long, looping overhand smash that caught Jesse on the shelf of the jaw and turned his head abruptly and tore him out of Turk's grasp. The tie rail caught Jesse across the small of the back. He arched his back, and then the tie rail split with a sound like a gunshot, and Jesse was lying in the dust of the street.

"Ain't that the old cook from next door?" one of the cowboys asked another.

The hard, calm look of power was in Turk's face. "That's me," he acknowledged. "And I know how to wring the neck of a chicken."

He told Ruby about it the next day when she found him soaking his bruised knuckles in a basin of soda water. "Oh, Turk. I'm just glad you didn't get arrested."

"Me, too, sweetheart. The town's buzzing with it—an old man taking apart that plug-ugly sissy." He massaged his fingers. "No law cares about that kind of brawl. It's given me quite a standing, though," he said, with not a little pride.

All the trauma of his earliest beginning was forgiven when JJ made his unassuming appearance. With a minimum of effort, Ruby gave birth on July 1, 1873. "He just fell out," she told Turk a few days later.

Olive was the only attendant needed, and her promise was fulfilled. "It was all such a miracle, I didn't even notice the pain," Ruby repeated. "It helped that he was just six pounds and a puny eighteen inches. Clara Brannigan had a tinier one the same week, and it took thirty hours of agony and a pair of forceps to bring that tyke into the world."

His grandmother declared JJ the most beautiful child she'd ever seen, while Turk secretly thought he looked like another species. Bald and red-faced, with blue eyes that bugged out like a grasshopper's, he had a high-pitched screech that could be felt as well as heard.

"I'll christen him myself," Ruby said when her mother asked about a church service.

Turk brought a sweet potato pie, pungent with cinnamon, and the Brannigans furnished their special brew of cider flavored with rose petals.

"Clara kind of invited herself," explained Olive under her breath.

Nobody cared that the ceremony was short and simple. Holding her son, Ruby said, "Because your daddy was Jack and my daddy was Jeremy, you'll carry both of those names. One you can live up to, the other you can live down. I'll call you JJ."

Olive followed up with an, "Amen," and the toasts were underway. The Brannigan baby was already chubby, guzzling greedily at his mother's full breast. Ruby noticed the milk bubbling around the infant's mouth and looked away quickly. Her own breasts were back to normal size already, and JJ fussed frantically whenever she tried to nurse him. She often wondered if there was anything in there, since he hardly swallowed at all.

Clara handed the baby to her husband and buttoned her dress; Ruby felt another pang of jealousy watching the couple. JJ wailed pitifully, and she knew she was expected to calm his cries, but she was embarrassed for the others to see the frustration of feeding time.

In the quiet of her bedroom, she tried to guide the hungry baby's mouth, but every time he latched on, his head bobbed back and forth in a frenzy, and he resumed his squall. A quiet knock at her door sounded just before it opened. Expecting Olive, Ruby was surprised to see Clara Brannigan peeking in.

"My first baby had a cry like that," Clara said, closing the door.

"You had another one?" Ruby asked.

"He came too early and was gone in less than a week."

Not knowing what to say, Ruby tried to shush JJ.

Clara said, "It must be hard on your own."

"I have Ma."

"That's how it was with my first, too." Sympathy was bright in Clara's eyes. "His pa died before we could get married. After the baby died, I ran away and then I met my husband. He doesn't know—nobody does. But I've been wanting to tell you."

Ruby's eyes glistened with tears. "Thank you, Clara."

"Another thing," Clara said briskly, clearing the air of emotion. "You don't have any milk, do you?"

"I don't know how to tell. But he cries all the time, and I don't think he's filling out yet."

Clara opened her dress again and took the baby. "Let me try."

JJ jerked his head around furiously, but Clara gently touched his cheek and, in a moment, he was suckling. Now Ruby's tears splashed down her cheeks. "It's too much," she hiccupped. "I can't do it all."

Clara held out her hand and Ruby took it. "Yes. You can."

6

When the last days of September were gone and the first ones of October were crisping the air, Ruby left Greenville. It was a good clear day, warm, with that smoky look in the distance that comes with the prairie autumn.

Clara had spent part of every day at the Dawsons', and Ruby had regularly walked JJ over to her pa's old workshop, which was rapidly becoming a snug home for the young Brannigan family. After the initial jealousy had worn off, Ruby was thrilled to see JJ's progress with his new wet nurse, and it bonded the two mothers in a trusting friendship. Olive and Clara promised the baby would be taken care of until Ruby was ready to send for him.

Nine passengers were stuffed inside the red and yellow stagecoach to Sam's Town. Five others endured the rocking on top, including the conductor and driver, hanging onto mail, baggage, and an express chest. Stops every ten miles provided a chance for Ruby to unbraid her legs from those of the old lady across from her.

"Pepper Junction lives up to its name as a six-bit stop." A middle-aged man told them about the home station where they'd stay overnight. "It's one of those towns that'll be blown away by a blue norther one of these days." He was thin, with a gray goatee and a windy, irritating voice. His accent was altogether Southern, and he wore a Confederate campaign hat, which lay far back on his head. Both thumbs were well hooked into his suspenders. Casting a furtive look at Ruby, he asked, "Where you heading from Sam's Town, young lady?"

"That's where I get off," she said, with dignity. "Got a little boy I need to raise on my own, so I'm tryin' to get me a stake, before I send for him."

"That town's run by outlaws, I hear," the woman directly behind Ruby said. Sitting back to back, it was hard to have a conversation over the creaks of the coach. "No law there," she went on, "but money flows the streets like beer from a barrel."

"Sounds like just what you need, girlie," the woman's husband injected. "Fill yer mug quick, and get outta town afore anybody sees yer there."

"Not likely, with this one," the Confederate said, appraising Ruby. "You need to turn around, old man; fill yer eyes with this sweet memory."

Pepper Junction consisted of about a dozen log huts; low, small, rude affairs, four-fifths of which were covered with dirt for roofing. Little, swift-turning whirlwinds spun the powdery dust in the streets as the coach pulled up to a corral about suppertime. A hand lettered sign read "Hot Food and Accommodations for the Weary Traveler," with an arrow pointing left. Ruby climbed down stiffly and took in the dilapidation around her.

Apparently, the rise and fall of the town had been swift. "After the cattle started coming through, things built up." A gray-haired man with a thin, black mustache lectured the passengers as he led them down the street to the Prickly Pear Hotel. "We had us a boarding house, a saloon, five general stores, a hotel, and a jail." There was a silence, and then he added proudly, "I served as deputy for a time. Name's Lund."

Late evening shadows heightened an atmosphere of abandonment, and he continued his history lesson. "During the summer season, the town was noisy—cattle bawling, horses' hooves—there were shootings and knifings most every night. When you heard one or two shots, you waited breathlessly for a third. A third shot meant a death on Juniper Street. Decent folks moved away, 'til we got things under control."

A heavy canvas curtain was the only door covering the entrance to the Prickly Pear. Large and mostly empty, the room had two wooden trestle tables close by an old cast iron stove. Next to an open fireplace, a single cot appeared to be the only bed in the hotel. Passengers lined up for a two-seater outhouse, which was far enough from the back entrance that the flies and pungency weren't noticeable.

The proprietor stirred some crushed eggshells into a pot of coffee and picked up his story. "Rough Creek is usually too low to paddle, but a few years back, a downpour overflowed it—cattle got caught in the flash flood, and so did some cowboys." He checked to see that the brew was clear of grounds and poured the coffee into tin cups.

"After that, the trail changed," the man went on. "Pepper Junction was off the map, and Sam's Town was in the right place to collect our business and our money. We been watching ghosts move in ever since."

Following a meal of fried chicken, steaming squash soup, and sourdough biscuits with pecan butter, Lund said, "The charge is six bits, two bits each for supper, bed, and breakfast." He graciously accepted their money. "Mighty obliged. Stagecoach folks is the only commerce we get here."

While the others spread out on bedrolls, Ruby sat at the table with Lund. "Been hearing tales about Sam's Town. Is it such a dangerous place?" she asked.

"Mind your p's and q's, and you won't have a problem. Get in Sam's way, and he'll run you over. Or, at least, his lackeys will."

Lund poured a shot of vinegar and drank it straight down. The mustache pinched over his mouth, and his nose wrinkled and twitched before he shook his head in a shiver. "Digestive cure," he grimaced. With a burp, he went on.

"Sam has some hoodlums, I'll tell you. To remedy our wild days, Pepper Junction didn't allow guns to be carried in the city limits. Cowboys saw the notices and deposited their arms with the sheriff or me—made things safer for everybody.

"Couple 'a Sam's boys came into town one day after the ban and jauntily filled them notices full of bullet holes. Well, we throwed 'em in jail. Sam sponsored a bonfire and burned it down, and course they got away."

Lund was bewitched by Ruby's attention to his stories. Women, especially beautiful women, were never so fascinated by him, and he found himself caught up, unable to stop rambling. Soft, pink lips parted in wonder at his tale, and rapt, blue eyes encouraged him to go on.

"Soon as the jail was rebuilt, Snake and Erly—that's their names—came in and tore it down, just to show they could. No other reason.

"It was rebuilt under day-and-night guard. Some kid with a stutter got hisself incarcerated for being drunk; he was freed in a few hours by those boys. They chased the jailer, broke the lock, and rode away with the kid."

"Why are they so loyal to Sam?"

"The way I heer'd it, Sam sorta' owns 'em. Stole a bunch 'a money from the Confederates and lit out with big promises to his boys. Long as they stay, they're paid—full-fledged renegades, I reckon. Sure you don't want to live in Pepper Junction, where it's quiet?" Lund smiled full on at Ruby, and she noticed a dimple in his left cheek.

Charmed, she teased, "I can cook up some prickly pear that would have this place live up to its name." Her red-gold hair lay like a flame on her shoulders and caught in the light of the fire.

"Ruby, you're the prettiest girl I've ever seen." Lund couldn't catch his words before they escaped into the quiet room.

"Maybe I'll come back here after a few months in Sam's Town—share my fortune with Pepper Junction." He laughed easily as she lightly caught his outburst.

Ruby liked Lund. Used to attention for her looks, she could tell when a man felt comfortable in her company and took pleasure in her wit, like Jack seemed to, and now this man.

Blowing out through puffed lips, she sighed and gathered her hair into the black ribbon from her wrist. "Time for some shut eye," she said, wondering how she'd fall asleep in this room full of bodily noises.

Lund curled up on the narrow cot and listened to the movements as she settled herself on the blanket. Her soft breathing a few moments later was the only sound he could hear.

Sam's Town wasn't very impressive looking as they rode in just after noon. It was a jumble of muddy streets lined with tents, tarpaper shacks, and crude buildings constructed of raw, unplanned lumber. Plank sidewalks ran in front of the buildings on Prescott Street, and a few lone pines loomed over them. Main Street was adjacent to Prescott, and when the stage turned the corner, Ruby had her introduction to the more established part of Sam's Town.

Main Street, a prong-shaped thoroughfare with three streets running parallel, was a double line of false-front buildings, most of them unpainted and graying in the weather. Here were the saloons, the honky-tonks, the stores dealing in firearms, boots, hats, and horse blankets; here waited the Calico Queens and the Painted Cats, ready to entertain the gallants of Texas. Overall, the peppery odor of new pine mingled with the smell of excited animals crowded in the corrals at the end of town.

Horses raised clouds of dust from the unpaved thoroughfare, and footsteps echoed on the wooden sidewalks. Knots of cowboys swaggered along these sidewalks, joking boisterously among themselves and shouting profane greetings to old friends. Under a tree, a black minstrel was strumming his ballads, luring a small crowd toward a crony who was bellowing out the bids for an impromptu horse auction. On a bare spot of ground at the other end of the street, two snarling dogs were locked in mortal combat, surrounded by cowhands betting on the outcome.

The Fat Chance Saloon was the town's dominant enterprise. Three men smoked against one of the hitching rails in front of it, waiting for the stagecoach. As it approached, they straightened from their casual poses and walked forward to the stop. They had the look of a semiofficial welcoming committee.

Hard laughter from a group of prostitutes rose above the tumult—four lusty women with dyed hair, wearing bloomers and bustiers without outer clothing. Ruby heard a rumble of voices, amplified by liquor, the rattle of poker chips, and a fiddle playing "Pop Goes the Weasel" on the balcony. Mostly men, the guests watched as a striking black woman sauntered in among the roughs and entered the saloon to hoots and hollers, breathing in the immoral atmosphere with gusto.

In the midst of this racket, there were contrasting islands of tranquility. Ponies waited patiently in front of the shops and saloons, some tethered to hitching posts but most restrained only by the fact that the reins were hanging to the ground.

On the veranda of the Empire Hotel, elegantly dressed men were sealing deals for the exchange of thousands of head of cattle and many thousands of dollars with a few quiet words, a handshake, and a drink. The sidewalks were strewn with silent knots of cowhands who, because of lack of money or their own temperate ways—or perhaps sheer exhaustion—were bypassing the seamier action in town, whittling thoughtfully with their jackknives.

Over the entire scene hovered the stern silence of disapproval that came from the town's respectable citizens. Although business depended on these visitors from the cattle drives, Sam's Town suffered from a basic schizophrenia about the element of rowdiness the cowboys brought with them.

Ruby swung down off the coach with ease on her own. The driver caught her with a hand on either side of her waist, handling her as if she weighed no more than a doll and then hoisted her scuffed, leather suitcase from off the top.

A pasty, yellow-haired man with a scar on his cheek stood slightly in front of his cronies and raised a hand in greeting as she stepped down. He came close to touching her red curls as they dazzled in the sunshine.

"Howdy," he said, with an imitation smile that didn't reach his chilly eyes. "Welcome to Sam's Town. They call me Sam Lester."

Ruby remembered all she'd heard about Sam, not just from Lund. "He's a rogue," Turk had said. "After a family called Prescott founded the town, Sam and his gang blew in from some place in Virginia—shot up the stores. Lester's boys have been riding roughshod over the whole town since then, and nobody's dared to stand up to them."

Nate Brannigan had added, "Sam is some sort of army deserter." He'd glanced at Turk. "Got his thumb cut off running from the Rebs. His hoodlums are stationed around, keeping tabs on who comes and goes."

Meeting the legend was a big disappointment. Lester turned out to be scrawny with a sallow complexion, standing about five feet nine inches, and weighing no more than 140 pounds. His eyes were milky blue, and his mustache was thin, a sickly tan color, and he coughed incessantly. Ruby felt an instinctive dislike for the man, and a shiver crept up her neck as she felt his gaping stare.

"This here is Snake," Sam said, nodding toward a burly man in a derby hat and a blue, silk bandanna. "And Haze." That was the ferret-faced man in the frock coat. "They're associates of mine. We been hopin' for some mail-order brides to arrive in town. You one of them?" His clammy fingers petted her cheek.

"No, I'm not," Ruby said, shuddering. She didn't want to continue this conversation. "Have you got a hotel here?"

"Yeah, kind of a high falutin' place. Or the boarding hotel. You can put up there a whole lot cheaper." Sam turned to point along the curving street. "Go on around the corner, past the general mercantile, and you'll see the Bosque Hotel on the left."

Ruby nodded. "Much obliged," she said, picking up her suitcase.

"If there's anything else I can help you with, young lady, come back here to the Fat Chance and ask for me. I'm sort of the unofficial mayor of Sam's Town, and my saloon is the temporary city hall, until I get a formal place built."

"I'll remember that," Ruby said. In reality, though, she wanted as little as possible to do with Sam Lester.

The boarding house was a large two-story frame building with a false front. Extending out from each side were small wings with walls made of canvas. In the winter, which was coming soon, it would probably be ice cold in those rooms.

A cadaverous man with a smile on his skull-like face stood near the entrance with a Bible in his hands. "Welcome to Sam's Town, ma'am," he said as Ruby arrived in front of the place. "I'm Reverend Kincaid, and if you have any spiritual needs to tend to, I'd be happy to help you in coming to the Lord. In the meantime, I'm collecting for our permanent fund for orphans, if you'd care to contribute."

"Sorry, Reverend. I don't have a penny to spare." Ruby wondered if the man was a burner for Sam. She had a feeling he was crooked, too.

Mrs. Randall, a prim, well-corseted woman of sixty-five, introduced herself as the landlady.

"Is there any work in town?" Ruby asked, as she signed the register and counted out the coins for a night's stay.

Mrs. Randall's almost invisible eyebrows pulled together, and she frowned. "Not unless you want to work for Sam Lester. Then there's plenty. He owns it all. Even took this place over."

"But he pays you?"

"Enough to keep us here, not enough to let us leave." She looked down at Ruby's signature and blotted the ink. The register went back on the shelf, and she searched the cubbies behind the desk for the heavy key hanging from a wooden knob. "We drifted west after the war and built us this nice little hotel here in Prescott—that was the name of town until Sam came."

"Then it is your place," said Ruby.

"Was. Sam and his bunch hightailed it into Prescott one day, shooting up a storm. One particular thug is called Erly. He rode his horse right through that door and says to Curly Bill—he's my husband—he says, 'I'll buy this place for a dollar.'" This was a story Mrs. Randall had told often, and she performed it well.

"He's yukkin' it up, but Bill holds his own. 'Looks like you don't have many customers,' the rider says. Then he picked up a china plate and threw it at Bill's feet. 'You better be lookin' to sell, cuz this hotel is worth less and less.'

"'I'm not gonna sell,' says Bill. That impudent outlaw shot Bill in the knee and rode his horse all through this lobby. 'I gotta reduce my offer now,' he said. 'The merchandise is damaged.'"

"Isn't there any law here?" Ruby asked.

"Law—Sam established himself as the head honcho by forming a lynch mob of his men, threatening anyone who opposed his takeover. No one bucks Sam, especially as he's surrounded by savages. Now, everybody's just got used to it. As long as things stay relatively peaceful, nobody cares who's running things. It's Sam's Town."

Ruby took her key, and Mrs. Randall said, "I'm surprised he didn't grab you right off the stagecoach. He's a lecherous lowlife with women, too. Why, if you'd come wrapped in a cocoon, he'd see through to your bloomers." Her rheumy eyes examined the travel-worn girl. "Wouldn't need to today, though. Your dress is almost invisible, stuck to you with perspiration like it is."

Embarrassed, Ruby pulled out her bodice and used her hand to fan herself. A flush crept up her chest into her cheeks, and she untied her red hair to let the air cool her scalp. Just then, Sam came through the double doors, leaving Haze to stand guard outside.

"Mrs. Randall helping you settle in?" he asked. "It's mighty warm in here." He stepped closer and blew on the girl's temples then pushed back the damp tendrils with the stump of a thumb. The sour stench made Ruby catch her breath, and she twisted away from his touch.

Sam went behind the desk and retrieved the register. "Ruby Dawson," he read. "Room thirteen." He came back around and leaned close to her ear. "Lucky thirteen, I'd say. Allow me to take care of your expenses, as a gesture of welcome."

"I'm obliged, Mr. Lester, but I'll be paying my own way." When she bent over for her suitcase, he cupped her bottom. She gasped. "You varmint!" Stepping back onto his toe, Ruby whirled around and walloped him with a loud slap. "I am not some strumpet you can stroke like a stray dog."

Haze burst in, his coat open to reveal a pistol, but Sam motioned him off. Putting a hand to his reddening cheek, he said with amusement, "Even stray dogs figure out who feeds 'em, Miss Dawson."

Doc Simpson stood outside his office, watching the dogfight. "The cattle men are no more welcome to me than a summer hailstorm," he told Spen Harris, who stepped out from next door. "The devil comes to town with jingling spurs. We're becoming like Abilene."

Spen had a ragged cloth tape measure dangling around his neck. "Freshly paid cowboys give me their money for new duds. I can't complain," he said, shading his eyes.

The two men were both about forty; both were bearded and well-dressed, but different in every other way. Harris came from New York City looking for money and thrills in the Wild West. As a clothier, his adventures were only vicarious through his customers, but he liked the spirit they carried.

The doctor had started out as a traveling veterinarian, but after rescuing an unconscious man from premature burial, he gave himself a promotion. Widowed and childless, he had become preachier than the preacher. "In Abilene, money and whiskey flow like water downhill," he opined now. "Youth and beauty are wrecked and damned in that valley of perdition." Spen wondered suddenly if Abilene would be a better place to set up shop.

Ruby came up behind them. "Excuse me, gentlemen, but I'm looking for work," she said. Simultaneously, the men looked across the street at a Mexican man standing outside the Empire Hotel. Six feet tall, weighing about two hundred pounds, he had no surplus flesh. A gun rested against his broad shoulder, and he stood erect, wearing a bright Indian blanket across his back, in spite of the warm autumn weather. Granite eyes felt hard as they slid past Ruby to glare at Spen and Doc Simpson and then back at the customers entering the Fat Chance Saloon.

Spen glanced at his neighbor and answered for both of them. "We've got no work for you." Simpson turned back to his office, and the tailor nodded at the striking young woman and stepped off the boardwalk into the street.

"Is there a restaurant nearby? I'm a good cook." She followed Spen past a paper sign tacked to the tying post that announced Dry Goods for the festive cowboy: Harris Haberdashery.

Walking faster, he looked back at her and said, "The restaurant won't be hiring, either." Almost trotting now, Spen caught up to another businessman and paid no more attention to Ruby.

Pictures of solemn cowboys in faraway places hung in the window of a Frenchman's photography studio. A line of patrons stood outside the door, patiently awaiting the chance to stand in front of a choice of backdrops—London, Paris, or Venice. Relatives back east would proudly display pictures of their boys, decked out in holsters and ten-gallon hats, posed in exotic settings.

Catching the attention of the photographer, Ruby said, "I'm new in Sam's Town. Are you hiring? I would be a dependable assistant."

"Je n'ai pas besoin d'un assistant," the youthful proprietor said, shooing her away.

"He might not want your help, but I sure would." A puncher laughed and made a crude gesture to his compadre and then sang, "Oo-la-la," in a high falsetto, grabbing at her as she made a nervous getaway through the crowd.

From the corner of her eye, Ruby noticed a buckskinned cowboy leaned back against the false front of the sheriff's office across the street. Silver buckles decorated his Stetson, which was black and creased on top, with rolled sides. He straightened like a soldier when a bull-shaped, bearded man wearing an old Confederate hat approached him on the boardwalk. The cowboy pointed at her with the stub of a cigarette, and the bearded man hollered something and crossed the street to the saloon.

"Don't pay that cowboy no mind," said a girl's voice. "That's Buzz Mills, our sheriff." A young seamstress sat in a partially open doorway stitching a shirt. "He's in Sam's pocket, just like everybody else around here."

"Can I come in?" Ruby responded, glad to escape the street for a minute. A bell on the door jingled when she pushed it enough to walk through. "I'm looking for a job," she stated with feigned confidence.

"I'm Sally," the girl said and kicked the door shut. "And you won't find work in this shop. Sam's already seen to that."

"Why? What have I done to upset him?"

Sally had yellow braids twisted in a dome on top of her head. Without the light from outside, Ruby noticed that she looked straight ahead while she traced her work with her fingers instead of her eyes. "You stood up to him. He'll never forgive you for that." Sally felt around for some scissors on a small table next to her.

"Sam has something on almost everybody in town," the girl went on, "a mortgage, a debt, knowledge of some private secret." She shrugged. "Nobody ever goes against him."

"How does he know what I'm doing here?"

"His spies, I reckon. Snake came in here an hour ago, said some girl had talked back to Sam. Told my aunt not to be hiring anybody new." She used a small wire to rethread her needle, pushing it through expertly. "See, Sam saved the shop when my uncle died, but Aunt Maude was obliged to pay him in some vile ways. He leaves her alone now, if she does his bidding."

"Well. I've got to find something. I'm a good cook. Is there a restaurant, anywhere? I've got a little boy to support back in Greenville." Tears choked her voice. "I need to get a job." Sinking down on the floor in front of Sally, she sighed. "I spent most all my money getting here, and I need to pay Mrs. Randall again tomorrow."

"You won't find a job if Sam's down on you. It's just a fact. But if you kowtow to him, he'll hire you. The Empire has a restaurant, and so does the Fat Chance. You'd get paid good at the saloon, if you were willing to be more than a cook."

"A dance hall girl?" Ruby asked, shocked at the girl's lack of propriety.

"Why not? They get room and board—meat every meal, so I hear. They're not all shady ladies, either."

"Even if they're not, folks think they are."

"Do you even know any folks here?" asked Sally. "Why should you care? One of the doves told me she makes $200 a month! More'n I make sewing homespun, that's for sure."

"Laws! You really know a fancy lady?"

"Sure do. Black Pearl." Sally nodded. "I made her a dress. Has a husband in Colorado and in a couple of months, she'll have enough to join him. And he'll never even know. Course, she says she just dances, but I suspect she does more'n that."

"I'd like to speak with Mr. Lester," Ruby told a Mexican girl the next morning at the Fat Chance Saloon. Thick, black braids reached her waist, which was tiny. Crimson ribbons hung loose over a plunging neckline and stood out against skin the color of coffee, well laced with cream. Ruffled petticoats were caught up in the back to show short, white satin pantalets. There was a hollow look in her black eyes, and she was careful not to show her teeth when she spoke.

"Thees way," she said with a Spanish accent. Respectable women did not come to saloons, and Ruby attracted attention.

"Tequila! Who's the chica?" a dark-haired man called out.

The girl whispered to Ruby, "Sam, he calls me Tequila, but my name is Tessa." She smiled naturally then and showed stained front teeth, which she quickly hid behind her hand.

Sam sat at a large, round table in the front of the room, where the unofficial town council held court. He didn't look up immediately—a decade of cowardice had frozen his nervous face into a vicious indifference. The cough he was constantly trying to smother started softly, like low gears meshing, and he seemed to be shaken with silent laughter. When he looked up, he put his bright, feverish glance on Ruby, and there was a murderous dare in him. Two circles of color stained his cheekbones above the stubble of his blond beard, helping the illusion of delicacy that was in his slight frame and thin hands. The coughing fit passed, and he snorted loudly, stood up, and acknowledged Ruby.

"The red jewel," he said. The flush faded, and his complexion was almost yellow in the dim light away from the window. "I had hoped you'd reconsider my offer."

"As you likely know, Mr. Lester, I need a job. Folks in town have been persuaded—by you—not to hire me," said Ruby.

"Sorry about the misunderstanding," Sam said to Ruby. "I like to look out for the well-being of newcomers to Sam's Town. Find 'em the right position, you see."

He led her over to a long mahogany bar on the left, which was overlooked by a life-sized painting of a nude woman. Her head was back, eyes closed, and her long black hair curled over her body, barely covering the parts the patrons were hoping to see.

Ruby had never been inside such a place. A dozen poker tables and three faro layouts were scattered throughout the spacious room, and some stairs at the back led up to a second-floor balcony. She could see rooms opening off the upstairs hall. Pot-bellied stoves sat in two corners to heat the large area in the winter.

Even this early in the morning, the main room was full of men, most of them hard-faced hombres in wool or leather vests. A buffalo robe hung over an upright piano in the back corner before the wall opened to a billiard room. The crack of balls echoed back to the bar. River rock was set in an adobe fireplace, which took up a whole wall of the second room. Calf hides and varmint pelts were nailed to the paneling, and a set of seven-foot steer horns adorned the cottonwood mantelpiece.

Pa would love all this wood, Ruby thought, forgetting her errand. The walls were of Louisiana cypress, the beamed ceiling of Texas red cedar. Framed mirrors hung at strategic places around the room, reflecting light and making the place seem even bigger than it was.

Sam pulled out a stool for Ruby and asked, "What's your pleasure, my jewel?" Without waiting for her answer, he called to a waitress behind the bar. "Two beers, Molly."

This girl was older, at least twenty-eight, and not as timid as Tessa. Early as it was, her lips were rouged and her eyes were ringed with dark brown paint that matched high-arched eyebrows. White-blond ringlets were gathered on top of her head with a circlet of pink pearls. Molly slid two mugs down the bar. "There you go, honey," she said without looking up.

"You don't know me, Mr. Lester," Ruby told him. "How could you possibly decide what job I should have?"

Flicking the stump on his left hand unconsciously, he said, "It's my profession to recognize skills in pretty girls. And, by the way, I'm called Sam by all of them." Brass spittoons were spaced along the floor next to the bar. With a practiced aim, he spit a wad of tobacco past the shoe Ruby rested on the brass foot rail and into the pot. He wiped his scraggly beard with a damp towel that hung from the bar, while a patron waited to dry the suds off his long-handled mustache on the same towel.

"The wrongs inflicted on working women are many," Sam quoted, fondling her knee through the blue denim skirt. "Shopkeepers have daughters to sell their wares and wives to produce their goods. Hideous, little creatures hawk vegetables in the streets for a pittance, sell toothpicks or matches; but not you, Ruby. You are a jewel."

Perspiration beaded on Ruby's forehead. The room was stifling, and Sam's words pressed in on her fears. Shifting away from his touch, she took a sip from the mug in front of her, and then a long, cool swallow. "And what skill do I have?" she asked dully. His answer surprised her.

"Making money," he said. "Do you wonder why my employees are unwavering? It's not because I'm likeable. It's because I'm generous. I pay well for loyalty."

Despair combined with the alcohol to deaden her scruples. She needed money, and why should her reputation matter now? Sally's words came back to her, "Do you even know any folks here?"

"You're a smart woman," he said, looking at her with a complete, interested coldness. Then he relaxed and smiled at her, which made the scar on his cheek more noticeable. Reaching into his pocket, he produced five $20 gold pieces. He took her hand, put the gold into it, and pushed her fingers shut. Watching her closely, he asked, "You like that stuff? You want a lot of it?"

Ruby looked at the money, and Sam sensed her weakness. "My girls are classy. No cussing, yelling, or beatings. I take care of you. You'll have a room with real carpet and a bed with springs and a mattress. You'll have nice clothes and decent food, good meat. I don't want no skinny, sickly women at my place."

"You gotta take a bath, mister," Black Pearl told the man standing by the bar next to Ruby. "There's a tub down the hall, and Tequila'll scrub your back and give you a shave. Wash your hair, too. I don't want no lice in my pillows. This is a clean house."

Tall and regal, the woman looked like a figurine carved out of chocolate. She turned her brown eyes on Ruby. Round as they were, the whites softened her appearance, as did the fleecy crown of black hair. "You're Jewel?" she asked.

"Ruby."

"We don't go by our real names, much. Most soiled doves are eluding the law or at least a peeved husband." Black Pearl picked up Ruby's suitcase and walked toward the stairs. "I read an obituary of a sprightly young bird called Louise in Dodge. Died of tuberculosis, it said. And then she turned up in Fort Worth, as rosy as a peach, going by the name of Lulu. She begged me not to tell a soul, since her daddy said he'd disown her after he killed her if he heard of her sharing her virtues again." Her teeth flashed a dazzling white when she laughed.

"How'd you end up here?" Ruby asked.

"Husbands. When I find one, I end up running away. I didn't have any in Sam's Town a few years back, so I figured it was a safe place."

"Didn't think anyone would want to marry a soiled dove, meaning no offense," said Ruby.

"Everybody wants to marry us, Jewel," Pearl told her. "We understand men, know how to make 'em feel special and loved. Course, most of them drink too much, lose their shirts regular in poker games, and frequent places like this, so they don't deserve good women anyway. And we aren't the kind of girls they want to take home to meet Grandma." She chuckled, and then added wickedly, "Especially if we already know Grandpa."

The freshly scrubbed cowboy was looking up the stairs at the women. Black Pearl set the suitcase in a small bedroom and then turned her back to Ruby. "Undo my buttons, would you? A man's fingers get fidgety, and I lose one every time."

"You have to take it all the way off?" Ruby asked.

"Sure. Been at this game a long time, and I'm efficient. I undress as soon as I can so my clothes won't get messed up or torn. And I make sure his boots don't touch the linens. I keep a canvas strip at the bottom of the bed so he don't blacken my sheets."

Reverend Kincaid, tall and thin in his black clothes, came forward to splash some whiskey into a glass for Ruby, taking the opportunity to replenish his own drink at the same time. She swallowed deeply, feeling the stuff go down like fire, and caught a glimpse of herself in the mirror next to the piano.

Her red, ruffled, knee-length dress was bell-shaped, held out by a colorful pink petticoat adorned with tassels. The pink silk bodice, adorned with sequins and fringe, left her white arms and shoulders bare. Sam insisted that his girls wear lipstick and rouge, feathers in their hair, and silk stockings held up by garters displayed often by the rustling skirts. Most of the girls dyed their hair, but Ruby's was acceptable to Sam in its natural state, particularly when she left it down in a mass of brilliant red curls.

She had a moment of wanting to laugh bitterly. This girl in the mirror would be unrecognizable to her mother, who chided her for wearing boy's overalls, worried about her freckled face and her sunburned neck. A straw hat had routinely kept her hair from the wind whipping the cornstalks that scratched her brown arms. Plus, whiskey was a man's drink. After her father died, it wouldn't have occurred to the two women to have it in the Dawson house.

Ruby set the glass down on the piano and saw the lust in the preacher's face. She hoped he wasn't a real preacher, just like she hoped she wasn't a real prostitute. But the girl in the mirror looked pretty authentic.

7

Ruby had been working a week when the government came to the Fat Chance Saloon. "Got clothes-lined here in Sam's Town," a smiley, gray-haired man told Sam Lester, taking a seat at the bar. Saliva collected in the corners of his mouth, and his lips glistened as he lit a pipe. "Don't let my tin star fool you. I look the other way when I'm out of Fort Worth. There's lawbreaking enough in Cowtown…"

"You Gentleman Jake?" interrupted Buzz Mills, his voice tinged with respect.

The older man stood up and tipped his hat to his buckskinned seatmate. "I am. Can I buy you a drink, Sheriff?" he asked, noticing the badge. "I'm meeting some local lawmakers here tonight, Slock Shuster and Clay Rutherford from Hood County and a couple outa' Erath."

At the end of the bar, Molly whispered to Ruby, "When the politicians come to town, there's money to be made. Watch Sam fawn all over them—he practically drools."

Buzz introduced Sam. "This here's the owner of the finest saloon you'll find out of Hell's Half Acre," he said, referring to Fort Worth's collection of bars, dance halls, and bawdy houses.

Sam snapped his fingers at Molly. "Our finest Texas bourbon for Gentleman Jake," he barked, arranging extra chairs at his personal table. "And, Jewel, get Jingle Bob at the piano."

"Erath County's where I'm from." Ruby panicked. "What if I know these politicians?" she asked Molly.

"Don't you worry about your reputation, honey. None of them remembers faces."

Slock Shuster watched the way the captivating redhead handled herself. Her slow smile went over to him, making him smile back before he took another drink. She sat at a table by the piano, with Sheriff Mills on one side and Doc Simpson, whose cheeks were vermillion-bright, on the other. Darts were flying over by the bar, and the whack of a cue stick rang from next door, but Slock hardly noticed.

Clay Rutherford, from Hood County, rose and proposed a toast to the new legislator from Erath County, a Dane or Swede or Finn something-or-other. This was the way it went for an hour or more, the room growing warmer and the talk livelier and livelier. Slock watched Ruby and swallowed free bourbon.

"You heard about the new branding law, Slick?" Rutherford had come up behind him. Shuster hated the nickname, although he took pride in his ability to change the minds of ornery voters.

"I'm about to brand me a filly," Slick said, pushing the other man against a table, his eye still on Ruby. The bourbon had taken hold. Vulgarity that Rutherford had suspected other times became a coarse gleam in Slick Shuster's stare. A purple strawberry mark ran from the underside of Slick's lean jaw to the leathery neck. Now the purple deepened; he spat a shred of tobacco off his lip and gave Clay a look of contempt.

"You and the other blowhards down here can consider laws. I'm here to break some."

Observing from across the room, Sam recognized Shuster's intentions. He walked over and made the deal. "Jewel caught your eye in the floorshow? Forty dollars for a second act upstairs—extra for all night." Slick's nostrils twitched with satisfaction, and he handed Sam a $50 gold piece.

"Come in," Ruby said. "Come out of the bright light."

When Slick passed through the door, she closed it quickly. He turned to find her resting against it, one hand on a curved hip. Her glance ran over him, top to bottom, then her lips softened and she murmured, "I'm glad you chose me." Indigo eyes watched him with interest, as his legs turned heavy. All the whiskey he had taken in during the evening began to have its way, grabbing at his stomach and threading his nerves. He removed his hat but then couldn't remember what to do with it and put it back on his head in slow motion. It felt crooked, and he laughed in a dimwitted way, fidgeting, exposing the purple birthmark under his jaw.

She said, "Do you want a beer?"

"Yes," he said.

She started to speak again but didn't, her expressive shoulders shrugging away the impulse. At that moment, she saw him pretty clearly for what he was—a patronizing, conceited drunk.

Liquid spilled over the bottle when she handed it to him; color showed on his cheeks. She held herself still and steady, waiting for his move, relieved when he slouched against the wall. Her expression relaxed, and she positioned a shoulder under his arm, hoisting his weight over to the bed. Mumbling something indiscernible, Slick Shuster was unceremoniously dumped across the mattress, where he would spend the night alone. Ruby spread the canvas cloth under his boots before rearranging his long legs. "I'll not have you blackening my sheets," she murmured.

Twisting her hair into a glossy red braid, she looked over at the snoring politician with loathing. *I'm too young to be so sour on men,* she thought. Tenderness washed over her as she remembered Jack's question. "Some schoolboy pull your ponytail too hard?"

It was strange she knew so little of the man who had changed her life. She felt near to him, even though she'd spent only a few hours with him a whole year ago. Maybe she'd made him up, like some character in a book, giving him attributes he didn't have. She guessed she'd find out more about him as JJ got older and she saw more of Jack through his looks and personality.

JJ. Oh, what a mess she was in. *Good reasons, bad choices,* she thought. Ruby was not a girl to cry or give way often, but she gave way then. And Slick Shuster slept through the entire, tumultuous affair.

A few weeks later, Jack Smith slouched lazily in a wired wood armchair by the door of the Deadwood Saloon, rolling a cigarette. Fort Worth, Texas, "Cowtown" as some folks called it, was the last spot of civilization on the Chisholm Trail. Cowboys seemed anxious to gamble away their paychecks before the long cattle drive to Abilene and the beef market up north. They came back in the fall to win it back before winter set in. It was a good place for a person to take stock.

Some shadowy things bothered Jack. There were the nights he dreamed of a farmhouse in flames, a little boy named Hank calling a man to come back. These dreams blended with a flame-haired girl pushing the blond hair off Hank's forehead as she wiped her own tears. He recalled the tears that dripped off his chin when he shot Autumn Red, the blood on the straw and the miracle of her foal. "We put stock in you, Jack." Silent voices repeated the phrase.

The dreams made the days restless and the nights wakeful for him. They created bothersome afternoons when he was not certain that all was well and uneasy spells that left him fretful and troubled about why such thoughts should come back to plague him. They were November thoughts.

"Smith! What the devil are you doing here?" a cordial voice asked. Jack got up effortlessly and shook the hand extended to him by his old boss.

"Frank Gollaher! I'm just passin' through. You?"

"Bringin' up the drag. Luke and I collected a herd of mavericks last spring, made a drive. Told our boys they could throw a real party for Cowtown before we head home tomorrow morning." Gollaher gauged his old employee. "I thought you'd have passed out at the end of a rope by now!"

Jack smiled and inhaled the tobacco. "No bounty on me, yet, Frank. C'mon, inside. I been hankerin' for a drinking partner."

The Deadwood was a decent establishment, noisy enough to signal a crowd. Tinny notes of a piano accompanied the clicking of a roulette wheel and the bawdy laughter and raucous talk of the customers and girls who worked there. The two men ordered some beers and after a healthy swallow, Frank set his mug down and pointed out a gray-haired man with a pipe. "That's the local law. Gentleman Jake, they call him."

"Who's the one with the purple birthmark?"

"Likely he'll be our next senator, though he's a condescending skunk. A rich, handsome, braggart who licks boots for a living. Name's Shuster."

The worst place for Slick Shuster was a saloon. Normally, personal ambition kept his mean temperament in check. Under the influence of liquor, he was a dangerous man, a threat to his own prestige. Well juiced with whiskey, he pawed the female companion of a scoundrel from Laredo.

"You are crazy as a loon," she said, shoving him away.

"Don't be so high-falutin with me," Slick said. "Sporting girls are my specialty."

"Do tell," she said with dismissal.

"I met a gal named Jewel at the Fat Chance Saloon. Polished her 'til she glittered," Slick bragged.

"Sounds to me like she'd take any guttersnipe and give him an hour for a gold eagle," Laredo said, escorting his lady friend out of the room. "Must have scraped the corral floor for you." The doors swung closed on the couple.

Jack had caught the end of the exchange, as had everyone else in the Deadwood.

Gentleman Jake sidestepped the politician and said in an undertone, "Jewel's a fallen angel from Greenville, the way I heard it. Some devil left her knocked up, and she made her way to Sam's Town. Wretched business."

"That scarlet haired vixen made me stay all night." Slick crowed. "She went crazy for everything I said—called me a 'sugar mouth.'"

With great restraint, Jack asked, "She's called Jewel?" The calm in his voice belied the churning in his gut.

"Swede Dobson from Greenville knew her as Ruby." Thrusting his hips forward, Slick Shuster proudly displayed a large sterling silver buckle. A brilliant red ruby was the centerpiece. "She's sure the jewel in my belt."

"You whoremonger," Jack snarled. "Coward..."

The Colt.45 seemed to leap from Jack's waistband into his left hand in a blur too fast for Frank to follow. Frank then noticed that Slick had a Winchester rifle in his hand. Slick seemed to anticipate what was passing through Jack's mind, for he ducked down behind the bar without attempting to use the rifle.

Instead of going around the end of the bar, where he could see the man, Jack took a rough guess at his location and fired through the end of the bar. The bullet struck Slick Shuster in the mouth and toppled him over on the floor.

Frank saw Gentleman Jake rushing toward his friend, pistol in hand. Jack's gun came up again smoothly, flame stabbing from its muzzle. The bullet went into the man's shoulder, rocking him back on his heels. He didn't go down, though, and Jack shot him again.

As he pulled the trigger, guns roared from both left and right. A bullet ploughed into the floor next to Jack's right boot. He kept turning, dropping into a crouch as he leveled his gun and drilled a slug through another man's throat. Blood fountained from the wound as the bullet's impact sent him reeling.

Frank Gollaher was nowhere near as fast as Jack, but he kept his head in a fight. He covered as Jack hurdled the pool of blood and the man struggling to get some air in his bullet-riddled lung. Jack heard the whistling as the air went right back out again. It was an ugly sound, as was the dying rattle that came from the man's throat a moment later. Gollaher shot at the bottles over the bar, and the tinkling of broken glass attracted the attention of the sheriff's men. It gave Jack the moment he needed to dash out the back door into the alley, where he'd left Big Red.

"Well, Red," he whispered into her mane as he jumped into the saddle. "You're an accomplice to murder now."

A gun cocked, and the sound was plain in the empty passageway. The first bullet whiffed by Jack's ear. He didn't hear the second one, but he felt the slug take him low and hard. He could see the blood soaking his shirt, and then great red drops dripped onto his thighs. Big Red leapt forward into the dark.

A vague bristle of warning went through Frank Gollaher; his horse snorted softly, and its ears went forward. The rifle slacked easily across the saddle, and he reigned to a stop by the roadside ten miles out of Fort Worth. He heard the approaching strike of horseshoes against the road rocks, and finally a rider materialized.

There was a moment before recognition when Gollaher dumbly marveled at the man's appearance. His bloody shirt was in ribbons, and a great, livid wound showed on his flat belly. His lean face was swollen oddly on one cheekbone, and his lips were thickened at the corner of his mouth. The hands atop his saddle horn were clumsily folded, and Frank noted that they were raw across the knuckles. But it was the gray eyes, defiant through their weariness, that disturbed Frank the most.

"You look like meat roasting on a spit," Gollaher said. "Thought you were dead."

"Almost was. I changed my mind kinda' sudden like, when I felt the heat from hell," Jack said. "I remember shots and a sizzling in my belly; I passed out right after."

Puzzled, Frank asked, "Who brought you clear out here?"

"This blamed horse saved my life. She must of found some craggy paths because I'm mighty scraped up; but even semi-dead, I knew to hang onto Big Red."

"Hate to admit it, but I'm not keen on being your friend anymore, Jack. Can't blame me since even hell didn't want you." Gollaher shook his head and looked off in the distance. "Trouble seems to boil up when you appear."

"Look, Frank. Why don't we let me die? November 2, 1873." He held out his hand, indicating an imaginary headstone. "Seems like a good enough death date to me." Gollaher looked back at the man, puzzled. Jack continued, "Give me a set of clothes for a proper burial, and I won't resurrect anywhere near Gollaher Ranch."

Frank understood then. "Haven't got anything worthy of burying, but you can have my extra outfit. I'll be home tomorrow, and I was planning to burn it, anyway." Frank dug through his possibles bag for a gray flannel shirt and some well-worn trousers. "It's good I'm tall," he said. Tipping his hat to Jack, he spurred the horse. "Git up, boy," he clicked, ready to ride off.

Jack's look stopped him. "Tore up my handkerchief for bandages," the injured man said.

"Blazes, man! You want my soul, too?" Frank stripped off his red cotton bandanna and handed it to the late Jack Smith.

8

November 12, 1873, Sam's Town

Leo Barlow looked around the saloon. At the head of the banistered stairway to the second floor stood a woman, a girl really, with the bluest eyes he'd ever seen. For a long moment, she and Leo watched each other. Neither of them spoke; neither of them moved. Then she smiled.

The tall, slender man glanced over his shoulder, thinking she meant the smile for Sam Lester, but Sam wasn't paying attention, his head close to a poker hand.

"Are you waiting for someone?" Leo said uncertainly to the copper-haired girl.

Ruby moved on down the stairs and came close enough that he could get the scent of her perfumed soap before she answered him.

"I've been waiting for you," she said.

Leo's breath stopped. The warmth in her blue eyes jumped the space between them and blazed up in Leo. He fought it down, smothering its wild flame by sheer will.

Wearing a feather-and-silk trimmed dressing gown, a lavish thing even by saloon standards, Ruby saw Leo's hazel eyes flick to the swell of her breasts and the curve of her belly. Deliberately, she moved her hips and shoulders so that the blue garment opened a bit more, the gesture of a woman who knows she's beautiful.

"Aren't you interested in why I'm waiting?" she asked.

Staring now at the soft whiteness of her long thighs, the bareness of her high breasts, he felt the blood driving up in him thick and dark. It was suddenly difficult for him to speak.

"I assume I look vulnerable." Leo looked away and cleared his throat.

She straightened, the movement closing the gown again. All at once, the seductive smile and the body shifting were gone.

"Sorry. I mistook you for one of Sam's—one of my friends."

A pulse pounded visibly in her throat, and she returned his bemused expression and turned around. At the foot of the staircase, she stumbled slightly, and one satin slipper slid off the first step. This time, the gown parted a little higher up, and he saw the wicked curve of her thigh again. She could hear the sibilant in-drawing of Leo's breath cut the silence between them.

"If you decide you want to be friends," she said, "my room's upstairs."

Leo was dumbfounded at this singular welcome to the Fat Chance. He tipped the new brown Stetson back on his head, whistling faintly through his teeth. New clothes were definitely worth the trouble, he decided.

Riding in from Barlow Ranch wasn't his usual Friday night activity, what with a mother-in-law in Fort Worth who expected him to visit his son on a regular basis. But this weekend, Mother Rounds was bringing the baby to him, determined to clean out his house before Thanksgiving. Leo had taken the extra night off to visit Sam's Town for supplies, to read a newspaper, and to hear the local gossip.

"Nice vest, Slim," said a tall, black woman about his age. Although she was dressed in a brown, gingham skirt and a blouse with a ruche-lace collar, he was sure she was one of the fair sisters who worked for Sam. Respectable women did not come to saloons.

"Red is your color," she said, admiring the shaggy wool material Spen Harris had called plush. Leo was a handsome man, still fit at thirty-one, with just a hint of gray fading his ash blond hair. But the calm look of poise was at odds with the sweet, bashful grin he flashed at Black Pearl.

"You gun shy?" she asked. He seemed baffled by the question, so she said, "You don't pack a gun."

"Bad men are confused by good men. When you're as good as I am, you don't want to tote a gun. It'll get you shot for sure."

"He's speakin' truth, ma'am," said an aged cowboy, swinging bowlegs through the entrance. "Lots of outlaws would empty their pistols on Mr. Barlow here, for his saintliness alone." He laughed and clapped Leo on the back in a companionable way. "Respectable men aren't trustworthy." The grizzled man turned away from the girl and said, "You ready to head home, boss?"

Black Pearl spoke over their heads to the red-haired girl coming back down the stairs. "Sam's about to have a conniption, Jewel. Keep him busy while I change, will you?"

Both men watched Ruby nod in understanding and hurry down the steps, her long legs exposed under the flashy blue wrapper.

"I'm not quite ready to leave, Jute," Leo told the old man. "I want to challenge that claim that I'm so respectable—become more trustworthy in your opinion," and he followed the redhead with his eyes.

Giving no notice when Leo approached the table, Sam fingered the Bowie knife with his left hand. It flicked off the stump where a thumb should have been, while his right hand slid to rest possessively on the blue silk that covered Ruby's knee.

"Mr. Barlow has a ranch just fifteen miles west of here." Sam greeted Leo obliquely. "Owns two full sections, 640 acres each, all the grazing land hereabouts. But he never graces us with his presence—fancies himself too good for us, Jewel." Sam turned and indicated Ruby by touching the knife lightly to the girl's neck. "This showpiece is the newest jewel in my box, Mr. Barlow, and by far the prettiest."

Leo kept his eye on the bully's threatening left hand, acutely aware of what he caressed with his right. Embarrassed by this public fondling, the girl made a move as if to rise, but the man's fingers clamped down hard, causing her to wince with sudden pain. After that, she sat quite still.

Perhaps, Leo thought, he should come charging to her aid, but it was hardly the place for misplaced chivalry, although he hated the way Sam treated the woman, whoever and whatever she might be.

"You're mistaken, Sam," Leo said. "I came in tonight looking for good music and good conversation." Looking right at Ruby, he asked, "Could I have a dance with you, ma'am?"

Ruby sipped at her drink and dabbed her mouth. "None of that tarantula juice sold here, sir. Would you like another one?" She was perspiring faintly from a polka, and cinnamon-colored tendrils curled at her hairline.

Leo wondered if she smiled like this at every cowboy who swaggered through the doors of the Fat Chance Saloon or if she could tell he needed encouragement to drop extra coins on the mahogany bar. The dance had cost him seventy-five cents and every drink was a dollar, but a night in Sam's Town wasn't often in his receipt books and he could well afford the splurge.

"Are you a boarder?" Leo asked, embarrassed suddenly, realizing what this implied.

"I'm staying here, if that's what you mean. But don't you go judging me. It's just for a while." Leo absently looked down at his calloused hands, wondering how they'd felt to her velvety skin. He was anxious to touch her again.

She was lovely to look at, flushed and youthful. Unwrapping a ribbon she had around her wrist, she tied back her thick, russet curls. "I've got a little boy back in Greenville," she said with pride. "I'm trying to get on my feet so I can take care of him."

"That why I'm paying a dollar each time you drink a glass of colored water?" he asked.

"You're not supposed to know!" She held in a giggle and pursed her lips. Her tone changed. "You're on to me, sir." Relieved, she confessed, "The idea is that you'll buy a drink for yourself every time you refill my glass, and I'll get a commission for both." She looked pointedly at his empty hand. "Don't know how I'll make a dime tonight, chatting up a teetotaler."

"Not a total teetotaler," Leo smiled at his rhyme. "But I like to keep my head in a place like this."

"Take it you're not a regular here at the Fat Chance Saloon." Ruby tilted her head with interest at the sun-browned face. "You're a puzzle." She sensed depths of experience and understanding in this man, forged into the calm of self-assurance.

Leo replied without cynicism. "Just because I don't throw back whiskey or gamble away my ranch?" he asked her.

"Laws! You don't gamble either?" she said with wonder. "No wonder Sam doesn't cotton to you!"

"Well, I dance," he said, shaking out his stiff right knee.

Tinny chords from the piano roused her sense of responsibility. Jingle Bob slapped the top of his instrument and announced formally, "Gents, balance your ladies onto the floor. I'm going to play you a waltz. Tickets, please."

Ruby teased the paper stub from Leo's pocket, tore it halfway through, and twirled out of his reach, sweet-talking him with her eyes. "C'mon, then. Take a turn with a fallen angel."

Molly, acting waitress for the night, brought them each another drink. "You're downing these at full chisel, honey," she said to Leo, with a wink at Ruby.

Leo twirled Ruby to a different corner of the room, where the floorboards weren't already damp. Leaning against the wall, he managed to pour the whiskey out without anybody noticing. "That's like throwing away a dollar," Ruby said. "Wish I had so many to spare."

"I'll have a new reputation around here," Leo laughed. "Boozer. Sam will finally treat me with respect." Enamored by the charm of this girl, he didn't think a few dollars in wasted whiskey was too much to pay for her company. "I've been saddle bagged by you, ma'am."

"Saddle bagged?"

"Shot through the heart," he explained. "It's something I say to my little boy."

"Oh. You're married," she said, with abrupt coolness.

"No, but I've got a little boy. Seems we've got that circumstance in common."

It seemed ridiculous to Ruby that she should care if this cowboy was married or not. After all, she was decked out like a trollop, flitting from man to man with silver dollars in mind. Still... "Do you take care of him?"

"Lives with his grandma over in Fort Worth. Has since Elsie—that's my wife—died a year ago. MJ was just six months old then. I see him weekends, tomorrow, as a matter of fact."

"MJ? My baby's name is JJ," Ruby said with delight.

"Manchester Josiah Barlow, after his grandpas. Name's longer than he is. Elsie thought we'd call him Josey for my brother, but it never stuck." He signaled Molly for another round. "Your turn. JJ stands for?"

"'Jilted.' At least that's how I think of it now." Ruby surprised herself with this admission. "I got saddle bagged myself a year ago. His name was Jack, and I figured his son ought to have one of his names, so I called the baby after his daddy and mine—Jeremy—one name to live up to, and one to live down." She sighed audibly through her bright pink lips. "Seemed fitting when I did it but a mistake now. Like most things I do."

Shaking her head as if to clear it, she took the new glass from Leo and sipped from it herself. "Getting maudlin, here!" Lifting the glass in a mock toast, she kissed him lightly on the lips.

Leo had seen the girl's face soften, the shadow of sadness when she spoke of JJ. What the blue gown exposed had caught his attention at first, but what the blue eyes concealed had captivated his heart. He'd been saddle bagged.

"Unless you're going for a second act upstairs, I got other places for Jewel," Sam told Leo after another dance. Somehow, Leo had forgotten what this girl actually did for a living. Uncomfortable, she looked away when he was reminded.

"How much? For a second act, I mean?" Leo asked Sam, surprising all three of them.

Sam's rate for an evening of pleasure depended on who was asking and how busy the saloon was at the time. Based on his knowledge of Leo's circumstances and the large crowd around the bar, Sam gambled. "A fifty-dollar gold piece will buy you an hour." His eyes widened greedily as he quoted the large amount.

The coin flipped from one hand to the other, and Leo took Ruby's hand in a protective grasp. Her laugh was delighted and rewarding, and he found himself gaining confidence in her presence as they went upstairs.

She drew the curtains and struck a match for a candle. There was a lamp in the room, but she left it alone. Over the potbellied stove, a hotplate held a coffee pot that was still warm. While Ruby poured them both a cup, Leo looked around, surprised at how clean and homey it was.

"I don't have any condensed milk, but I've got sugar." She dipped a small cube into the steaming liquid and sucked it clean. "That's how my daddy introduced me to coffee," she told him and kicked off her slippers. "Carried sugar cubes for the horses and the kids in town..." she sucked in her lip and swallowed, then went on, "...said I was his sugar mouth." Turning her back to Leo, she started to take off her blue gown.

Now he was staring at her like a fool, feeling the light touch of her hand like fire on his face, wanting to rise and flee, and not really wanting to either. Then she leaned forward slightly, and suddenly, he was holding her and kissing her clumsily. It was like being snatched away by a raging river in flood. He held her fiercely, and she was encouraging him, twisting and fumbling.

He panicked, losing courage and desire abruptly. He'd been about to do a despicable thing. He'd misunderstood. What he'd taken for fondness was just passive acceptance of the fate she was used to; here in this room, this place, she did not expect anything decent or good.

He found himself standing above her, guilty and ashamed. He tried to speak, but the words wouldn't pass a sudden obstruction in his throat. He watched her rise, bring order to her clothes, and dust off pieces of mud on the bed where his boots had been. She fluffed up the pillows and lifted her hands to her hair.

"Wait, ma'am...Jewel..."

"My name's not Jewel. It's Ruby," she said flatly, facing him. "I'm different than you think—don't you judge."

"I'm not judging." With fumbling hands, he retied the ribbon fastening for her and said, "You are different than any woman I've ever known. But I want to know you better before … " his eyes flickered down to her bosom, " … before that."

He felt strangely old, yet filled with a tenderness such as he had never known before. Muscles in his neck clenched, and he cleared his throat. "What I'd like to find out from you, ma'am, is whether or not it will be worth my while to come back." Leo thought she might laugh, being spoken to so artlessly.

Instead, she said in a low, trembling voice, "I would like for you to come back. I'll be waiting."

She looked at him for a moment longer. She would have liked to kiss him again, and perhaps he was expecting it, but it wouldn't have seemed quite right. There was a lot to be settled between Ruby and her conscience. There were things that had to be studied out before she could live with them comfortably around a man like Leo. He collected his new brown hat, turned quickly, and walked out of the room.

Taken sideways by a wall of wind later that night, Jute and Leo took shelter in a shallow cave close by the river. "Let it blow itself out," Leo said and hobbled their horses for the rest of the night.

Jute started a small fire. Preempting the conversation, he said, "I don't think we ought to talk about you and the woman, boss. It ain't really fitting. There's things that won't stand a straight answer, and what's between a man and a woman is one of 'em."

"You liked her, though, didn't you?" asked Leo.

"Sure. She seemed a right nice lady."

"You call her a lady. That's sort of funny, under the circumstances."

"No, I don't reckon it is. Not the way I see things."

The wizened cowboy fussed with the coals, shifted his legs, and finally got out the rest of his reply.

"Let's just put it this way, boss. I've knowed whores I'd take my hat off to and respectable women I wouldn't spit on."

"Well said, old man." said Leo soberly. "Folks are more what they are on the inside than what they are on the outside. And it's easy to see through 'em, don't you think?"

"Yes, sir, I do. It's what I meant about Miss Jewel."

"Her real name's Ruby, Jute... Ruby. Like her hair." They sat still again, watching and listening to the flames.

"I reckon most of us don't get a second chance," mused Leo. "We don't get to be our better selves. Folks just expect us to keep on being, and we live down to their expectations. It's a shame."

Leo had no background with a woman like Ruby Dawson. He had never been through the painful, boyish hungering after the sight and feel of a girl's body. Too work-pressed to worry about sneaking looks and feels, he had always reasoned that when he was ready to be a man, he would be one. In consequence of this innocence, Ruby devastated him.

Elsie had been a different experience. He'd needed a wife, and she'd needed a husband, and that was that. Their marriage had been without passion from the beginning. She told him that a wife's lack of warmth was normal for a well-brought-up lady. Curbing desire was a man's noble responsibility. Her miserable pregnancy came about because he wasn't noble enough, and when she suffered from heat and nausea, followed by a terrorizing delivery, he felt responsible. Her resulting depression and death had added to his guilt. Finally, eighteen months later, he was able to let it go.

Beginning with that first night, Leo could not put Ruby out of his mind. The pleasure of looking at her had been matched by the pleasure of her company. No woman had ever affected him as this one did; none had ever stirred him so deeply or made him realize how much he was missing in his life.

His thoughts followed every movement of her voluptuous body, whether he was awake or asleep, to the point of obsession. Leo was not the first man to be enamored to distraction by a woman, but this experience was the first for him.

Thursday afternoon, he told Jute, "Look after things. I'm going into Sam's Town before I go over to Fort Worth."

"Glad to see you perking up, boss," said his old foreman. "Been a while."

"Seen something you like last time you were here?" Sam was hunched forward on a stool, his eyes red and watery after a coughing spasm. Wiping his mouth with a dirty bandanna, he snorted and spit into the brass pot next to the bar. "You'll have to wait your turn. They line up for Jewel." His wink was vile. "Unless you want some variety. Tequila over there," he jerked his stump, "she's a vixen. Lives up to her name." The pretty Mexican girl had a swelling bruise on her arm, and the look she gave Sam was filled with loathing.

Just then, Ruby's door opened and a young man's face, browned by exposure and heavily bearded, peeked out at the landing. A fringe of unkempt hair, still damp from the mandatory bath, stuck out at odd angles. He quickly covered it with an old wool hat, worn and weather-beaten, the flaccid brim falling limp on his shoulders, and folded back in front against the crumpled crown.

Likeable under any other circumstances, Leo found him contemptible now. The boy stomped his feet until his trouser legs fell to their customary length, just above his ankles, showing a pair of curiously contorted shoes. Hitching up red suspenders, he came down the stairs.

"J'ai paye cinq dollars—haf eegel—a Jewel, Meester Lester," he said self-consciously before he swung the doors open and went out onto the boardwalk.

Conflicting and irrational thoughts rose in Leo's mind. He'd paid $50, and this kid had paid $5? And for what? Ruby was worth much more than $5! On the other hand, Ruby should not be for sale at any price. How much of the money did Sam keep? What a thug! He wouldn't pay...

"Three double eagles will guarantee an undisturbed evening, Mr. Barlow," said Sam. His soft, clammy hand was out, palm up. Leo was ready to dispute the exorbitant sum and defend her honor all at once when Ruby walked out, carrying an empty coffee cup and an armful of sheets, and bent down to lock her door. The red hair was a soft cloud of curls around her face, and the fantasies of the long week burst from Leo's heart.

"Ruby..." She looked down, and her blue eyes caught fire; smiles wreathed her face. Sam caught the coins in mid-air, and Leo took the stairs two at a time.

Leo could not keep his hands off her face and hair, and it was only with the greatest effort that he refrained from pawing her clothes off. He pulled back and said, "I'll not have us start out backwards."

Coffee was poured, and Ruby magically produced a sugar cube. She soaked the white cube and placed it between Leo's lips, letting her finger stay inside while he sucked the sweetness out. Then she took the cube from his mouth and dipped it in the coffee again before she slowly popped it onto her own tongue.

Stray red strands of hair stuck to her lips, and Leo brushed them away. She set the cup down and pulled her hair back with the black velvet ribbon.

Watching the ritual, Leo said, "Does Sam provide silk gowns and velvet ribbons to all his girls?" Just a drop of jealousy poisoned the sweet flavor of the room.

Without looking at him, she paused, then said, "I'm sorry, Leo. I forgot who I am. For a few minutes there, I felt like a regular girl."

When she turned around, he saw tears glistening in her blue eyes. "Maybe you didn't forget who you are, Ruby," he said. "Maybe you remembered." With an effort, he didn't touch her but said, "Tell me who you were when you were a regular girl."

Self-conscious, she bit her lip, but Leo's eyes were warm and encouraging.

"I helped my daddy build coffins, of all things." She glanced over to see his reaction, then sat down on the bed, folding her arms around her knees. "He was actually a furniture maker, and I helped him cut cottonwoods, dry logs—I wove a lot of hickory bark for chairs, I can tell you!"

"Go on," said Leo. He put his hand on her arm. "I like listening to you talk." She relaxed back into the pillow and looked up at the ceiling.

"One time during a diphtheria epidemic, Daddy worked all night, making five caskets for the Bentley children. The five of them died in the afternoon and were buried the next day. I held the light for him that night as he made those coffins, and it was morning before he finally completed them." Ruby babbled on like a brook, with twists and turns off the path. A half-hour later, she was still talking.

"A year ago, I thought they'd both die of cholera, but Ma came through. Somebody needed to support us, so I went to work for Turk. He's a cook."

"Is he a good cook?"

"Only if you're hungry," she giggled. It came as a shock to discover that they were both laying on pillows while she rattled on about himself. She threw her legs over the side of the bed and started to rise. "I didn't realize..." she said, embarrassed. "It's time for you to leave."

"Do you want me to?" he asked.

"No, but it's not like we're having an ordinary conversation. Sam will expect a half-eagle for another hour."

Leo leaned up on his elbow. "It doesn't seem fair that you had no say in the arrangement, but I actually bought you for the whole night."

Relieved, she lowered herself back onto the pillow. "Nobody would believe the abnormal things we're doing in here." She turned to face him, and said, "Tell me about your ranch."

"It was a real nice place before my brother died, but it's not much now."

"And you run it all by yourself?"

He grimaced. "It isn't so much a question of running it as of keeping things from falling apart completely. And I'm not alone; I've managed to keep a crew of sorts, kids, and old men..."

Shifting, he said, "Got a man—Jute—who can hardly move any more. He helps out a bit. Don't say much. Says he came to Texas because there's no questions asked, no answers expected."

"Sounds like Turk," Ruby said. "What was your pa like?"

"There's a man. My daddy's voice was as soft and low as a lullaby—would break the heart of Lucifer himself to hear him and Ma sing harmony." He told her then about his sisters, Josey's harmonica, Nataki. "She said our music would make the angels weep."

"What'd you do?" Ruby asked, picturing the scene.

"Strummed. I got a guitar. We sang all the old Kentucky songs to the Texas wilderness, to while away the wintertime darkness."

He told her about watching the lightning chain at eight years old, when they first settled the ranch. "Nothing but the wind and the rain to argue with," he said. Lost in his own memories, Leo said, "After Ma died of the measles, just before my daddy followed her, he said, 'I tell you boys, if either of you remember how your ma taught you how to pray, get down on your kneebones this night and tell Him up yonder you're beholden for the land he give us.'"

Chagrined at his rambling, Leo rolled over and looked at Ruby. "I oughta' save part of my breath for breathing." He was talking to her as he'd talked to no one in years.

"You're good company, Leo Barlow."

"Guess if you're going to spend your whole life with yourself, you need to learn to be good company."

The mood changed subtly. "Will you do something for me, Leo?"

"Yes, ma'am."

"First, don't call me ma'am. And second, kiss me. It won't obligate you to anything, I promise. It's just that I never get kissed simply because a man likes me. I think it would be nice."

Kissing her this time was new. In the old, safe, slow way of learning how another is, Leo lifted his head and leaned over her face. Questions were in her eyes—did he like her? Would he leave her? His rough-skinned hand brushed hair away from her soft mouth with tenderness, and he lowered his lips gently onto hers. The other kisses had promised things to come. This kiss was its own promise. No probing, delving, or clutching. Just trusting. It was honorable, hopeful—new.

9

For Ruby, the days waiting for Leo's visits were endless. Between the hours of her shameful duties, she reproached herself—the reprehensible choices she'd made to be in this bleak circumstance horrified her, but she was trapped. The one thing that Sam demanded above everything else was loyalty—poor Tessa was an example of that.

Too cowardly to handle beatings himself, Sam had set Erly and Haze on Tequila when her brother came to take her away, bloodying her nose and breaking her ribs. Snake had gone with Sam's brutal bodyguard, Bolte, after the brother, and he bragged afterward that they'd "swung that Mexican from a hemp necktie." *Bolte was the Mexican who deserved hanging,* thought Ruby. His menacing presence, standing guard outside the saloon night and day, was a terrifying warning to Sam's other soiled doves.

Unconscious of male scrutiny, Ruby swept upstairs to her room, head high, eyes downcast. A man coming along the corridor breathed an apology and stood close to the wall to let her pass. He paused in front of the door to suite three. It opened and closed softly, and the sound of giggles reached her through the flimsy panels as she entered suite two.

Outside her room, she could pretend she was a respectable workingwoman, making a living to support her son. Inside the room, Ruby was a soiled dove, receiving no respect from anyone, least of all from herself. Standing there, she saw her face in the mirror and told her image, "You're well dressed, well fed, you're even clean—well as clean as soap and water will make you. There may be a few small spots on your soul that won't scrub out. In any case, it's a little late for you to get finicky now."

Someone knocked lightly on the door. She opened it to the phony preacher. She had for him the same contempt she had for all men these days, except Leo.

"Boss, you have a fever," Jute observed one day. Leo was leaned back on Rascal, woolgathering, a leg thrown over the horse's neck, with his good knee crooked about the horn. The empty stirrup flapped in the early December wind.

"A man sits back to roll a smoke, and he's branded as sick in your book, Jute?" He laid the small brown paper above his knee, sprinkled on the tobacco and then, without a change of position, rolled it with the ball of his thumb. A dab of saliva and the cigarette was working. "Ought to cut out your tongue for talking to the boss that way. Jute the mute." Leo smiled at his own joke, as he scratched a match on the sole of his boot.

"You're chilled as an old maid in that empty house of yours, and you're hot as a chili when you ride off to Sam's Town." Leo looked at Jute with interest. The old cowboy continued, "Seems like you're old enough to take your medicine."

"There's a potion for this malady?" Leo asked.

"Marry her." Jute made the pronouncement with authority. "Only way to get you back to work."

Bolte's red Indian blanket finally matched the weather as he stood watch between the Empire Hotel and the Fat Chance Saloon. Leo roped his mount to the tie bar and actually tipped his hat to Sam's Mexican bodyguard in his eagerness to see Ruby. Bursting through the doors, he found Molly on her knees, emptying the disgusting spittoons, and Tequila washing glasses, polishing away tobacco stains.

"Where's Ruby?" he asked. It hadn't occurred to him that the housekeeping fell to these girls, never having come so early in the day.

"She's cleaning the toilets," said Sam from the bar. He spat into Molly's clean brass pot just as Ruby came in from the back. Hair tied up in a black turban and wearing stinking leather gloves, she carried a bucket of filthy rags needing to be soaked and then washed.

Seeing Leo, mortification colored her face. "Jewel doesn't shine quite so brightly in the morning," said Sam. "That's when I use her for other things."

"What are you doing here?" she groaned. "I'm too dirty—go away!" Leo turned quickly and walked out of the saloon.

"You didn't have to humiliate me in front of the man," Ruby said.

Sam sneered. "He's carrying some romantic notion about you. There's nothing as predictable as a man who lives alone in the Texas wilderness. Besides, you've been putting on a few too many airs. It's funny how the minute you give a woman a fancy dress, she's got to try to live up to it." Mistrust was in his eyes. "That's all right for customers, Jewel, but don't you put on any airs with me."

"Airs!" she said hotly. "I haven't a shred of self-respect left. I'm smart enough to know there's no future in a life like this. You can rant and bluster and threaten me all you want, but it's not what's making me stay. I've given away more than my body these past weeks. I've given my soul. Only an insect like you would have me anymore, and I know it."

"You're so high and mighty, in love with a rich farm boy. You were shabby and broke and hungry when you came to me, but you still acted like you were doing me a favor, like a princess in exile. That's what I noticed, Jewel, that look: a princess condescending to mingle with commoners. You don't fool Sam Lester. I knew you smelled quick money. You thought you could step down to my level and haul up enough to buy back your respectability. I think you're beginning to catch onto the fact that you've bitten off more than you can chew. You sold yourself to a Confederate instead of starving honorably, like a lady should."

She hit him then. Her own violent reaction took her by surprise. She hadn't realized how deeply his sly voice had cut and probed, searching out the weakness in the defense she'd built around herself.

Feeling the harshness of his weak jaw against the glove, she took pleasure from the rough contact. An instant later, she was on the floor, and the whole side of her face was oddly numb, except for a burning, stinging sensation. Half-dazed, she didn't quite understand what had happened. Then she heard his voice.

"You use your hand on a man and expect him not to strike back? Get up!"

She put her hand to her bruised cheek, incredulously. It was the one thing that hadn't happened to her. Despite the men she'd met here, she'd never before encountered deliberate physical brutality. A man who got a little rough when he was drunk wasn't the same thing at all. Usually, he'd be ashamed and apologetic and very generous. But there was no hint of regret or apology in Sam Lester's face; and she realized that the capacity for violence was what she'd sensed in this man, what she'd feared, and now that she'd made the error of calling it forth, she had no idea of how to cope with it.

He took a step forward. She saw, aghast that he was going to hit her again. Picking up the bucket of rags, she threw it at him.

Snarling, he grabbed at her, but she ran upstairs to her room and locked the door.

Tessa said quietly, "You can come out, now. He's gone to Fort Worth till tomorrow." Ruby pushed the heavy dresser aside and turned the key. "I've fixed you a bath, but you can't let Bolte see you. He's downstairs."

Ruby gathered a few clean clothes and said, "I thought he'd kill me."

"Not Sam. He's probably scared of you. But Snake, Erly—that's who he'll send to do it. And they are devils." Tessa blocked the view, while Ruby rushed down the hall to the small, tin bathtub. "You're too popular here for Sam to let you go. He'll leave you alone if you don't cause more trouble. I know."

Not big enough to relax in, the tub was adequate to get the stink from Ruby's hair and skin. Purple already stained her cheek, and her eye puffed out almost to her hairline. Regular clothes covered the assets she was required to show off these days; she wished she had a veil to hide the rest of her.

Exhausted by emotion, she locked herself back in her room. By the time Black Pearl knocked with a tray of food, Ruby was becoming frantic. "Will Sam beat me again?" she asked, almost clutching the older woman in her frenzy.

"He's not so bad, if you heed his rules. He's worried you'll turn on him; he can't handle that—that's when he gets mean."

Pearl set down the tray and bustled around the room, picking up an empty beer bottle and some coffee cups. "He'll seem to forget the whole thing, so pretend you have, too. Act normal-like and flatter him a bit. Toss your hair; use those long eyelashes. Long as you don't rile him up, he won't bother you again."

Black Pearl slid a note under the door about nine o'clock. *One of your favorites will knock on your window at midnight.* It had to be

Leo. Ruby had no other favorites. When the tapping came, she put out the light, opened the curtains, and let him in.

"Your eye," he said, touching the soft spot under her lashes.

"Leo," she began, "you can't be here like this. Bolte is downstairs, and I'm being watched until Sam comes back tomorrow." A small amount of pleasure showed through her discomfort. "I ambushed him with crap cloths. It was a great satisfaction." One side of her mouth went up in irony. "But I'll pay for it."

He'd waited long enough. "I want you to go out that window with me," Leo said with intent. "I aim to get you away from Sam."

"And then?" she asked, watching his face with a curious look.

"Why," he said, "then we'll be married." He sat down on the bed.

She said, "Leo Barlow, you're a fool!"

He looked at her in mild surprise. She stared back, annoyed. He thought he'd never seen anything near as lovely as she looked, standing there with her long hair loose about her shoulders. There was a funny, tight expression about her swollen mouth and eyes, as if she were hard put to keep from crying.

He was calm. "I see nothing foolish in what I said."

"You don't want to marry me!" Gulping air, she shook her head, bewildered.

"As for want to," he said, "I reckon I'm a better judge than you are."

"You're just a man smitten by a saloon girl. Even Sam said it. It's got nothing to do with marriage, with two people living together day after day, year after year."

He grinned and said, "Of course I'm smitten; that's why I want to marry…"

She went on without heeding him. "You're going to spend your life among people in this town. They know what I am! A man wants to be proud of the woman he marries! You can't marry a little trollop and take her away from an outlaw—a bully—just because you feel sorry for her."

Leo reached up and began to wind a lock of the long, chestnut hair about his finger. "No need to be so hard on yourself, Ruby."

She took his hand away. "Hard? I know what they'll say, all those good people! Hard? There's nothing like fine, righteous citizens for hard!"

"The Barlows owned land here before folks settled Prescott, long before Sam Lester came and took over the town. I've never consulted that thug on anything, and I certainly don't need his approval on getting married. I reckon the folks of Sam's Town will be civil to Mrs. Leo Barlow, whoever she may be, or we'll just pull their town down and build us a new one with better manners."

Ruby's mouth trembled and then composed itself firmly against this weakness. "You see!" she said. "Now you've wiped out a town full of people because of me."

He chuckled. "It was a pleasure, ma'am. You want Richmond or Atlanta razed to the ground, just say the word."

She stared at him blindly for a moment and began to cry, the tears running down her cheeks unheeded. He stood up to touch her, but instead, he closed the curtains again, throwing the room into darkness. Then he sat back on the bed and drew her down beside him, still crying.

"You don't understand," she gasped. "You...you just don't understand what kind of a person...you don't know what I've been!" She went on quickly, before he could speak. "Oh, I know what you're thinking. You're thinking I'm a tragic victim of fate whom you're going to save from a life of shame. Well, I've always managed to keep some such notion, myself, until today. I've told myself that somehow I'm finer and better than the girls who...who work in...I've seen myself as a clever, brave, free soul...brave! I'm a coward, Leo. When Sam hit me this morning, there was nothing inside me but...but jelly. And I realized suddenly that I've been a coward, running from anything I'm afraid of to anybody who'd promise to take care of me..."

He said, "That's not cowardice, Ruby. That's trust—that's a brave, hopeful quality. I won't misuse it."

She drew a long, ragged breath. "Can't you see? I'm bringing nothing but trouble to this marriage."

It was a capitulation, and he kissed her gently. "Go to sleep now," he said. "I'll stay. In the morning, early, before Sam gets here, I'll take you down to the ranch. You'll be safe with me."

Ruby got up, shivering, and began to pack hastily in the darkness. The cold dawn after the warmth of the night before symbolized marriage to her. Leo was still asleep, still in the spell of the fairytale that had lulled her into fantasy. She wondered when he would realize she was gone. She knew Sam would destroy her if she left, deliberately, slowly, savoring each step in her downfall. She couldn't let him destroy Leo, too.

The chair she had tilted against the door made a clatter as she pulled it away from the knob. Leo gave a deep sigh and turned over. She stood there a moment longer. It had been a beautiful dream: a husband, a home, a father for JJ. The stairs creaked in the early morning quiet as she crept downstairs. She looked out the window at the dark, endless prairie, wondering how she'd dare venture out there alone.

Abruptly, she turned up the lamp and walked across the room to a mirror. Her face looked back at her from the spotted glass, disfigured by Sam's blow. Only a man in a poorly lighted room could have found her attractive, she reflected grimly, as she pushed back her hair and tied it up with the ribbon from her wrist. The bruise would heal, but there would be other blows, now that the man had discovered the potency of the treatment. She had to leave. He'd probably beat her half to death when he learned about the whole marriage idea.

"Ruby." The voice was soft and sad, and she looked up to see Leo on the landing outside her room. "Ruby, don't you trust me?"

"I didn't want you to feel obliged, Leo. I figured you'd regret your words and not know how to take them back." Suddenly, she buried her face in her hands and began to cry helplessly. "I seem to fall into traps...I don't want you to be trapped with me. The shabby truth is that I'm a harlot. It's unforgivable."

Leo came down the stairs and said, "Haven't you heard the story of the prodigal son? He did some riotous living but got forgiven. The Bible says 'he came to himself.' I reckon you've come to yourself. You've given up your riotous living, and you can come home. Barlow Ranch can be that home."

By then, she was in his arms, and she knew she wouldn't ever leave them.

10

December 2, 1873, Barlow Ranch

It took most of the morning to get to Barlow Ranch from Sam's Town. "When we moved here from Kentucky, no living thing was moving through the vastness, except the lizards. Skulls and whitening bones of buffalo were scattered everywhere," Leo told her as they traveled.

"Pa was tenacious. The land was covered by buffalo grasses—broiled by the sun in summer, it cures on the ground to a sort of hay that's good for cattle."

The landscape changed, and they followed a stream toward a magnificent stand of pines. The house itself, a one-story, flat-roofed stone affair with a long, deep veranda, squatted under the big trees. Off closer to the creek were clustered a barn, corral, and sheds that made up the working ranch. It had the rich, worn look of something used and old, and as Ruby saw it for the first time, she understood why Leo loved it.

There was a second stone building midway between the house and the barn. "That's where my brother Josey lived," Leo told her.

"I never cleaned it out. I've used it to store whatever I don't know where to put. And there's an abandoned mill in that stand of cottonwoods," he said, pointing toward the woods. "Mormons left it some twenty years ago."

The trees nearest the house were old, with thin yellow leaves still clinging to the branches, but those further back were thick, tall, and straight.

The bunkhouse, blacksmith shop, and smokehouse all had a raw, unfinished look, built from weatherboard and cottonwood logs. "That's Jute's territory. I'm planning to hire more men, pick things up a bit." Their horses pulled up in front of the house. Leo said, with a mixture of pride and hope, "My folks saw promise in this place."

Ruby's hands trembled but not with cold. She wanted to touch him, smooth the work-worn furrows that creased his forehead. He took his hat off, pushed his hair back, then put it back on again and held out his arms. "Can't break their promise," she said.

The guilt Ruby wore like a woolen cloak seemed to fall from her shoulders as she stepped into Leo's house and looked around. Potatoes in sacks, bushel baskets of carrots, parsnips, and turnips all sat on the kitchen floor; shelves of dry onions with shining skins, squashes, and cabbages—dried dill, sage, and mint hung from the rafters next to copper pots in barely controlled chaos. Six ladder-back chairs, with seats of woven hickory bark, surrounded a heavy oak trestle table.

Two steps down took her to the spring room. Leo had worked out a system of waterworks so that cold water, collected from a spring, was captured in a large barrel and piped into the kitchen sink.

"Running water!" Ruby exclaimed. A tin tub hung near the barrel, and a huge kettle sat on a woodstove, which heated the room and the water for a bath.

Puncheon flooring in the parlor was covered by straw, under a faded but still colorful rag rug. Two daybeds sat at an angle. Feather pillows of various sizes, covered in patterned muslin cases, were scattered on these couches and on the floor nearby. A frayed quilt was thrown over an old Boston rocker in the corner, next to a stack of books as high as the roll-top desk, which was littered with crumbs.

"Are you rich?" Ruby asked, without subtlety; the ranch house was twice the size of the Dawson farm.

Evading a direct answer, Leo swept his Stetson in a broad arc. "Why, my dear," he said with an exaggerated bow, "haven't you heard of the Ashby's of Kentucky?" He raised his eyes. "You're lookin' at one."

Ruby mock curtsied, with a skeptical lift of one brow.

"It's true," Leo said. "But Ma's branch of the family was Quaker, missed out on the cotton fortunes, being against slavery and all. Still, we got the goods." Leo swept his hat around once more. "This here is the cause of my daddy's death." Ruby's eyebrow went up again. "'Totin' this plunder'll be the death of me' was his chant all across the Texas plains. Ma reminded him of it every time he laid on this fine feather bed."

Leo pulled clothes from beneath the lumpy covers and stuffed them in a carved wardrobe already overflowing with unfolded linens. Just off the bedroom was a smaller room, furnished with a narrow bed set high off the floor, a trundle stuffed beneath.

"Room for a woman here," he said. "And a couple of young 'ens?"

They were in the kitchen when Jute knocked and stuck his head in the door. "Boss, you got unpleasant visitors. Askin' for Miss Ruby."

The men were already off their horses. Haze's hands were rope-calloused, and he chewed tobacco with a patient violence. It bulged his sunken left cheek and seemed to draw his small eyes even closer together by widening his face. He stank of horse sweat and its sweet, acrid smell—mixed with the even sweeter smell of the chaw—clung to him like a sickening aura. A man of average height, he had narrow, slanting shoulders that set his big head in bold and ugly dominance. His gun was holsterless, attached at the end of a strap, and usually concealed beneath his sleeve. Now it was exposed and raised inside the open frock coat.

"B-B-Barlow? S-s-Sam wants his pr-pr-property back."

"Stealing from Sam Lester has put you in a fix, Mr. Barlow." Snake stood next to his pony and pulled his Winchester from its scabbard, relieving Haze of the guard. The latter walked up to Leo and kneed him in the groin. Leo twisted forward, writhing in agony, and Ruby, crying out like a wounded animal, crouched to help him. Haze grabbed her arm and jerked her toward the horse.

The muzzle of Jute's carbine barrel bit into the small of Snake's back. "Unless you want a bullet-smashed spine, get off this land," the old cowboy said. Haze let the girl go and instantly turned to protect Snake.

"Careful, now," Jute told him. "Bein' paralyzed would make your partner ornery."

The two outlaws hefted themselves onto their horses and backed down the driveway. "J-J-Jewel made a d-deal with S-S-sam," Haze shouted.

"Stay out of Sam's Town," Snake bellowed and fired his gun into the air when he was safely out of range.

Leo was on his feet now and stumbled back into the house. "Sam Lester will not intimidate me!" A foreign harshness was in Leo's voice. He raised his fist to slam it down against the table but checked the impulse. His anger evaporated as quickly as it had built up; he scoffed at himself and at Jute's expression.

"What's the matter, old man?" asked Leo.

"Why, nothing," Jute said. "Nothing at all. It was just—well, for a moment there, you had me scared. I thought you was going to turn out human after all, with a temper and everything."

"Ma used to say temper is a weapon best handled by the blade. Can't throw it around without getting hurt yourself."

"You keep your temper, Leo Barlow, but I'll not keep mine!" Ruby was in the grip of a fury that made her lower lip tremble; her blue eyes darkened with anger. Leo could see the thin dusting of faded freckles across the bridge of her small nose. There was wildness and rage in her face that burned passionately, a fierce intensity that made her, at that instant, more alive, more beautiful than Leo had ever seen her.

"His property? I'm his property?" Unconsciously letting her hair down, Ruby stretched the ribbon tight between her hands. "I'd like to hogtie Sam to a tree, watch him try to loosen the rope without a thumb...I hate that man!" Kicking one of the pillows seemed to release some of the wrath that had built inside her over the last months.

"You can kick him—he's here." Leo was looking out the window as Sam rode up.

Startled, Ruby bit her tongue and grasped Leo's arm, tightening her grip. "He'll take me back, Leo. He will...I can't go back there. I can't." Her words had a whimpering, pleading quality to them; her bravado melted like snow in the desert.

Deliberate and calm, Leo opened the door. "News travels fast, I see." Without hesitation, he stepped out on the veranda to face the sallow man. "I've informed your henchmen that they are not welcome on my land, and the same is true for you."

"Just trying to do their work for 'em, is all," said Sam. He looked past Leo to Ruby. "Don't like you takin' so lightly of your word, Jewel. Thought we had an arrangement."

Leo put his arm out to stop her, but she stepped around it. "I was earning a road stake, Mr. Lester. Just staying till I could send for my boy." Her voice was unwavering. "I'd be obliged to call things square between us."

Sam's face contorted with outrage, the scar a bright plum. "You're askin' for trouble, Missy." Sucking in air through tobacco-stained teeth, he said, "You're no more'n a guttersnipe, you and your high-falutin' dandy, here. Always thought himself a bit too good for Sam's Town. He got no grit—he ain't worn a gun in his life, and you thinkin' he'll look after you?" His shoulders shook convulsively, and a phlegmy rattle rose from his throat. Clearing his lungs with a loud snort, he hocked the mucus on Leo's boot. "Don't show yourself in my town. My boys have orders—shoot to kill."

Sweat came out on Ruby's forehead. Infuriated and terrified, she sunk down on the floor in a heap of skirt. When she'd collected herself, she looked up at a rust-brown shotgun hanging on a deer antler rack over the fireplace. "That's all we've got?" she asked.

"Pretty much," Leo said, unruffled by Sam's tongue-lashing. "Grandpappy brought it from England. It has outside hammers and percussion locks—not real efficient for killing men with six shooters." Pulling Ruby to her feet he said, "Ma named it the 'Last Resort.'

"After that tirade, I'm sure of one thing," Leo continued. "We're not going into Sam's Town for Reverend Kincaid to marry us."

That thought sent Ruby into convulsive laughter. "I know Kincaid a little too well, and he is not the person he pretends to be." With that thought, she sobered. "Neither am I, Leo."

He grabbed her hand and twirled her under his arm to a mirror hanging by the door. "Of course you're not—what woman would just pretend to be Mrs. Leo Barlow, when she could be it for real?"

He untied her ribbon and fluffed up her red hair. "Pretty up, sugar. You're getting married!"

Just beyond the Barlow woods, there was a small clearing, where a broken down covered wagon sat in a heap. Beside it was a spartan cabin being constructed from the wood of the carriage itself. The canvas covering had been remodeled into a makeshift roof, and the wheels were propped on stumps, covered with planks to serve as worktables. Leo pulled up the buckboard and called out to a man named O'Brien.

Immediately, a thickset man ducked out of the shack, wearing a dirty flannel shirt. It was missing a button so that some of his ample belly showed where it bulged against the garment. He had a close-cropped salt-and-pepper beard and a thatch of graying hair that stuck up in wild spikes. O'Brien ran his fingers through it now and squinted toward the bright orange sunset. "Mr. Barlow," he said, pleased, shooting out his hand, "right nice to see you!"

"Looks like you're making progress, O'Brien." Leo turned to Ruby and said, "Sold off some of my land last month. This is our newest neighbor. And he..." Leo looked with hope at the man, "...he is a preacher."

O'Brien tipped his head in mock modesty. "A renegade preacher, chased out of my own church because I confessed certain doubts," he said to Ruby, "but a preacher just the same."

"We're looking for just such a man as yourself," said Leo. "For the price of a bath and a catfish supper, would you consent to marrying us tonight?" Ruby looked as surprised as O'Brien. "Ruby makes a fine cup of coffee, and I'll send you home with a cow for your trouble."

"My preaching days are far behind me, Mr. Barlow, but I still know the right words." With a reassuring smile at Ruby, he said, "I'm bona fide, ma'am, no worries there. And I'm hungry to boot."

Pulling himself into the back of the buckboard, he rested his head on the rail and looked at the darkening sky. "Can't think of a sweeter way to end the day."

Leo turned his face to the silent stars then caught the gleam of the lamp and felt his belly go tight, and his breath grow short. He did not remember the porch steps creaking under him as he waved off O'Brien nor the panel of the front door swinging inward beneath his hand. He did not even remember carrying her across the room. He only remembered—and would remember always—the bedroom lamp lighting the satin cream of Ruby Dawson Barlow's silky shoulders.

Ruby put her arms about his neck, regarding him thoughtfully. "When you do this, my dear," she said, "when you do this, it's always nice to tell your wife you love her."

He tried to speak, but now the words would not come. She smiled and drew his head down. Her lips were warm and responsive, as he'd remembered them, her arms receptive, and her hands held him close. Tonight, there was no feeling of shame or guilt, or even any great sense of urgency. When they overbalanced, in each other's arms, and fell to the bed together, the rope springs let out a great sigh; and suddenly, they were lying there, looking at each other in the lamplight and laughing. She sat up presently, pulled the ribbon from her hair, and shook it loose. It fell about her shoulders, shining redly, the way he'd first seen it.

"Ruby," he said, watching her.

"Yes."

"I love you," he said.

"Yes," she said. "And I love you, Leo."

He kissed her lips lightly the next morning and allowed his hand to trace the shape of her cheek, firm and smooth to his touch. It seemed quite natural to take this liberty, until she stiffened slightly against him. He took his hand away.

"My apologies," he said, a little hurt.

She laughed softly and took his hand and replaced it where it had been. "Don't be silly. You just… Sam bruised me there, that's all."

He knew a little pang of jealousy at the thought of the other men she'd known. Apparently, she sensed it because she said quickly, "Don't think of me in that place, Leo. I can't bear the look in your eyes."

Resolved, he changed his mood. "Are you ready for your honeymoon, Mrs. Barlow?" Horses sounded outside the kitchen window, and Jute poked his head inside. "I'm too old for your early morning escapades, boss," he complained. "Wagon's ready, packed for a few overnights."

"Time to meet our sons," Leo told his new wife.

MJ cried when Leo took him from Elsie's mother. It always took a while for him to warm up to his pa, remember who this tall stranger was. "Say howdy to your new ma," Mrs. Rounds said to the baby, verging on tears herself.

Even though Ruby had been a mother for six months, she was awkward around the toddler and tried to hide her nervousness. She was glad he was wailing in his father's arms rather than hers, glad to be the one carrying baskets of paraphernalia to the wagon.

"Are you widowed as well, Mrs. Barlow?" Mrs. Rounds asked.

Leo knew his mother-in-law would eventually hear the gossip. He stepped around it now by saying, "Ruby has been alone since before her son was born, Mother Rounds. He has needed a father, as MJ needs a mother. We'll both be forever grateful to you for seeing to him this past year." Kissing her downy, creased cheek, he said, "You've given him a fine start."

The baby howled again as he realized he was being hauled away; his grandmother pecked the top of his blond head and let the new family leave.

Olive beamed at her new son-in-law. "Welcome, welcome. We've needed a man in this family." Then, bobbing her gray head up and down at JJ, she said to him in a singsong tone, "But you'll always be my little man." JJ's toothless grin widened at his grandma. Leo and Ruby each held a baby, looking as domestic as a couple could. "Three days married, you two have your hands full!"

"You're welcome to come home with us, Ma," said Ruby hopefully, with a quick glance at Leo. It was obvious to Olive that her daughter's new husband was already overwhelmed with family.

"After you're settled, I'll get the Brannigans to bring me for a visit. Fifty miles is a long way to travel at my stage of life." To Ruby, she said, "put JJ on a cup already. Should be fine if you've got a cow."

"Lots of cows, ma'am," Leo reassured her. MJ was asleep in his arms. "Don't you worry about your grandson, Mrs. Dawson."

Ruby left them to walk over to Clara's and say her good-byes. "You have the gift of goodness, Mr. Barlow." Olive said. "I'll go to sleep in peace tonight, knowing my daughter has you." Taking the sleeping baby from his arms, she went on, "Jeremy would have approved."

"There'll be talk, Mrs. Dawson—shall I call you Olive?" She nodded her consent. "Olive. There'll be gossip. Ugly words will be said about Ruby's stay in Sam's Town. It was a bleak, wretched time for her, but it's done with." Leo said it with finality. "And I'll get her some help for the babies—folks are moving in round about us. Bound to be a young girl needing work."

In the end, it was an old man who needed work. Ruby's reunion with Turk came just in time. "Lightin' out," he said, without explanation, indicating an old chuck wagon stacked high with his goods. A discussion was underway with Len Grove about a horse trade.

"Old Buck here, his front leg's gettin' a little gimpy," Turk told Len. "If you're interested in selling that colt, I'd be interested in buying—maybe."

"I'd sell my wife first," Len replied.

"I'm not interested in your wife," Turk said.

Len looked at Buck and then at the colt. "He's a handful. You a good rider?"

"Not unless I have a good horse," Turk said. "Look, is he for sale or not?"

The little gray looked as surefooted as the buckskin had once been. Turk spoke to it, and it flicked an ear to listen. This was a good horse, steady and quiet.

A deal was struck, and Len led Buck away, noticing Ruby for the first time. Leo could read the young man's mind and stepped in front of Ruby to block his stare. "Leo Barlow," he introduced himself, with composure. "Ruby's husband."

Len touched a finger to the brim of his hat and glanced at Ruby. "Best of luck to you," he said, subdued by the coolness of the older man.

"Dead?" Ruby was saying when Leo turned back to the conversation. "Jesse's dead?"

"Yep," Turk said. "Nobody noticed him missing for several days. Stink couldn't get past the corral."

"How did he die, anyway, Turk? Did he fall, or get shot or what?"

"No bullet, no blood. They found him dead in his blanket—dead as could be."

"Kinda' like that bad man from Abilene?" Ruby asked.

"Kinda," Turk said.

"We're hiring Turk," Ruby announced instantly. It was the first time in their short marriage that Leo had seen her tenacity. "We need him," she implored when she saw his resistance. "You're wanting to hire on extra men. How're you planning to feed them? Turk's manned a chuck wagon, trussed up buffalo, baked pies with desert weed...you should hear his stories!"

"I'm sure I will," said Leo, assessing the cook. It was easy to see Turk was in love with Ruby, which, considering his age, Leo regarded as an asset. With Sam Lester's threats hovering over the ranch, the Barlow family could use an extra set of defensive eyes. "What's your specialty?" he asked the old man.

"Six-shooter coffee—strong enough to float a pistol," said Turk.

When Ruby took over the team later that day, Leo noted her handling of the horses with approval. She was so different from Elsie, he thought, more feminine in many ways but with skills she would have deemed masculine. Elsie had been all emotion and dependence; scared of the wild land he loved, afraid to step out of his shadow. Ruby was spirited, stubborn, and she spoke her mind—forceful traits that made her more feminine somehow.

The streak of humor in her matched his—cheerful, tolerant, sometimes ironic. Her lightly freckled face, with its wide, soft mouth, honest blue eyes, the vibrant, red hair that he always wanted to touch, the young, slim, knowing body; these things gave her a lushness that Elsie hadn't shown. Ruby's recent past had added experience to her natural understanding of men—not just their dreams of passion but their dreams for life, their desire to make something lasting and worthwhile.

After Ruby and the babies were sleeping in the wagon, Leo found Turk hunkered down before the fire smoking a cigar. The light made plain the long, half-bitter lines of the man's face, the thin pressure around the lips.

Turk was near sixty, small, tough, and wiry, showing the knocks of life. He had ash-white hair and the steadiest brown eyes Leo had ever noticed in a man. His language was colorful, with a southern twang, and, because Ruby did, Leo trusted him immediately without reservation.

"Night-owling," Turk said. "Nothing like a prairie sky at midnight."

By day, the cloudless winter skies had been gunmetal blue. By dark, the blazing stars were low, growing in size and whiteness until Leo could hardly believe they were real. The frosty stillness carried a coyote's bark so clear and sharp that it made the short hairs on the back of Leo's neck rise up and shiver him in a grand, fearful way.

Cigar finished, Turk asked, "When did you arrive in this wondrous country, Mr. Barlow?"

"Back in 1850. People were flooding into Texas like a spring river then. We got swept along."

Leo harrowed the earth with his heel, sniffed a handful of dirt, and sifted it through his fingers. "My folks loved this land. Bet their muscle and grit on it—dug mesquite sprouts for heat, watered the crops with sweat. Started ranching soon after, gathering the wild cows and branding them for our own."

"Texas longhorns—tough to eat and tough to handle," said Turk.

"Texas greenhorns, just as tough to handle." Leo was getting around to his subject. "Don't know what you've heard about Ruby these last months."

"Word gets around—a coupla' boys from Greenville talked pretty loose about seeing her at the Fat Chance. Course, Jesse spread that manure thick." Turk ground the cigar butt with a vengeful boot.

Leo said, "Sam Lester has sic'd his rowdies on her. Jealous as all get out. Banned us from town, which means supplies will be harder to get. We'll handle that all right. It's her safety I'm worried about. Wish she'd lay low for a bit." The fire was dying, and Turk couldn't see Leo's face, but he felt the unease. "Sam won't forget this humiliation anytime soon."

"Holding that girl back will be like hanging onto the wind, Mr. Barlow. The little boys and the ranch ought to keep her close to home, though, at least long enough for this to peter out."

11

Barlow Ranch

"Do you go to church on Christmas?" Leo asked Ruby. It hadn't dawned on either of them that families were celebrating the holiday all around them. Their own private celebration of family had eliminated all thoughts of the season.

"We used to," she said. "I kind of gave up on churchgoing when the churchgoers announced publicly that I was going to hell. Takes the fun out of the sermon." She smiled ironically. "Did you go?"

"Not that I remember. There wasn't even a church to go to, and Mama's religion was branded heretic, anyway. Course, she taught us. For a while, the Bible was our only book, so she taught us from it. We read it, then copied it so we'd learn to write and spell. We memorized passages, acted out performances."

He took on a spooky voice and sleepwalked across the room to her rocking chair. "I'm Lazarus, come forth from the dead," he moaned. *"Lazarus has seen the dead!"* He grabbed the back of the rocker and tipped it until she almost lost her balance and dropped the sleeping JJ on top of his brother, who was drowsing under a quilt by the fire.

"Leo!" she said, lurching. "Stop that!" Her feet caught hold of the floor, and she settled herself. "We had no such antics in our Sunday school," she told him, soothing the baby. "It was all dour-faced people in black, glaring at children who wiggled their noses at the strange smells. But, you may give our little family a Christmas sermon, Brother Barlow. Our first tradition."

She relaxed back, and he told the familiar story, by heart. "And it came to pass in those days…"

When he came to the part about Mary, "his espoused wife," Ruby said, "I never thought about it that way. People scorned her because she wasn't married. I know how that feels."

"More important, so does she."

Just three months into their marriage, Ruby already knew she couldn't broach her subject until after Leo was fed. While he washed, Turk put some spring onions on the table, fried up in bacon. There was little talk between them, at first. Ruby had patience, holding her words for the right moment.

Leo pushed aside the black toast with disgust. "I'll just have coffee," he told Turk.

"Leo," Ruby said. "Turk is a cook. He knows when bread should be soft and when it should be burned. Just trust his judgment." Her new husband rolled his eyes. It was nerve wrecking, her watching him eat.

When the first edge of his hunger was gone, Leo told her about moving cattle across the river that morning. "Erly and Snake were drifting around. They want to know what we're up to, I guess, to report to Lester."

She wasn't listening. "I hauled the babies to the pond today, thought MJ could dip his feet, first warm day and all..." she was rambling, stalling. "The stink was vile, and the sod was gone."

Leo wasn't sure what this had to do with anything. Ruby continued, "The Zabalas' sheep have nibbled the grass to its roots, their hoofs chop the roots and the grass dies. We gotta keep 'em out of there."

"Shall I stand and wave them off with my hat, sugar?" Leo asked, wondering where this was going. The Basque sheepherders had always grazed their animals on his land.

"The pond keeps the pungency of wet wool, and the cattle won't go near it for days after a flock of sheep come through. It's why we need a fence."

Before her husband could protest, she hurried on, "The sheep men don't care that our animals sniff and snort and gallop madly away. Just the smell of sheep is a curse on our land."

"It's a good thought, Ruby. It is. In fact, we've thought of it before, but the cost of materials and labor..." Leo glanced up at Turk, who was clearing away the supper. The cook wore a, "Good luck, pal," kind of expression, and Leo grabbed a slice of burned toast before he leaned over to pick up JJ.

An evening routine had been established as the new family adjusted to each other. The babies were playing on the floor a few nights after Ruby mentioned the fence, and Leo had forgotten the conversation. MJ concentrated on threading wooden beads on a string, while JJ swiped the colorful balls and stashed them in his mouth for a quick getaway. Propped on a pillow, Leo dug between sharp little teeth to pull one out and let the baby crawl back to MJ's collection.

"We went over the ground for thistles again today," he said, "and got most of it planted. With three good rains, we'll get two thousand bushels of wheat and barley."

"If we don't get hail," Ruby replied. "Or sheep."

A pencil scratched as Ruby did some arithmetic. "Leo, how many acres stretch between us and Zabala's?" She looked surprised at his surprise and protested, "I promised I'd help. I know about fencing, is all."

Leo sat up straighter, ready for a discussion. Ruby continued, "Our cattle wander over to Zabala's, and they never come back. He keeps them and we lose money; plus, he uses our cropland for grazing and putrefies our water, and we lose more money."

"I don't want to start up any range wars, sugar. Those wire strands chop up the free grass of Texas."

"That's the problem. Zabala thinks it is free, but it's not. It's yours—ours. Fences keep range wars from happening according to the government. And look here." She pointed to his newspaper. "Barbed wire: Glidden's brand is 'light as air, stronger than whiskey, cheap as dirt.'"

"You're as sappy as the trees out back," said Leo. "That ground is still hard with frost. Best to put it off another few months."

Leo lifted the posthole digger and brought it down hard against the rocky ground. The blades didn't penetrate very far into the stubborn dirt. With a sigh, he lifted the digger and then slammed it down again. Pulling the handles apart, he lifted them and turned to empty a pathetic amount of dirt onto a pile that seemed to be growing with infinite slowness. Then he threw the digger on the ground and said with uncharacteristic anger, "Blast, I hate digging postholes!"

Jute stacked the wooden posts and stepped forward. "Lemme work on it for a while—you can unload that roll of wire. I got some brawn left in me."

The early summer beat down mercilessly on the two men. They were stripped to the waist, revealing fish-belly-white torsos. Leo's was hard and muscular, while Jute's was saggy, spotted with age, but still powerful.

Despite having no shirts on, they still wore their hats. Jute's headgear was curled and weathered, showing vestiges of age, like the man it shaded. Leo's hat was the plain, flat-crowned brown. He just wanted something to keep the sun from his eyes today and the rain off his neck tomorrow.

The semi-arid valley was bordered by low hills on the south and the pine tree stand on the north. Barbed wire had now been strung from the hills to the mesas that marked the Barlow boundary.

Leo sat down for a second on the wagon's lowered tailgate and pulled off his work gloves. He wiped sweat from his face, which was tanned to a permanent shade matching that of saddle leather. "I don't see why somebody had to go and invent that blasted devil wire in the first place," he complained.

Jute dug the posthole digger into the ground. The blades grated in the gravelly soil. He grinned over at Leo.

"It's your wife buying it!" he said. Then he went on, "I reckon there won't be near as many range wars."

Leo shook his head. "Folks'll just find something else to fight over."

"Well, ain't you a gloomy cuss today. Look at it this way... you're out in the fresh air, ain't you? You ain't wearin' an apron, stuck behind some store counter somewhere, or sweepin' up in a saloon. Nobody's shootin' at us, either."

Leo tipped his hat back and gazed off into the distance. "I'm not so sure." Pulling his glove on, he slid off the tailgate and went along the side of the wagon until he could reach over and grab a roll of barbed wire. "Sam's boys are always skulking around just out of sight," Leo said. "Bought these wire coils over in Greenville, and there they were, just watching. Sam's jealous nature brings out the exasperation in me. I'd rather buy from him, high prices and all, just for the convenience. But his crazy ban on us going into town sends us elsewhere. Then that sets him off, too."

"Look, boss, he hates anyone who stands up to him. You always have, which irked him from the start. But your little red-headed gal, to boot?" He chuckled, thinking of Ruby, and Leo relaxed a bit, too, reminded of his wife's spunk.

"Sam detests courage. Take his contempt as a compliment, boss."

Ruby put JJ on the kitchen floor and hung up her bonnet. Glancing toward the daybed, she saw several inches of snake disappear behind it. *"Leo!"* JJ started crying at his mother's scream. She snatched up Turk's cleaver and, with a war-hoop, killed the rattler before her husband burst through the door.

"He was three feet long!" she said, knowing Leo would have carried the varmint away on a broomstick. "I'm getting my own gun," she said, shaking with shock.

Leo picked up the wailing JJ and looked back at MJ, who had followed him from the yard. "Son, we'll make you a hat band from the skin. See them rattles? You'll be a music man." Grinning at his wife with pride, he asked, "Now where are you going to get a gun?"

Wearing denim trousers and a long, loose, gray shirt belted at the waist, Ruby looked like a sixteen-year-old boy. She lifted JJ into the wagon, adjusted his hat with rawhide drawstrings, and cinched him to the wooden bench with a blanket and leather belt. Turk had packed well for the four-day journey, and she was exhilarated by the prospect of her adventure.

"I'm not happy about this, you know," grumbled her husband.

"Laws, Leo, I'm a grown woman, taking my boy to see his grandma. I wasn't born in the woods to be scared by an owl. How'll I raise heroes if I'm a nervous biddy?"

MJ climbed on the wagon, expecting to go along. "C'mon, son." Leo put him on his shoulders. "Guess we're batchin' it this week." He leaned in so they could kiss Ruby and JJ good-bye, and she popped a sugar cube in each of their mouths.

"Brought 'em for the horses, but you boys need a little sweetening up." She pulled a blue bandanna up over her nose to collect the dust and gave the whimpering baby a sugar to suck. "Hyah!" she yelled to the horses. "Don't worry none about us!" she called out, and they trotted down the driveway.

After a night at the Prickly Pear in Pepper Junction, Ruby arrived in Greenville the next afternoon.

"Ain't this a sight!" Olive Dawson said over dinner. "This baby eats left-handed!"

"Does everything that way," Ruby replied.

"Already needs a haircut, and he's not yet a year old." His besotted grandma brushed the thick blond hair out of his eyes. "Not a trace of red, and no curl, either. Are you sure he's yours?" she teased.

"You pulled him out, Ma. You ought to know."

Olive heaved a tranquil sigh. "It's sure been a year. But you're happy now?"

"Married to an Ashby of Kentucky?" At her mother's questioning look, she said, "Oh, Ma, we have such fun! He's good, and kind, and he's forgiven me for ... well, for everything. And he loves this little huckleberry."

Olive listened with content as Ruby praised her husband. "He's taken to Turk, too. Neither one of them wanted me riding over here alone. But I'm not afraid of Greenville. I already know nobody likes me—don't need to please a soul."

"Folks have a bit more respect here, just like I knew they would. Even Grace Dobson and that wretched Holt woman asked kindly about your Quaker husband.

"Leo's not a Quaker, Ma. His mother was, is all," Ruby protested.

"Seems to be known as one. Knows his Bible, they say. Anyhow, it ups his reputation. That, and the fact that he's polite and handsome ... and owns a big ranch." Olive sounded like a schoolgirl, and Ruby giggled. "Some of the men are dubious about a man who won't carry a gun, though," Olive said. "Think it's timid, cowardly."

"There's not a speck of yellow in that man, Ma. I've never seen a man like him. But he doesn't adhere to violence. He says if you want peace, quit fighting."

"Must be a challenge for him, living with you!"

"Can't say I've taken up his philosophy. He calls his gun 'a last resort,' and it's so old I don't think it would fire even then. So I'm planning to take Pa's .44 home with me. Need something to shoot snakes." She told her mother about the rattler then, and they complained about crows and rats and worried about Indians.

"I don't hold with shooting folks, but sometimes, you need to look like you could," said Olive, remembering some Cherokees that came by regularly in the early days. "We gave 'em food, let 'em water their horses, and they were friendly enough. Your pa said it was because he'd shot back the first time they raided. They knew he could, so they showed respect."

After supper, Olive mixed the potato water with flour and sugar for a sourdough start. It was still light, so Ruby took care of her second errand and rode over to Shack's lumber mill for some fence posts. Shack greeted her cordially and gave her a good price on the posts and some coils of wire to try out.

"Nate Brannigan's got your daddy's business well in hand," he told her. "It's good to have a finish carpenter in town again. Don't get much business from up your way, though. Sam Lester has cornered that market, even with his high prices."

"I'll let folks know you'll be fair with them, Shack," Ruby said. "My husband's sold off a lot of land, and families are moving in, needing lumber."

Shack had inherited the lumber mill thirty years before and watched his customers siphoned off as they came under Sam's control. "I'll send some supplies over to your place; see if you can sell anything for me. We'd both make a profit and still beat Sam's price."

Fog was thick the morning Ruby left Pepper Junction for Barlow Ranch. Lund was concerned, but she wanted to set off early from the Prickly Pear. The six-bit stop was worth more than that; he had packed her a lunch for the same price.

Sun peeked through the leaves as the fog began to evaporate. At the moment of a cloud passing, Ruby could see beyond some cottonwoods to a limestone ridge. Relieved to see the familiar path, she suddenly picked out a motionless horseman silhouetted against the skyline at the crest. Even at the half-mile distance, she recognized the towering bulk of the rider. It was Snake. She did not need to turn her glance to the low ridges surrounding the little meadow. Those other grim, still watchmen would be there, she knew. Her heart sank chillingly within her.

O'Brien was outside working on his new cabin when Ruby passed by. "Sent for my wife and kids, Mrs. Dawson," he called out, excitement in his voice. "They'll be here the end of summer, for sure. What with the Carters and the Anthonys moving in, we'll have a real town here in Barlow Woods."

The hammer and saw were comforting sounds, and Ruby's fear dissolved in the joy of a safe arrival. "Shack's in Greenville is sending me a load of lumber next week," she told O'Brien. "If you're interested, it'll be for sale."

"Thank you, kindly, ma'am. I'll watch for it." He looked around at the tall trees. "Plenty of lumber right here, if it weren't so hard to process."

MJ burst out crying at the sight of his mother. The bravery of separation had overwhelmed him, and he clung to her shoulders for consolation, burying his face in her red curls and breathing in her familiar scent.

JJ had slept all afternoon in the rocking wagon and was full of energy when he was finally released from his harness, dodging between Leo's legs in a stiff-legged, tumbly toddler gait. Turk and Jute both greeted her, unharnessing the horses and hauling off the wood and supplies.

"My girl's not scared by any owls, I can see that!" Leo said, full of pride and relief, hugging her close. "I shouldn't have doubted your mettle."

Ruby pulled out the .44 and said, "I got my own protection now. Snakes better keep their distance."

"They're running for their holes right now, sugar. Any trouble on your way?"

Anxiety was swallowed up in confidence. "Nothing I couldn't handle," she told him. "And guess what? I'm starting a lumber yard!"

Ruby worked Vaseline into her shoes. "The leather cracked," she explained to Turk. "Must have dried 'em too quickly."

"Heard some news while you were away, sweetheart," Turk announced. Leo pulled out a chair and sat down with her, letting Turk continue. "Jack Smith is dead."

The words hung in the air, while her body reacted: the quick intake of breath; eyes widening; head tilting slightly, wondering; heart stopping for just one beat. A repertoire of emotions played out across her face, and then she took hold of the words and answered softly. "I'm glad," she said. Her thoughts went to JJ. "Now my boy can make a good name for himself." Putting her hand on Leo's, she said again with finality, "I'm glad."

It was quiet, and then she asked what had happened.

"Gunfight over in Fort Worth. Killed some politician over a woman, others got in the way, and then the sheriff shot him making a getaway." Turk watched her take in the details of his report. "Jack Smith was a bad man."

Ruby looked out at the perfect evening. Little, yellow violets had lifted their faces above the ground, basking in the lap of spring. And the sand lilies! There had never been so many before, dotting the land with their purity as the dandelions had strewn it with gold. Meadowlarks drenched the air with melodies most mornings, and even blossoms that usually had no fragrance smelled daintily sweet.

Leo caught her expression and said, "There's good here, Ruby. Ma used to say, 'the earth is full of the goodness of God.'"

"Do you believe in God, Leo?"

"Can't help it. In my darkness I prayed, and now I see light."

Ruby looked around at her new home. "My darkness is melting away, too. The peace of this place has rubbed off on me. I'm finally happy, Leo."

12

Summer was typically dry and hot. By August, the wheat and oats were mostly in the shock, and lush green pasture grasses gave promise of fat and healthy herds of cattle. "Looks like a plentiful harvest this year, Boss," Jute told Leo one afternoon.

The next day, Jute began seeing strange silvery spots circling in the sunny skies. "Damn cataracts," the old man said, rubbing his eyes. Thoughts of blindness terrified the cowboy all day until some of the hired hands mentioned seeing the silvery circles, too. They were millions of grasshoppers in flight.

Toward evening, they began dropping to the earth. "Hoppers!" yelled Turk. "Save the garden!" In minutes, the hired hands were digging for potatoes, picking cabbages and turnips, plums, and green apples. Insects fell like giant-sized flakes in a snowstorm, crawling over the fields in a solid body, eating every green thing that was growing. The hillside looked as if water were running down it, the hoppers were so thick. When they had eaten the fields bare, leaving not a sprig of grass, they piled up on the new fence posts and ate the bark. They ate the leaves off the fruit trees and seemed to relish the green peaches but left the pits hanging.

Wings beating on the roof and sides of the house terrified the children, who screamed as the creatures writhed through their hair and down their shirts. Ruby tried to secure the house, smashing them with a broom after shaking them out of the bedding. Turk spread gunnysacks over the precious vegetable patch, but the grasshoppers ate right through. They ate harnesses, window curtains, hoe handles, and even each other. Leo tied strings around his trouser bottoms to keep the pests from crawling up and biting his legs.

Lighting upon trees, the hoards broke limbs under their weight. Barlow Ranch was littered with cottonwood and juniper branches, alive with the bugs.

Jute and his men dug trenches to bury the critters, lighting fires to burn them out, but the flames were covered and smothered by grasshoppers piling a foot deep or more.

Leo's efforts to save his crops were futile. The wheat and barley vanished in a few hours, plants denuded to the stalks. Within days, the trees and prairies were as bare as midwinter. The cattle and horses stood by helplessly as the pests crawled all over their bodies, tickling their ears, eyes, and nostrils.

Mrs. O'Brien and her children had traveled by train to Fort Worth. "It was horrible," she said. "A dark cloud of grasshoppers landed on the tracks and stopped all the trains. Grease from the crushed insects set the locomotive wheels to spinning, and we couldn't move an inch!" The terrifying experience had held them up for days and with the nightmare on O'Briens' land for a welcome, the family thought they'd arrived in Hades.

Fresh water was polluted by the bugs, and the cows and chickens that had gorged on the hoppers were useless as food, as were the fish in the streams. The meat smelled and tasted like grasshoppers. Overnight, the Barlow Ranch was in ruin.

"There's a bounty of fifty cents a bushel on the critters," announced Jute. His cowboys fastened boxes on wagon platforms and drove around the fields until the crates were full, hoping to earn enough to cover their wages. Mr. Zabala, who had an abundance of the insects, chased the men with a pitchfork when he discovered them "poaching grasshoppers" on his land.

"See? Barbed wire isn't the solution to everything," Leo reminded Jute. "Folks'll always find something to fight about."

It was only a week later, although it seemed like a year. Leo was beating the hordes with a shovel when he smelled a storm. A sudden clap of thunder jolted the cattle, and they became a monstrous force plunging through the dark afternoon. Hurling the shovel, he jerked off Rascal's bridle and let the horse run for home then loosened his metal spurs and threw down his pocketknife. Friction of the speeding cattle caused weird, blue flashes to quiver at the tips of their long horns just before the lightning struck the ground and set the grass on fire. The grasshopper plague was over.

Faced with a hard winter, Barlow had to let his men go. Food was the major issue. Until the soil was cleaned up, there could be no planting—any harvest before summer would be a miracle. Rather than see them starve, Leo had turned the cattle back to the land, where they'd fend for themselves. Even Jute left the ranch after years as foreman—without a crew, there was no work for him,

September was gone, and great stringing flocks of gray Canadian geese were moving. Their lonely cries kept Leo awake and anxious during the long nights. After supper one evening, restless as always these days, Leo left the house and walked up through the undergrowth to the edge of the county road. He stood a long time looking northward toward the abandoned mill. The air was taking on the feel of autumn. Finally, he noticed he was not alone.

"Nobody round here's got any seed," Turk said. "Sam Lester's sent east for some, and he's already jacking up the price daily, afore it even arrives. I've managed to salvage some of the food in the root cellar, but we're in for a hungry spell." Absently, Turk bit off the end of a cigar, swiped a match against his boot, and got it going.

"Hoped I'd get through life without kow-towing to Sam, but I guess it's got to be done. I'll go into town tomorrow." Leo kicked the dirt ruefully and swore. "This situation is bringing out the worst in me," he said, and swore again. "I never swear."

Ruby was adamant. "I'm going," she said. Knowing he'd lose the battle in the end, Leo decided not to fight it. "It'll be faster to leave the wagon here."

Turk saddled the horses and brought them around. "I've packed up a lunch and other necessities," he said.

When Leo saw the firearm, he said quietly, "Take it off, Turk. I'm not riding into town with a rifle on my saddle. That's asking for trouble isn't it, when I'm known not to pack a gun?" His voice took on a kindly tone, and he shook the cook's knobby hand. "Look after the boys. I'll bring her back safe."

Bolte stood in his old position by the Empire Hotel, surveying the street from under the wide brim of his black sombrero, when the Barlows looped their reins over the tie rail in front of the Fat Chance Saloon. They'd noticed Erly's Confederate cap tailing them from five miles outside town, the man decked out in his sheep-skinned chaps.

"Sam's got a gunman ready for each of us," Ruby had told Leo, tension creeping into her voice.

"Not much to brag about, shooting an unarmed man and a woman," Leo reassured her. "Pay them no heed."

Now they swung through the doors and sat down at the table next to Sam's. Molly's curls were just as brazen, her lips just as red. Her painted eyebrows rose in disbelief when she saw Ruby but unsure how to greet her, she busied herself behind the bar. Over the crowded tables, across the noisy room, cold, observant blue eyes in a bronzed, pockmarked face watched them with resentment. The ever-present bulge of tobacco in Haze's cheek dripped juice over his insolent lip, and he opened the frock coat conspicuously to display his gun.

Nausea rumbled Ruby's midsection, and her chest warmed the bile that rose in her throat. Dread overwhelmed her. She looked at Leo for backbone just as Snake whipped an arm around Leo's neck and hauled him roughly backward out of his chair and toward the bar. In the same motion, he pulled an Arkansas toothpick and brandished the knife at Ruby as Leo kicked against the arm lock, twisting loose of the hold. Snake fired from the hip, right through the holster's tip without pausing to withdraw the pistol. The bullet splintered the wood of the table, inches away from Ruby's elbow.

Sam came down the stairs, snorting, red-faced from a coughing spasm. "Now, boys, let's let our guests explain themselves before we remind them of their undesirability." He snapped his fingers at Molly. "Just one beer." He sat at his own table and motioned with his stump for Leo to join him, calling Ruby over with a swing of his greasy, yellow hair. He swallowed his beer, shook as he held in some hacking sounds, and cleared his throat.

"Jewel," he taunted, "I hardly recognize you. You were such a beauty." Producing the bowie knife, he flicked it on his stump and then touched the point to her throat. "Freckles, creases," he looked at her hands, "blisters...what a shame," he finished. Looking at Leo, he smirked. "Hear the hoppers wiped you out."

Assertive, with poise, Leo answered, "Not quite, Sam. The crops and cattle have taken a hit, but I still have land, lots of land. I'm here to make you an offer." Snake made a move when Leo opened his wooly vest for a document but retreated as the man unfolded a large map. "The sections colored in yellow are the prime parcels," Leo explained. "I would like to trade one of them for enough seed for a thousand acres."

Sam looked at the map, and pointed to a few bits colored red. "I have to admit I'm interested, Barlow. Are these areas for sale, too?"

"No. I can't sell you those acres—they're worthless." His finger trailed to a section just off the county road. "This is the choicest spot. It's in the pines, with an old lumber mill ready for restoration." Ruby sucked in her breath. She couldn't stand to have Sam so close to her home.

"This is what you want to sell me?" Sam asked.

"It's by far the best land I have. You would get a good return on such an investment, I can assure you."

Sam went back to a large red tract, not attached to the rest of the property, in the direction of Sam's Town. "And why isn't this piece available?"

"It's called Pot Hill. The Indians deemed it haunted. There are some warm springs up there; it's covered with hot pots, most of them dry. But the legends make it off bounds. It's worthless. I'd never try to sell it—wouldn't feel right."

Snake was hovering behind the conversation and caught Sam's attention. Pushing away from the table, the man took his cronies to the other corner for a hushed discussion. Molly came over for the empty beer mug and gave Ruby a quick hug. "We don't blame you for leavin, honey. We blame ourselves for stayin." Ruby asked about Tessa and Pearl. "Tequila's upstairs. She's all right. Black Pearl got caught again. Sam sent her over to Fort Worth for an abortion. They gave her prussic acid…" her voice trailed off as Sam came back to the table. "She died," Molly mouthed to a stunned Ruby.

"Tell me more about Pot Hill." Sam narrowed his eyes. "I don't really trust your kindly concerns. Seems it would have a good view across the valley." He looked back at his boys. "Snake's heard the old legends. Says they were invented to keep the hot pots secret. Either you're a fool or a fraud, Barlow. Those hot pots would be fine recreation for my boys here."

"Mr. Lester, for the seed I'm needing, I couldn't sell you that land without being called a cheat. I'm an honest man, Sam, and I'm telling you the mill property would be your best bet."

"I'll make the deal for Pot Hill," said Sam. "That's my only offer."

"You men are witness to this transaction," Leo said to the crowd that had gathered. "Against my explicit advice, Sam Lester is buying Pot Hill in exchange for seed for a thousand acres."

Riding out of town, Ruby observed, "As usual, Sam got what he wanted."

"So did I, sugar. Ma always said bad men are confused by good men; they don't know how to believe the truth."

"Looks like he got his hilltop, his lookout, and his hotpots. 'Fine recreation for his boys,' he called it."

"Oh, they'll enjoy it this fall, all right," Leo told her. "And they'll fit right in come spring. That's when the hot pots fill up with snakes."

13

July 1881, Barlow Ranch

July 1, 1881, was JJ's eighth birthday. "Ever seen a red horse?" Leo asked his son, pointing to the filly. "She's a fiery one. And the bay is fast, or the pinto. You can have your pick." The mustangs had arrived the day before, and Leo had promised JJ his choice.

"None of them's as fast as Pepper," MJ bragged, nuzzling the black and white colt he'd gotten the year before. Without warning, a dun stallion attacked the red filly, using his front hoofs to strike hammer-like blows. She bit back, and the stallion reared again, kicking viciously. It was then that Leo noticed the twitching and the bald spots on his hide.

"I got a bellicose horse over in the corral," Leo called to Turk, herding the boys back to the house. "Must be locoed—ate some rattleweed or purple loco. Keep these kids inside."

Tightening his grip on MJ's hand, JJ asked, "What's locoed?"

His brother shook him off. "Crazy. That horse was plumb crazy!"

"Did you know Turk here is an expert on crazy horses?" Ruby sat MJ down with a pan of peas to shell as a distraction and commandeered JJ to measure him for a new shirt. "Tell them, Turk."

Clouds of flour rose as he heaved a pile of dough onto the table, and he started the tale. "My first job as a wrangler was to round up a herd of horses that had been eating locoweed. Some of 'em had gone into fits, some lay groaning, some foamed at the mouth, and some had fallen dead. Me and another man shot two horses that couldn't stand up, and then we gathered up the cripples and made a start for the ranch, 180 miles due south."

Kneading the dough put Turk in a rhythm. "They was bad locoed and half-starved, most with a skin disease that eats the hair off and leaves the shivering creature exposed. They had swollen, running nostrils and wheezy breathing. Three long weeks of these melancholy beasts, and I was plum near crazy myself."

MJ had lost track of his peas, and JJ stood with his arms in the air, draped with pattern pieces. "So? So, what'd you do?" JJ asked.

The old man's Adam's apple bobbed. "We happened on a town just a day short of the ranch. One of those towns that looks like it'll up and blow away with a good breath of wind. But it had a saloon. I still had a half-eagle, so I went in and asked for the strongest stuff they served. Figured me and my partner deserved a night of forgetfulness.

"It was the worst tarantula juice I ever tasted. We was laughin' and weepin' and drowning our sorrows while we was bedding down our sickly herd, and I dropped the bottle.

"Next thing I know, we were marching and singing right up the trail to the corral, those drunk horses following like we was in a parade. We were welcomed like heroes. Drink cured us all, I guess."

Ruby had unpinned JJ by the time the story was over. "Is that true, Turk?" the boy asked skeptically.

"Truer than an outright lie," Turk said. He swept the flour out the door and saw that the ruckus was over. O'Brien was walking away from the corral with Leo.

A hound dog, likely abandoned close by, was digging in the yard. "That mangy trespasser is waiting for a handout again." Flailing the broom, Turk yelled, "Shoo, dog! Get out of here!"

MJ shoved back from the table, "No, Turk! He comes to see me!" The door banged against the house, and MJ jumped the steps. JJ wasn't far behind. The puppy was a curious dark blue with various-shaped black spots—a bluetick coonhound, Leo had said. His ears were mostly black, thin, and set low on his dark head.

"He is the slobberiest dog I've ever seen," complained JJ as he knelt down next to his older brother. "How can you stand all that drool?"

MJ didn't answer. "He's got a scent, Jage. Look at him."

The dog sniffed and then ran around a stand of bushes before he scratched the ground and started digging furiously.

"I think you've all been munching on locoweed," Turk said from the door. "Another day, and you'll be foamin' at the mouth."

Leo scooped leaves out of the watering trough while Ruby swept them off the porch. Autumn breezes dumped piles in the slight hollow surrounding the house, and it was a daily chore to keep them from blowing inside.

"Shack's delivering some supplies from Greenville," Ruby told her husband. "O'Brien and his boys are coming over to help." In the past seven years, fourteen families had moved into Barlow Woods, and the need for lumber had multiplied greatly. Ruby went back and forth a few times a year, but Shack's wagons were better equipped to haul the big loads. Recently, he'd suggested she get the old mill back in production for lumber, since the demand for barbed wire and fence posts was taking over his business.

Being the middleman for Shack had been a boon for the Barlows at just the right time. After the grasshopper plague, it had taken Leo a good five years to build up a herd and get back on his feet. Her small income kept them from starving.

"I'm fine," Ruby had said, working in the fields. "Growin' up on a farm, I did most of the plowing from the time I was ten years old. I must have walked thousands of miles behind an old mule." However, she was glad when they could hire a few hands to help out. "I'm not going to be some dependent ninny, though," she told Leo. "Ma was helpless without Pa. And I was helpless before you." Her arrangement with Shack gave her some security.

"The posse is out again," Shack's deliveryman told her nervously when he pulled up. "Some fat man in a derby is patrolling the county road with a squirrelly runt I could smell from twenty yards. Said they don't like me doin' business in this part of the valley."

There was a light explosion of her out-sighing breath, and a faint frown turned her pink lips down. Even with a straw hat shading her blue eyes, the red hair bushed out around her face. She shoved the hat off her head impatiently and tied back the mass of curls with the black ribbon she wore around her wrist. "Those hoodlums are the bane of my existence!" she burst. "I'll come to Greenville next time," she reassured the man. "And I'll pay you extra for your trouble today."

More and more, Sam was pressing in on any success they had. The snake pit property had been seen as just another affront, which of course it had been, but Sam had been warned fairly and actually could be living right next door, if he had an ounce of sense. Horrors!

An old woman pulled up in a dray fit for hauling a big load of lumber. Ruby recognized her as the landlady of the Bosque Hotel. "Mrs. Randall," she said, "you may not remember me, but I stayed at your boarding house in Sam's Town a few years back."

"Course I know you, Miss Ruby. You scandalized the town for a couple of months: bright, young treat you were, full of hope, then victimized by that scoundrel. Turned all respectable now, I see." She said it with pleasure. "Guess everybody does, eventually. Turn respectable, I mean... except him. Hear you're all but mayor out here."

"No, no... but what are you doing in Barlow Woods?"

"Got unnecessary for the varmint. Curly Bill, that's my husband, he died finally. Sam, that lily-liver, scared of an old woman—had his Mexican come over and all but shoot me out 'a the boarding house. My home for over fifteen years! So I came over to Barlow Woods to live with my daughter." Well corseted even in old age, the woman's top-heavy form barely moved, even when she hefted herself out of the dray.

"You are still a grand fountainhead of gossip in town, Miss Ruby. Hear all about your lumber business, how you purloin all Sam's customers, and about the folks movin' in from all over, former slaves even. Don't that beat the Dutch? Sam hatin' 'em like he does?"

"Knew Sam hated everybody, Mrs. Randall, but I'm not sure who you're talking about."

"Why, those cotton pickers from Mississippi, the Ramseys. Least they used to pick cotton. Now they're planning to grow it, right here on your land. Could make a pretty penny! They have plenty to say against Sam and his daddy—knew the old man when he beat and raped his slaves. He expected his boy to do the same. Young Sam got a shovel across his face when he tried." Mrs. Randall laughed out loud, holding her solid middle. "Imagine how many folks will be glad to hear that tale!" She made her purchases, and O'Brien's son, Patrick, loaded the wood on the flatbed of the wagon.

"Hanging me a nice shelf tonight," the woman crowed as she handed Ruby some coins. "Glad to have some conveniences out here. Sam's Town is awful far to haul goods and awful expensive, as well. Hope other businesses will spring up, fly in Sam's face, so to speak, like you folks have done."

After Mrs. Randall left, Ruby walked up to the abandoned mill. As far as she could tell, it was left with all the equipment in good order. The structure itself was disintegrating; a wall collapsed, and the roof caved in. Tall pine trees surrounded the building, and the stream crashed below a dilapidated paddle wheel. Taming the water would be the real challenge, she knew. Wondering if Nate Brannigan would be willing to reconstruct the place, she turned her mind to face the real problem, Sam Lester. In any other circumstance, this kind of venture in a growing community would be a lead pipe cinch. Why was she so afraid?

"You're going to make me swear, and I never swear," said Leo, when he heard Ruby's plans. Turk tilted his chair against the kitchen wall, scratched his middle-aged paunch, and enjoyed the growing warmth of the late summer sun. It had been a fine Saturday morning until this crazy woman he worked for and lived with announced another out-and-out war with Sam Lester.

"It's like spitting in the man's face," Turk said. "He'll have to spit back, and Sam has got breath like a double-seater, sweetheart. Starting up that mill will be going head-to-head with a monster."

"We've got almost sixteen families living here now, moving in every day," she argued. "Somebody's got to start a lumber mill! There's demand! Think of what's to come: stores, taverns, coopers, we'll need blacksmith shops, a livery—and we've already got the trees and the mill right here! On our land!"

"It's true, Ruby," replied Leo. "But Sam thinks he's laid claim to all that business, and every time you tweak his nose, he gets madder. Let somebody else do it."

"Are you two telling me that Sam can continue to browbeat this family? He's a bully, a spider with a sticky net. I'd like to knock him to the floor and obliterate him with my boot. I'm not looking to him for permission."

And so, the Barlow Mill came to life.

The winter of 1882 had been mild enough for Nate Brannigan and a few hired hands to restore the deserted building. The saw blade was sharpened, ready to slice logs into boards, as soon as the stream was cleared out. Now, spring rains promised a torrential runoff, and a millwright from Nova Scotia called Fontaine had set the gears and agreed to run the mill day-to-day.

"Can we go up and see the saw after breakfast?" JJ asked. "Pa's there. We won't get chopped up or anything."

Ruby had set firm rules about the boy's boundaries and the sawmill was off limits. "The blade and stream are like fire, excellent tools when they're controlled, treacherous when they're not," she'd said. Like all little boys, they were drawn to danger, but unlike some, they were unusually obedient, and Ruby didn't worry. Not quite seven, JJ was already sensible and trustworthy, though skinny as a fence post. "There's chores first," she answered. "And you haven't touched your breakfast."

The kitchen was warm from the fire, and there was a fine smell of bacon frying and coffee steaming. Eight-year-old MJ was a good eater, and he leaned into his food, downing an egg and five strips of bacon, plus a couple of hotcakes. Dipping a sugar cube in her coffee, Ruby sucked its sweetness and dipped a couple more. "Here, sugar mouths," she said to her little boys, who loved this morning ritual.

MJ could not have presented a more appealing picture as a wide-eyed, wandering, barefoot boy. His beaming, slightly bucktoothed smile would have melted the heart of a limestone head marker. "I saw some ghosts in the yard last night," he said matter-of-factly to his younger brother.

"Did not!" JJ scoffed, alarm mixed with suspicion. "You never!"

"Did so. They was scooting 'mongst the trees, jingling, like their death chains was rattling. One of 'em had a long, dark cape flowin' around him, and their faces glowed, light flickering by their eye sockets—"

"Mama," JJ interrupted her musings, "are there such things as ha'nts?"

"Don't know, JJ. Your pa believes in ghosts, he says. I wouldn't want to meet up with one."

Turk was just starting in on a chicken. He was at his storytelling best with feathers flying from his greasy hands.

"I remember when Bud Thompson's face was plastered with his own brother's brains. Horse stepped on his head." He had the boys' attention.

Ruby muffled a gag. "Turk! You say the most unappetizing things while you're fixing a meal!"

"Bud went to bed that night, and a ghost came calling, all empty headed and bloody. 'Give me back my brains... give me back my brains!" He wiggled his gelatinous fingers in JJ's petrified face and laughed.

"Turk, was that true?" the boy asked.

"Truer than an outright lie," the old man answered.

Outside, Trespass heard boots scrape and came roaring out of his barrel ready to take somebody's leg off. He got his nose belatedly full of Leo's smell and was instantly on the ground squirming and barking, wetting himself in abject apology.

"Scroungy mutt," Leo said, rubbing the dog gently with his stiff leg. His limp seemed more pronounced when Ruby stepped out the back door. She was wearing a faded blue cotton housedress, and her sleeves were pushed up to her elbows, revealing the golden brown of her arms. Her red curls were awry, and she pushed them off her forehead. Leo put his finger to his lips, and she knew not to make a fuss about his appearance. "I'll need some breakfast, Turk," he hollered. "Start burning some toast. Be in in a minute."

"That's a bad cut on your arm," Ruby gasped. "I'll fix it. And there's a fresh shirt on the line."

Leo was grateful for her tact. He'd stopped to wash at the creek, where he'd scrubbed the blood from his face. There was nothing he could do about his clothes or the cut.

Turk returned to the door with Ruby. He nodded at Leo but stood blocking the view from the house. Ruby had a basin and hot water, salve, and rags, and she bathed Leo's arm, afterward wrapping it up. Leo submitted in silence, stretching out his tender knee. Turk went back to distract the children, and Ruby tied the bandage and put the cap back on the salve.

"Who was it?" she asked.

"Didn't see a soul. But Sam Lester was behind it. I went to check the steps Brannigan finished yesterday, and Fontaine had been setting those gears. The steps collapsed under me. As I stumbled around, I saw the main belt had been slipped off its pulley. It could have burst the big wheel apart! Don't know what all damage there'd have been if I hadn't gone there this morning."

"Ha'nt's, JJ called them." Ruby thought back on the kids' conversation. "Leo, I think MJ might have seen them. He talked about ghosts, one with a long, dark cape. Bolte and some others were here in the night, I'm sure of it." Thinking again of her children, she asked, "Leo, do we need to have guards around?"

"Form an army to fight Sam's army, you mean? A battle is not what we want, Ruby."

"But fighting back might be a necessary evil!"

"No matter how necessary, it is always an evil. Never a good." Leo changed his shirt and left the sleeves down to cover the wound. "Brannigan can fix the steps; the millwright will fix the gears. And you fixed me." He held out his arm as evidence. "The damage will set us back a few weeks, but I see sawdust in your future, sugar." As always, Leo smiled at his little wordplay, just as the two boys escaped Turk's surveillance.

"Pa, why do we have to muck out the barn?" JJ wailed.

"If you're big enough, you're old enough," Leo said, his stock reply.

Shoving each other playfully, their sons stumbled over Trespass, laughed hysterically, and tagged it toward the corral, jumping hay bales, tussling over the shovel, tossing and catching a stick between them. A running argument over whose horse was fastest, MJ's Pepper, or the red filly JJ called Cowlick, filled the air with words as familiar as floating dandelion seeds.

"I think we've actually got three puppies," Leo said, looping his arm over Ruby's shoulder. "You lot have saddle bagged me."

Leo went outside a few days later and stepped down off the porch. The roses around the steps were in bloom, and their scent was strong in his nostrils. He could smell the rich, fresh-turned earth in the garden patch, and somewhere, a magpie screeched. The air was hot, but in the distance, thunder rumbled. Soon, it would be raining on their crops. A few scattered drops fell, and the wind began to pick up. Looking south, Leo watched a dark cloud that seemed to twirl around on the prairie. It took a second to register in his brain, but then instinct took over. "Tornado!"

Within minutes, the air was filled with bricks, barrels, boxes, and boards, which were blown about like chaff. The dust so clouded the air, as to shut out the light of day. Wind lifted ten-pound boulders and a two-year-old mule colt off the ground, and a squawking flock overhead may have been geese, maybe jackasses.

The tornado, with its fearful roar and death-dealing funnel, was terror to the Barlow children.

Settling the boys in the storm cellar, Turk reassured them. "Your folks'll be all right. Your pa has gone to sing to the cattle, settle 'em down. They can't all fit down here with us, you know."

"Where's Mama?" JJ whimpered. Turk was wondering the same thing but comforted the little boy with soothing words. Then, to distract himself as much as anything, he said, "Did I tell you about the storm in 1860?"

MJ held a blanket over his head as protection—dirt sprinkled through the slats from the commotion outside. "Tell us," he said.

"The twisting motion of the wind drew all the milk from one farmer's herd of cows and sprayed it into the air. It became mixed up with small pellets of hail and made a downfall of ice cream. Some pretty big hail fell that day. One chunk stuck itself in the ground when it melted and afterward, we had us a fine new boating pond."

"Is that true?" asked JJ.

"Truer than an outright lie. Right, Turk?" answered MJ.

The wind had died down, and the roof of the storm cellar was lifting up. Ruby stood, a foreign creature, sickly white from the dust and rain, grasses, and leaves sticking out of thick, tangled, wet hair. "Thank God!" she said, when she saw her children.

Clamoring up the ladder, MJ yelled, "Pa!" Leo was running from the corral drenched in the downpour but untouched otherwise.

"It missed the barn completely!" he called out with relief. "And only one section of the corral went down.

The twister had zigzagged a swath through the ranch and left most of it intact. The stone house had taken the brunt but survived, except for the porch. Loss of life was limited to a few unsuspecting chickens and the peach tree that fed the grasshoppers almost six years before.

Ruby had been hanging a flannel sheet out to dry. "It sailed off like a giant kite, and I was holding on so tight I almost went, too!" After the fact, it all seemed a grand adventure, and Turk had magnificent details to add to his collection of tall tales.

MJ gloried in the fact that his pa had saved the animals. But that was the very fact that troubled JJ. Why had he run away from them at such a moment, the youngster wondered. Did he know it would be safer in the barn?

Turk dug out his special box of imported cigars and offered them all around in celebration. "Not on your life, young man!" Ruby said when MJ reached for one, but even she accepted a small puff from Leo's when he held it out to her. "After the grime that swirled around me today, this is like breathing a summer breeze," she said.

14

June 1882, Barlow Ranch

"If I've drunk with you, I can't kill you. That's the code," the nine-year-old explained to his big brother. "And if you're a gunslinger, you gotta keep your nerves in hand." JJ showed off a quick draw technique with his well-used wooden gun. "Holsters just get in the way," he said, "unless you fire from the hip plum through the leather."

"You're just saying that because a holster falls right off your spindly hips," MJ retorted.

"Am not! Tucked in my waistband, I can feel the pistol without even looking." He stuck the gun into the front of his trousers and demonstrated how fast he could pull it out left-handed and shoot a bad man. In this case, the bandit was a target carved into the peach tree stump with a pocketknife. After the tornado, it had taken almost a month for the boys to chop up the branches for firewood. This was the first chance JJ had had to put his etching to use, and he was disappointed not to be using a real gun.

"See?" He swung around and stood sideways to make himself a smaller object. "Some day, I might wear a holster as a decoy and trick some jasper." JJ twirled and drew. "Bang! Bang, bang!" Practicing the move was a major part of his daily labor. He was intent on becoming a fast, accurate shot and continually begged his mother to let him shoot rabbits or quail for supper with the .44. Ruby agreed it was a crucial skill and allowed him to shoot occasionally, in spite of Leo's objections.

"Take a try." JJ handed the wooden replica to MJ.

Squinting, MJ pretended to pull the trigger. "I can't even see the stump clear, let alone the bull's-eye. I'd rather have a fishing pole, where the target comes to me."

"That's cause you're a chicken. Like Pa."

"You take that back!" Without pausing, MJ toed around hard and fast and, with a youthful savagery, drove his fist into the center of his brother's face. The blow budged the boy's jaw by a fraction of an inch. Blood from his nose made twin rivulets over his lips. MJ felt the wind of two blows he managed to avoid before a glancing force rocked his temple and JJ's elbow slammed him brutally in the stomach.

The older boy's arms wrapped around JJ until his little brother bellowed and wrenched free, and then JJ smashed his knuckle under MJ's chin. MJ's teeth clicked together on his tongue and he howled, diving toward JJ's knees.

Both boys were in a sobbing frenzy when Leo jerked them to attention. Clamping them each by the back of their shirt, he hauled them to the trough and dropped them in. "Maybe you boys should soak your heads for a while."

JJ came up sputtering, fists flying, and his father shoved him under again. "Not long enough, I take it."

"But, Pa…" MJ started, coming up for air, "JJ said something downright vile."

"Was it true?" Leo asked.

"No, sir."

"Then learn to ignore it." JJ was scowling at his brother under a dripping mop of blond hair. Leo used his son's hat to dump another stream of cold water over his head. "Learning to ignore insults is a sign of manhood." He splashed more water in their faces and baited them, "'Course I'm talking to a couple of waterlogged whippersnappers."

Diving over the fragmented porch in a fever to join the melee, Trespass let out a bawl. Then he dropped his bony rear into the mud by the trough and began to scratch. Leo sloshed some water on the blue hound, and the boys howled as he streaked back to his barrel by the smokehouse, yelping. Thoroughly drenched, Leo straightened his stiff knee, wrung out his bandanna, wiped the remaining blood off JJ's nose, and went back to work.

Having forgotten what the brawl was all about, the boys went back to their game. "Are you packing a gun, hombre? Hand it over," MJ told his prisoner, in a deep voice. "I'm the law around here." JJ spun the carved weapon on his finger and held it out to his captor, barrel first.

"You'd be dead, fella," said Turk from the door, plate in hand. "Any gunslinger worth his salt would flip that gun in the fraction of a second, and its muzzle would be pointing right at you, his trigger finger ready. Shuck your weapon, Jage," and he held out the plate.

The boys ran to the kitchen and took the hot biscuits Turk offered them. "How do you know so much about gun fighting?" asked MJ. "You're a cook."

"On the trail, the cook is second only to the boss, and there's a few bad men that sign up for those rides." His Adam's apple jumped, and his brown eyes sparked. "I always told them if I caught them in my chuck wagon, I'd kill 'em one of two ways."

"What were they, Turk?" JJ settled down for a yarn.

"I'd either shoot 'em or poison 'em." He shook off the temptation to sit down and expand. His arthritic knees would have a tough time getting him back up.

"Shoot him or poison him—that's what I'd like to do to that mutt! Get him outta my domain," Turk said, kicking Trespass out the back door. "And go feed the chickens. They could starve to death while you're shooting each other." He shooed them toward the ever-waiting chores and tossed Trespass the last of the biscuits.

Ruby sat by the front window of her house and considered her reflection in the September twilight. Evening shadows in the sunset glow polished her skin and caught her hair on fire. It was a full ten years since the girl that stared back at her had disappeared into womanhood. September 1872. What a long time ago, it seemed, since Jack had ignited her fantasies. She hadn't gone where she intended to go, but she'd ended up where she intended to be: a home, a husband, and children.

Leo was hardly the husband she'd imagined for herself back then. Instead of just a prince, she got the whole castle. He was her fortress: secure, solid, and indestructible. Deep sun wrinkles now creased the corners of his hazel eyes; the dark, blond hair was graying at the temples and thinning on the top. Squatting down to listen to children or ploughed earth, riding Rascal long hours to round up longhorns, hauling lumber from the mill—these things had bowed his legs, slightly stooped his back, and stiffened his joints. Long gone was the spry cowboy of his youth. But Leo lived in that rare grace of self that could keep his identity intact through any ordeal. He did not depend on outward props to shore himself up; heartache, circumstance, and violence could not eradicate the moral, gentle habits of his upbringing.

Jack had been a mirage. Leo had been a well, hardly visible from a distance but with the depth and purity to restore her. She hardly ever thought of those ugly days anymore. Leo had broken off that part of her life like he would the wormy end of a piece of corn. When it was gone, it was forgotten, and he just saw the golden, fresh promise she held inside.

Ruby had not quite forgotten. Why did she still think about Jack? JJ's wavy hair was as blond as Jack's had been black, but the boy's complexion was almost bronze after a summer in the sun, like his father's had been. And he had an agile, easy stride, his long legs promising height. Her son was why she remembered Jack with a fondness he didn't deserve. She felt sorry he never knew about JJ and the traits the boy carried inside, without even being aware of it. JJ's tenderness toward Cowlick, his own red filly, and the way he talked to her, reminded her of the night she'd been introduced to Big Red. The boy's humor was different than Leo's; he bantered in that light way Ruby remembered. The left-handedness came directly from Jack, and she chuckled to see how he tucked a gun in the front of his waistband. How could he have inherited that?

JJ was smart. Not like MJ, who loved to read his daddy's books, try experiments, and do figures in his head; JJ was smart about people. He could read situations and moods. He was volatile, more likely to throw a punch than discuss a principle, but he was learning to keep his temper. Leo had told him that men are like steel—when they lose their temper, they lose their worth. Peacefulness did not come as naturally to JJ as it did to his older brother. Ruby wondered sometimes if Jack would approve of the way she and Leo were raising his son. Since he was dead, she was able to imbue him with favorable qualities, and she liked to think he'd have come forward eventually and treasured his son.

MJ interrupted her thoughts. "The O'Brien kids are going to start school in Sam's Town," he said without preamble. "If I promise to get my chores done, can I go, too?"

Leo was right behind him, signaling Ruby not to answer. "What if we set up a public school here, right in Barlow Woods?" he asked MJ. "We could go the whole hog, science, history, maps for geography..."

"Where, Pa? Who'd teach it? And who'd come?" MJ voiced the same questions Ruby had.

"How about Uncle Josey's house? We could get that fixed up. I've got books we could start with, until we can order new ones. And there's no better teacher in the world than your mama."

MJ looked skeptical. "She's already taught me everything she knows," he said. "Why can't I just go to regular school?"

Then Leo gave the ultimate enticement. "You could design the whole school yourself."

"Jage!" Arms already in motion, MJ spun his foot and leaped an inch off the floor with a pivot. "Jage! We're making us a school!"

"A school? I don't want a school!" was JJ's less enthusiastic reply. "So we'll have to sit and read all day long?" The back door slammed.

"Sorry, sugar," Leo said to Ruby. He slacked onto the daybed, legs outstretched, feet crossed. "There's no way in tarnation Sam will let our boys go to school in town, but I couldn't tell MJ that. So I came up with an alternative. Seems a good one, though."

He saw her queasy excitement, and teased, "You've always had a hankering to be a real schoolmarm, I know it. Give you a chance to charm another wrecked outbuilding into a going concern. This ranch will be a town in itself when you're finished with it."

Between the house and the barn, Josey's old, stone-faced cabin was hidden in a cluster of pines, on the edge of a small meadow fronting the stream. Inside, two rooms were lined with peeled logs, weatherworn to soft silver. A sunny east window illuminated spider webs and birds nests, which the boys wiped out the first morning with brooms.

"Jage! Want to shoot some rats?" Ruby asked. Nothing could have pleased the boy more. She and MJ swept the screeching critters out the door, and JJ picked them off with the .44 as they ran for the trees.

An old roll-top desk was emptied and the papers burned, along with perishables that had long since perished. "Mama, there's newspapers stuck on the logs in here." MJ said from the smaller room. He crooked his neck and read, "Women's Complaint Tonic."

"Looks like they chinked the logs and then pasted whatever paper they could find to keep out the bugs. We'll replace the chinking, repaper, and whitewash over the top to make the rooms brighter."

Boards and wood blocks were hauled from the mill. JJ made a bookcase along one wall, and MJ built a wood box for the potbellied iron stove. A long bench lined the opposite wall, with a blackboard at the front of the classroom.

"Uncle Josey must have been just like Pa," said MJ, digging through stacks of smelly books. "He's got an atlas, something about Greek my-tho-lo-gee..."

"You say it myth-ology," Ruby said. "But these are all mildewed. Sorry, Uncle Josey," she said and dumped them on the fire. By mid-September, the room was very pleasant. There were curtains at the windows, and a wooden clock echoed a slow ticking through the quiet.

Ruby planned a trip to Greenville for desks and a pair of spectacles for MJ.

"Tuck that butter in the milk box before we leave, Jage," she said, carrying a basket of food to the long buckboard. JJ lifted a chunk of earth behind the house, where a box was buried, and rearranged the cream and buttermilk to wedge in a bowl of fresh butter as a horse pulled up in front.

"I got you some students, Mrs. Dawson," O'Brien called to Ruby. "Six families are willing to sign up their kids."

Ruby walked out onto the new porch.

"Sam's going to take a hit," she said, "and he's not going to like it. Us Barlows are used to skinning that skunk, but do the rest of you want to get on his bad side?"

"It can't be no other way out here," the man said. "It's stick together or get starved out. Or rained, or hailed, or tornado'd out, or whatever. So when Sam threatens you, he threatens all of us. You can skin your own skunks all you want, but when those same skunks are stinking up our land, they ain't exactly your skunks."

Ruby looked at him, her face muscles working. She swallowed hard and waited until she was sure she could talk steady.

"I'm pleased to hear it, Mr. O'Brien."

The trip to Greenville was much easier for Ruby these days, now that her sons were old enough to help out and keep her company. Cowlick and Pepper were tied to the back of the buckboard, while their young masters debated the horses' strengths. "Pepper inherited all his size and speed from Rascal," MJ said, referring to Leo's horse, Pepper's sire. "He's a thoroughbred."

Ruby raised her eyebrows and said, "About as thoroughbred as Trespass is. We know he's a dog, and we know Rascal's a horse. So Pepper's a thorough horse—you can say that much."

JJ stood up in the wagon, held out an arm like a circus announcer, and said, "My horse, Cowlick, is a thoroughbred mustang. Born of the wind and desert, red as a winter sunset, wild as a..." he thought about it and then finished, "...wild as a child." He smiled at his rhyme.

"Bravo!" Ruby said. "You're as poetic as your pa."

"My brother, Jage, the thoroughbred," MJ declared, in the same circus performer's tone.

It was time, Ruby suddenly knew. Leo had said they should wait for a natural moment, and you don't get more natural than thoroughbred. "I don't think anyone's a true thoroughbred," she said.

Her sons were listening, and she sprinted on like a racehorse with blinkers. "How would you account for red hair, or long legs, or buckteeth if everyone was a thoroughbred?" She could see they weren't following her words.

"Those horses, for instance," she said, indicating Cowlick and Pepper. "They don't know who their pa is, or their ma. But you've raised them, fed them, taught them things like gentleness ... that's what's important, isn't it?"

"I wouldn't call Pepper gentle, Mama," said MJ. "He stomped that sidewinder good! You don't want a gentle horse, anyway ..."

"Cowlick could stomp five sidewinders at once ..."

"Boys! I'm talking about being thoroughbred or not being thoroughbred. Anyways, I'm telling you that horses, and people, sometimes have parents they might not know about. And other families take them on and become their folks."

"Like we did with Turk?" JJ asked. Clearly, she was being overly subtle. Maybe the timing wasn't right, after all, but Ruby was too far into the skirmish to retreat now.

"Tonight, we're staying at Grandma Dawson's house," she began again. "She's my mother."

"I can tell," said JJ, "because she always says 'laws' just like you do."

"Laws, JJ! Quit interrupting!" Calming herself with a deep breath, Ruby said, "MJ, remember when we visited Grandma Rounds?" It might be better if the idea dawned on him spontaneously. He nodded. "Whose mother is she?" Ruby asked.

"Pa's?" Confusion crept up on him. He knew exactly where Grandma Barlow was buried on the ranch. "Whose?" he asked now, the answer sneaking through the uncertainty. His shiny eyes clutched at hers. Panic deluged Ruby's gut. She shouldn't have done this without Leo. It was wrong, cruel even. "Aren't you my real ma?" he asked.

Tears bubbled up, dribbling over his eyelids at first, and then gushing down his smooth rounded cheeks. The precious overbite showed over his bottom lip as he sucked it in, gulping air, clasping overlapped fists to his chest with a slapping sound. Ruby's arms went around his quivering shoulders, and she tucked his head into her neck, weeping with this son of her heart. JJ looked on miserably, knowing this revelation affected him, too, but not sure how. His own tears started, and he was soon leaned around his brother, grasping his shoulders in a bear hug.

"Let go! You're digging in my neck, Jage!" MJ shook off the younger boy's embrace, annoyance balancing his heartbreak. There was a momentary tussle, and then Ruby wiped her nose and passed the handkerchief down the seat.

"Let me explain. MJ, Pa was married to a wonderful woman named Elsie. They had you, but after that, Elsie died. So Elsie's ma, Grandma Rounds, took care of you until Pa married me. You weren't even two yet, so I've been your mother almost your whole life."

"So does this mean he's only a half brother and I'm a whole?" JJ asked.

"No," MJ shoved him. "I'm as whole as you."

Ruby had to complete her mission. "JJ, you have a story, too. When I met Pa, you were already born. So he adopted you."

"You're adopted!" MJ said with glee. "I knew it! Didn't I always say you had to be adopted?" His own status was already forgotten, as he laughed and pummeled his younger brother playfully.

"I don't want to be adopted," JJ moaned. "Why can't we be a normal family?"

And then Ruby knew how Leo would handle this. "Remember that Christmas story in the Bible? God was Jesus's father, but he needed somebody to raise him?"

"You mean Joseph?" JJ asked.

"Joseph married Mary. I think that means he adopted her son."

"So Jesus was adopted." The idea dawned on MJ spontaneously.

"Seems like it," Ruby said. She thought Leo would be pleased with how it all turned out.

"Josey's got specs now, Grandma!" JJ burst threw the door of Olive's house. After a stop at the mercantile, MJ was in a state of wonder at the vividness of the surrounding world.

"Don't you look fine," she told him, giving Ruby an affectionate hug. "So grown up, too."

"I'm taller," JJ bragged, cornering his older brother for a back-to-back.

"Nate's going to help me load some desks for the school," Ruby said and left for the workshop.

"I know you're not really my grandma," MJ said matter-of-factly. "Mama said we were old enough for our whole story, so she told us everything. JJ's adopted."

"You're adopted, too. By Mama, remember?" JJ added.

"My real ma died, and so Pa married Mama and JJ, and so that's why I'm shorter than JJ right now, on account of his bein' adopted. I'll grow later."

"Laws, MJ, you have got it all worked out," Olive told him. He skipped out to help choose the desks, and JJ sorted through a stash of coins Olive had in a jar.

"Was my real pa tall?"

"I guess so. You must take after him. I didn't ever see him."

"You didn't? Was he already dead? Mama said he died."

"You can be proud of that, too, JJ. He was shot defending your mother's honor."

"He was? Was he a gunfighter? *Josey!* My real pa was a gunfighter! He died in a shootout!" JJ was out the door with the scattering of coins and the crash of a jar. Olive already knew what would come next.

179

"*Ma!*" Ruby caught the door almost before it had shut. "What did you tell him?"

"They said you'd told them the whole story. I thought he knew, so I wanted him to have a part to be proud of," Olive said from the floor.

Ruby picked up a wayward half-dollar from under her foot and handed it to her mother. "Well, I didn't tell them everything. I let them assume I was married, and I didn't mention Sam's Town or any of that, or even Jack's name. JJ worships gunfighters, so I guess that won't do much harm." She sank into a chair. "Will they hate me for my past?"

"They already love you in the present. Don't go kickin' yourself. Everybody has secrets."

"I never found out any of yours," Ruby said.

Her mother smiled. "That's 'cause I'm good at keepin' 'em."

The trip home was slower, with the wagon topped with fifteen desks. JJ and MJ rode their horses, impatient with the sluggish pace. After a night at the Prickly Pear, Ruby let the boys practice with the Colt. MJ was amazed at how his aim had improved, now that he could see what he was aiming at. But shooting was still JJ's skill. He practiced drawing the weapon and squeezing off shots at cactus berries, hitting each one dead center.

"Look in those weeds, Jage," Ruby whispered. "There's a grouse." JJ dropped to his knee and fired once. He kept his gun trained on the fallen bird until he reached it and held it up by its neck.

"Next time, we're bringing Trespass," said MJ. "He'd have every critter in these bushes treed, and JJ could bring them all down. Have us a right barbecue!"

"Something's stinkin' up these parts," Ruby said. They were an hour away from Barlow Ranch when the odor became obnoxious. From somewhere close by, she heard a rustling, and then the more obvious sound of someone relieving himself before mounting a horse.

A fleshy man with a derby hat appeared on the road ahead of them. It was Snake, Sam Lester's hoodlum, stalking them alone.

"Looks of them desks, you must be expectin' some pupils," he said. "What would you want with a school out here?" He watched Ruby but addressed his question to MJ.

"Well, sir," MJ said. "My brother and I, we told our mama we wanted to go to school. She said we weren't invited to the one in Sam's Town, and Pa said to build our own. Talked to some of the other kids, and they think they'll like ours better'n Sam's. It's called Barlow Woods School."

Ruby quirted the horses and tried to get past the ugly man. Snake opened his coat and raised an old Enfield rifle. "Never liked schoolteachers much," he said. "Used to fancy I could find one in the woods like this. Specially a pretty one." He prodded Ruby's bosom with the tip of the gun, ignoring the boys in his lust.

Sweat beaded JJ's forehead and his mouth was utterly dry. He tried to swallow and could not. He pulled the .44 out of his trousers and pointed it at Snake.

"Don't make a mistake, sir. I'm a good shot," said JJ. "I am going to protect my mother, and if I have got to shoot you, I'll do it. Lower that gun, or I'll pull this trigger." Snake mocked him with a sneer.

JJ shot an old beehive a few feet from the man's head, startling his mount, and he dropped the rifle. "Now, get off your horse and stand in front of me." Snake looked at Ruby as if she should reign in her son. Another shot hit a bird's nest, scattering feathers and twigs over Snake's skittish horse. The boyish voice hit twice as hard, "Stand in front of me!"

Snake's knees bent and dust squirmed up around his boots when he jumped down and planted himself in front of Cowlick. "Now run," JJ said. He pulled Cowlick into a slow trot and watched the fat man turn to run with the angular, shambling gait of a rider who had never walked more than fifty feet at a time. Snake turned his face back, showing a strained anxiety, and his breath deepened. Sweat rolled off his face. He sawed his arms back and forth, and his head jerked up and down, and when he sucked in air, it was like a gusty cry. He looked back at JJ once more, caught his foot on a rock, and fell flat.

"Keep running."

He struggled to his knees and to his feet. His head kept dropping on him, and JJ saw his legs shake. His mouth was round and wide, faintly purpling at the edges. But he flung himself into a run and went another hundred yards, each pace dragging him lower and lower until his whole body was in a crouch. When he fell, utterly exhausted, he rolled over, half-unconscious.

JJ swung his horse back to Ruby with a born sureness, with more confidence than he had ever known, but he collapsed into the child he was soon after the encounter. Later that evening, he came to his parents. "I want to carry a gun."

Leo looked at him with amazement. "What balderdash! You're a boy! What's more, you're a Barlow, and Barlows don't carry guns."

"He saved my life, Leo." Ruby said. "I don't know what would have happened out there."

"He's just ten years old. He's not old enough," Leo told his wife.

JJ stepped into the conversation. "I'm old enough to know what matters."

"What matters? You don't know what matters, to me, to your ma."

"I might never be that old. But I know what matters to me. I don't want to be some puppy-dog like Trespass, followin' folks around for a handout, hopin' to be looked after and protected. I want to be sure of myself. Have folks trust me."

"That's quite a speech from a boy who's never even read a book. Shooting isn't the way to respectability. You got a lot to learn, son," Leo said. "A gun should be a last resort."

"What if it came time for the last resort? What if I was all out of every other resort under the sun? Wouldn't you hope when I got down to the last resort, I'd know how to use it? Pa, you always say if I'm big enough, I'm old enough. Didn't I prove I'm old enough with Mama?"

Being right so often hadn't given Leo much practice in being wrong.

"Look, JJ," said Ruby, "you come to school in the mornings, and I'll let you take my gun into the woods in the afternoons." She looked quickly at Leo, reminding him with her glance that it was her pistol and her son. And her life he'd saved today.

15

September 1886

MJ was fourteen, a grand time in the life of any boy. He had shot up, though he was still shorter than his brother, and he was strong, with hard muscle laid over his rawboned frame. Near-sighted hazel eyes were already wrinkled from squinting, but his spectacles gave him a sharper perspective on the world. He was finding out where he stood.

One of the earliest things brothers try to find out is who's the favorite. And one of the earliest things MJ had found out is that he wasn't. Oh, he felt loved and approved of, even trusted and admired. But everyone adored JJ. His raffish twinkle usually started folks smiling. The flamboyant and airy lack of responsibility in the boy became, against all reason, a kind of virtue. JJ's humor was inexhaustible. As much as one boy ever worshiped another, MJ worshiped his younger brother.

He'd missed him on this trip to Greenville, the first time he'd made a cattle drive alone. Not alone, exactly: twenty cows, a dog, his mount, and a packhorse. Trespass trotted proudly beside Pepper, two feet off the ground, all sixty pounds of him, with his pointed tail held high. The coonhound could trail the horse for hours unless he caught a scent. Then he was off on a chase that ended with braying and drooling when he'd treed the raccoon or fox, while he waited for his master to praise his efforts to high heaven.

Even though MJ carried the "Last Resort" as, well... as a last resort, he wasn't anxious to use it to kill the dog's captive for no good reason. He was not comfortable with the gun, but his glasses made him accurate, a combination that pleased both his father and his mother. "We'll leave him be, Trespass," he told the dog, after a celebration of hugs and slobbery kisses.

MJ had tied a tiny bell around the hound's neck so he wouldn't spook the small herd at night with his infernal digging. They got as used to the sound as they were to MJ's tinkling spurs. Trespass sang right along with the boy as he quieted the cattle along the trail back to Barlow Ranch. "Git along, little dogies," he crooned in Leo's clear baritone to the accompaniment of the blue dog's baying.

"You crazy old mutt. You know we're almost home?" Trespass howled to announce their arrival as they paraded past the O'Brien cabin, down past their house, and into the corral.

"You lowdown mavericker! You thievin' my cattle again, boy?" With a whoop, JJ leaped on the back of his brother's horse, attacking MJ in a Texas wrestle. They had the common knowledge that they were tough, but who was toughest on a given day depended on who could pin who. Sliding to the ground, MJ had trouble putting down his younger brother and might never have made it if Trespass hadn't leaped in and begun licking JJ's face and nipping him in the side till he hit his tickle bone. That got JJ to giggling so hard he couldn't fight, and MJ was glad to press the boy's shoulders flat into the dirt of the trail and quit while he could.

They got up, knocking the dust and twigs off themselves to cover the awkward spell that was bound to set in when big boys had carried on too catnippy for their ages.

As always, it was JJ who got to talking first. As they walked toward the barn with Trespass nipping at their legs and pawing for attention, he chattered a blue-tailed streak, as if they'd been separated for a month instead of just a few days.

"Ain't you had nobody to talk to, Jage? That cowlicked filly a' yours stopped listening to your chatter?" MJ asked.

"I don't like folks insulting my mare," JJ said, doffing his brother's head. "We have right fine conversations. She's smarter than you, and she don't even have to go to school. Fact is, neither do I—least not tomorrow!"

The boy whooped again and took off running toward the mill, with Trespass at his heels, and MJ yelling, "Hold yer horses! What's tomorrow?"

JJ knew he was different than his brother. MJ was like Pa, and he'd learned to be careful dealing with him. Fearlessness, daring, grit: these were characteristics JJ aspired to. He thought of MJ as bookish, steady, and earnest, but he couldn't actually treat him that way. Who'd want to be seen as drab? But that was what Pa admired.

Already peculiarly handsome, JJ walked like a young lion—large, loose, and still a little awkward in his growing strength. Instinctively, he was taking control of his form and his ideas, flexing his independence. JJ had also wondered which of them was their father's favorite. But if boyhood questions aren't answered before a certain age, they can't ever be raised again. Happily, he didn't worry about it anymore. Pa always said he'd have to make his name for himself, anyway.

His grin was as warm as it was quick. Sandy hair, faded to blond from the wind and sun, fell across his forehead into his eyes, and he brushed it back to tuck under his black hat. Pulling the .44 from his trouser tops, he shot at a small wild pig in the brush. "Pork chops for breakfast!" he cheered.

Leo came out of the mill when he heard the shot. He was past worrying about JJ having a gun. With Ruby's encouragement, the boy practiced every day and was now a dead eye, his left hand almost a blur twirling the pistol around and between his fingers, tucking it in and out of his trousers.

"Pa!" JJ said. "Tell Josey what we're doing tomorrow!"

Nodding with approval at his own idea, Leo said, "You're starting your own herd, son—marking those new cattle with the MJ brand. It's not too early to have a stake in the Barlow Ranch."

"I've got him by the horns," yelled MJ. "Burn him! I ain't got all fall to wait!"

JJ grinned, stepped back to the fire, and pulled one of the two stamp-irons out of it. He rapped it expertly on a rock, knocking off the wood ash to see the color underneath. It was a rose-gray, just right.

"Hold him!" he yelled back, lost in the pleasure of excitement. "Here goes!"

With a flourish, he started the smoking tip of the stamp-iron toward the bull's rough-haired flank. He never finished the motion.

"Drop that iron," said a dry, tight voice behind them.

Then, with bitterness dripping from it, the voice went on, "Reach high and pray hard, kid."

JJ neither reached, prayed, nor dropped the iron.

Instinct kept him still until the first wave of blind anger had swept over him. When it was past, he turned slowly, the iron held low in his left hand.

"If you want this iron, Mr. Lester," he said, "you come and get it."

He let his eyes wander over the riders siding up next to Sam. There were four of them, three familiar looking and one JJ didn't recognize.

"You're a boy, Barlow," Sam Lester's rasping voice said. "I would advise you to do as you're told. So I'll say it once more. Drop that iron."

"Josey," JJ called to his older brother, ignoring Sam. MJ was edging clear of the fire.

"Erly," Sam said to the fourth rider, "you had better see to the older boy."

Erly grinned. The gray-skinned man moved quickly in spite of his girth. A cross-slung holster held a heavy revolver with a notched grip. With his Confederate hat and his slouchy vest, JJ decided he was trying awful hard to get himself taken for a killer.

"Sure," Erly answered. He moved his horse around the fire. Coming up to MJ, he was still grinning. "You going to make trouble, boy?" he said.

MJ looked helplessly at JJ. Erly hit him across the head with a Colt's seven-inch barrel. MJ collapsed, and his slack form went into the sun-baked earth at a bad angle. There was an audible giving of bone, and MJ lay loose and still.

JJ made an animal sound deep in his chest and came for Erly with the stamp iron.

"Stretch him, Woody!" snapped Sam to another man, and the riders spurred their horses forward.

It was like running a calf from a chute. The riders had their loops shaken out on the first jump, built on the second, laid down on the third. JJ got no more than halfway to the grinning Erly before the first rope was whipped tight around his ankles. His own momentum threw him flat on his face. The force of the fall shook him hard, but in a split second, he was pulled to his feet, standing in front of Sam.

"We could drag you back to your house face-first, with your brother trussed up like a deer, but we'll save you that embarrassment," Sam said. "Just tell your mama that we haven't forgotten her."

Turk had remedies for rope burns and headaches. He made a salve of turpentine, sweet oil, and beeswax for JJ's ankles and rubbed an aloe vera plant on both their faces. MJ was given a tonic of charcoal dissolved in water, mixed with a few drops of whiskey, and was now sleeping off his concussion, his broken arm elevated. Laudanum was saved for bedtime. The horror of the event was settling on the family, along with relief at the outcome. After hours of pacing, nursing, and reassuring, Leo just wanted to be alone.

The dry rattle of the cottonwood leaves came to him, and he smelled the bitter, pungent odor of desert brush that came off the ranch with the stirring of wind. He let the night settle on him, but it didn't alleviate the pitch and roll in his belly.

Leo had always been very sure about certain matters. "Peace of mind only comes to peaceful people" was an adage he'd learned in boyhood—he knew it to be true. Resentment, spite, and revenge were what he had on his mind now. And to him, few things were more bitter than feeling bitter.

Ruby threw a wrap around her shoulders and followed him out to the porch. There was a chill in the air, and when she looked toward the hills, she could see orange sunlight touching the very tops of the pine trees she loved. It was a melancholy sunset, as all fall ones are, with their promise of winter coming.

"Leo, it should have been me they trussed up, pummeled with a gun; me that fell through the stairs that day at the mill. This brutishness has been directed at me all along, but you're the ones who always get hurt." Her face shone like a lamp in a dim cellar, and he saw something tender and vulnerable that he had not seen before. She swallowed and mustered her words carefully and then spoke them. "I think I should go." At his instant protest, she said, "I have thought mighty strong on this all afternoon. If Sam thinks he's won this battle, he'll leave the rest of you alone." Drawing a deep breath, she squared her shoulders and went back inside.

Leo followed her into the kitchen. His wife stood resolute by the table, slim, her arms folded across her chest. Her attitude was solemn, her face grave, rational, faintly defensive. JJ sat up on the daybed and said, "I heard you, Mama. It's me they were after 'cause of how I bedeviled Snake that time. You can't go, Mama. Tell her, Pa! It ain't her fault!"

"Listen here, Ruby. Us Barlows came to this spot in 1850. Twenty-four years later, it was still just a spot. You saw it. A place lived in by ghosts, a victim of isolation. Corn was planted, but cows ate all the corn—no fences. Logs were a nuisance, jamming the river, making floods—no mill. No school, because there were no children, no families. We've built a town out here—you've built a town out here, Mrs. Barlow Woods. Over my dead body will you abandon us!" Leo's face was flushed as he finished, neck clenched in that uncompromising way of his. He flexed his right hand and shook out the tenseness.

"Barlow Woods is going to be a big town; but big or small, it's going to be law-abiding," Leo finished.

"Trouble is, Leo, if somebody has trouble out here, he can't call the sheriff... there isn't any sheriff. He can't have his case judged by the law, because there isn't any law. He can't appeal to anybody or anything, except his own sense of right and wrong. But, then, that's deemed to be breaking the law." Thoughts of leaving were gone. Ruby's thoughts were now on her home of a dozen years.

"Sam thinks he can do anything he's big enough to do, no matter how it tramples on other folks' rights," she continued. "Some people can reason a thing out and settle it fair and square. Others understand nothing but force. So what do we do?" Ruby's assessment was accurate, and Leo was reminded of the viciousness of this morning's attack on the boys.

"Do you believe in killing people, Pa?" JJ asked.

"No, son. But I believe when people live in a society with other folks, they have to abide by the rules of that society. When a man crosses those rules, he's liable to judgment."

"So, who does the judging?" JJ asked.

"The law. Ultimately God. He expects us to use the weapons we have: forgiveness, mercy, tolerance."

"And guns," stated JJ.

"Sometimes, a man's venom poisons himself more than his victim, Jage. Those men aim to drag you into a war. Have no part of it."

"You can be as peaceable as you want, Pa. Josey was the one bashed over the head; I was the one cinched up with a lariat." Leo was slow to condemn, so slow that JJ wondered if the actions and morals of people meant anything to him. He had the greatest impulse to use words on his father like sledgehammers, to change the light in his eyes, to waken and shake him to the ache in his gut. But Turk's laudanum was taking effect, and his other aches were finally drifting away.

Erly had an assignment to assess the situation. Late that night, he snuck up to the Barlow home, with hopes of seeing the results of their attack on Ruby's boys. Like a jolt of lightning, a sound took the man off his feet. He had two seconds to vault back onto his horse.

The bullet caught Erly twisted in his saddle. It entered low in his left side, ranged up between the ribs, deflected against the right shoulder blade, and burst out high under his right armpit. The rupturing of its exit tore his lung in passage.

His next memory was of his horse stumbling. With the last flash of consciousness, he wrenched himself free of the saddle. He fell sideways and heavily away from the animal. Waiting for the jolt and crash of the ground to rush up and smash him senseless, he felt, instead, the life-saving shock of cold water. He knew from that, and from the distant feel of the moss and the sliding rocks under his numbing hands, that he had fallen into the stream.

He struggled clear of the creek's shallows and the next instant, the mud of the creek bank was reaching for him. He came to it gratefully, belly first, head twisted grotesquely to the left. There was no movement and no sound, save where the slowing pump of his heart lifted the bright blood up into his throat from the torn lung and pushed it through his clamped teeth out upon the waiting clay. Erly's body was found behind the schoolhouse the next morning.

The notch-gripped pistol was missing from Erly's cross belted holster, and it never did show up, even when Sheriff Mills came out to collect the body. No inquiries were made, and it was apparent that nobody in Sam's Town would miss the gray-skinned man with the confederate hat.

Turk's treatments had the boys' healing and in that way of youth, the torture was already a memory, stored away with grasshoppers and tornados, to be revisited only in nightmares.

After tying a fresh dishtowel around MJ's neck to serve as a sling, the old cook set a pan of soaked pinto beans on the table and rubbed his arthritic knuckles. "Mash," he instructed.

"What are you making?" MJ asked, first snagging a fresh Granny Smith from a bushel basket near the door. His slightly bucked teeth pierced the apple with a squirt of juice that caught on his chin. Mopping it up with the same hand, he sat down to his task.

"Red Bean Pie."

"With meringue?" asked JJ.

Turk's Adam's apple worked up and down under his long johns as he nodded with pleasure. "Nothing better than a chuck wagon special," he grinned. "Served it the night Poker Brown got shot. It was his last meal. Did I ever tell you about Poker Brown, the gunslinger?"

JJ didn't even notice the bowl of apples placed before him and the paring knife Turk slipped into his hand. He just started peeling as the tale began.

"Poker carried a .45 peacemaker rather ostentatiously, bragging about the number of men he'd brought down. Fifteen murders before he was twenty-five he was credited with. Claimed he'd kill any card shark who cheated him in poker. Got to be a challenge. Every time we hit a town, men were lined up at the saloon waiting to cheat Poker Brown.

"That night, we pulled into a place called Newton on the Chisholm, just south of Abilene. Poker ate my stew and biscuits, finished with some Red Bean Pie, then hustled himself off to find some cheat to plug. Found one, too, using a mirror.

"His gun cocked when it cleared leather. A sound like that echoes through a packed saloon, and the crowd gathered to witness a killing. The first bullet whiffed the cheat's ear. Steadying down, the cheat braced himself and shot Poker through the shoulder, which knocked him to the table. He did not go down; .45 or not, you have to hit a man right through the heart or the head if he's big enough or mad enough, and Poker was both.

"Just then, Poker looked down at the cheat's cards. 'You have a full house,' he said in wonderment. The cheat looked around at the crowded room and said, 'I sure do.' And that was the end of Poker Brown."

"Is that true?" asked JJ.

"Truer than an outright lie," Turk chuckled, pleased to have his apples peeled and his beans mashed.

"Seems like gunmen aren't afraid of anything," said JJ. "Ready to shoot just to prove their mettle."

"Stupid don't mean brave," Turk replied.

"Don't know, Jage," said MJ. "Sam's men looked pretty locoed to me the other day. Why would you hang your honor on tormenting weaker folks? Why not do something good, like be a doctor or build a railroad? Shooting seems a waste of time.

"Maybe you'd be protecting something. Maybe you'd be a guard. You don't have to kill the person, but sometimes you gotta' make 'em think you could. Right, Turk?" MJ asked.

"There's good men and bad men in every profession, that's for sure." The old man dug out a cigar and pulled on his plaid vest. The boys followed him outside. "Can't always tell who's who in the killing category, though. Saw some cowboys once, a tight little cavalcade of riders expecting no trouble." Trespass loped over and slobbered happily. MJ smoothed his glossy blue coat, which felt coarse under his fingers.

Turk's homely face had a distance to it. "They rode as tired men ride, lounging in their saddles, greeting folks with a, 'Howdy, John,' or the tip of a hat to Mrs. Jones. There was dust on their horses and dust on their clothing and dust on their beards. They were the good men."

Trespass was busy digging, but his thin, black ears were ever listening for a squirrel or a rabbit, ready to chase it down, earn a sugar cube and a loving tussle with his master.

"Just like that mutt, they were hound dogs, out hunting their prey. Another dusty batch of cowboys rode toward the men. It was only their guns that had no dust. There was no humor in them, for they were men to whom killing was a natural business. These were the salty pick of a lawless bunch who rode for the highest bidder."

Trespass came to attention, his large round eyes fixed, and then he let out a baying cry, like a short howl. Twitching his nose, he took off in the direction of the mill after some critter or other who'd finally take refuge in a tree.

"Didn't matter in the end who was a good man or a bad man. A bunch of 'em ended up dead." Turk booted the stogie into the dirt.

JJ brushed his shaggy hair back off his golden brown face. "Is that the end?"

"Nope," said Turk. They listened to Trespass bawling in the distance.

"Anybody can shoot a gun," Turk said finally. "And with practice, he can draw fast and shoot straight. What counts is how you stand up when somebody's shooting at you." He waited for JJ's unvarying question, which didn't come. So he answered it anyway. "That's the truth."

Six weeks had passed, and Turk declared MJ's arm healed. Without the sling, he was free to roam the woods after school with his fishing pole, while JJ hunted wild turkeys with the help of the dog. The hum of the saw attracted the boys, and since they couldn't find Trespass or his quarry, they decided to look in on Fontaine. Six men, all from Barlow Woods, chopped the pines, hauled the logs, and watched over the giant wheel, keeping the stream clear so the gears would not jam. The millwright kept the pulleys and belts in good repair. Ruby didn't like her sons to be near the immense, ear-splitting saw, but they were regular visitors just the same.

Fontaine greeted them in his usual distracted way. "I'm shutting her down for the night. It'll be a bit smoky in here when I put out the fire. You might as well go home." Smoke settled in the mill, and he bustled into the adjoining shed. It seemed to get thicker, suddenly so dense they couldn't see.

Choking, JJ grabbed at his brother, who had gotten down on the floor to feel his way out. "I can't find the door, Jage." MJ was wheezing, gasping for air. "Which way is the door?" The roar of the fire and the incessant high pitched whirring of the saw drowned out his voice, isolating JJ, even though he could still feel MJ's arm.

A howl broke through the commotion of the thundering flames, then another howl. Scrambling toward the familiar sound, MJ shouted into the dark, "Trespass! Keep barking, boy!"

They didn't realize until they were out that they were both screaming like banshees. They'd been crying, too, and their sobs turned to gasps as they hit fresh air. Out of the cacophony of the inferno, they heard riders and a high rebel yell of triumph well away from the trees.

Smoke from a blazing wagon whipped about in the wind. A front axle burned through and the loaded wagon crashed down, splintering wood and driving red sparks. Ruby raced up the hill and saw the roof of the mill mushroom into a scarlet wall of fire. Smoke and flames were spurting from broken windows, and fire was bursting through the dry shake roof, spewing smoke, flames, and whorls of red embers. Through the veils of hot, drifting smoke, Ruby saw her sons wandering aimlessly it seemed, hanging on one another, wretching, keening in anguish.

Leo was in the corral when he noticed something in the trees, a queer patch of evening sky that was lighter than the rest. When he heard the first shot, he stood up, listening for a distress signal. Two more shots evenly spaced sounded through the crisp air, and he grabbed the reins and headed toward the blasts. As he rode faster, it grew brighter, and when he smelled smoke minutes later, he was sure of it; the mill was on fire. It lighted up the whole night so that everything was made plainer than by daylight. The lumber had caught in the mill, and the framework of rafters, a cherry red, was ready to fold on itself.

And then, with relief, he saw Ruby and the two boys. They were at the periphery watching the blaze. Only MJ wasn't watching. He was bent over the sprawled shape of what looked like an animal—it was Trespass.

Leo felt a slow wrath at his helplessness, just as the rafters fell and a great spout of sparks funneled up into the night. The fire flared brighter now, and movement caught his eye. He saw something move through the dry trees as he peered intently. Presently, it moved again. It was a horse that vanished with its rider into the outer circle of darkness.

Smoke sifted from the charred timbers, where once the mill had stood, and curled wistfully around Ruby. Now there was only desolation, emptiness, and death. The small, green valley lay still in the night, heat emanating from the burned timbers. *So this is the way a dream ends,* she thought.

Two horsemen waited beside their saddled mounts, watching the Barlow road. Presently, a third horseman rode up through the growing moonlight to join them. There was a muttered exchange of greetings, after which the newcomer paused and asked, "Where's your trained ape at?"

"Snake's gone to Abilene," grunted Bolte. He then added bitterly, "He ain't the same no more."

"He's the s-s-same," rasped Haze. "I allus s-s-said he didn't have no real g-g-uts."

"Yeah," said Bolte. "Only you never said it in front of him." The men split up then and rode for the county road before heading back to Sam's Town.

The county road was as far as Haze got. Dismounting to wait for the others, he felt himself whirled around by his collar, and something smashed into his jaw like a weight. Sprawled on his back in the dust, his first instinctive reaction was to streak for the gun inside his coat. Then he saw Turk, solid, stocky, his face blazing in fury, with murder in his eyes.

"Get off this place!" Turk said in a thick voice. He stepped up to Haze and slapped his face once with his palm, once with the back of his hand. "I'd string you up for this myself, you cheap lackey, if I had one shred of evidence. But Mr. Barlow has this strange concept of law." Haze tripped over his feet, his jaw throbbing already.

"Get off this place now, and stay off!" Turk growled. The uneasy nicker of his horse caught Haze's attention, and he heard his own blood pounding in his ears as he mounted bitterly. He looked around for Bolte and Woody, realizing he'd been abandoned. Blood welled from his mouth, and he spit it out, gingerly touching a molar where Turk's fist had crunched his face.

16

It was the tenth day of April 1887, Ruby's thirty-third birthday. By the calendar, she was middle aged; by any other witness, she was a radiant, vibrant woman. But her feelings that morning were those of a girl as her handsome husband burst through the door.

"Birthday news, sugar," Leo sang out to Ruby and tipped back his hat. Her red curls caught the spring sunshine streaming through the window, and he suddenly grabbed her waist and waltzed her around the kitchen. "Rubies would not do justice to your hair, Mrs. Barlow," he said, twirling her under his arm.

"What happened to you?" she asked, laughing at his exuberance.

"I got saddle bagged by your beauty!" He bent and kissed her suntanned nose. The freckles had faded over the years, leaving her skin a light bronze that seemed to last year-round, and her figure had filled out just enough to soften into feminine curves. Blue eyes sparkled between tiny smile creases; happiness had settled on her nicely.

"Shack brought the new gears over from Greenville," Leo reported. "So Fontaine says the mill will be operable within the month. Ma used to say when a door closes, somewhere a window opens—gotta think it's true. After just six months, Barlow Mill will be better than ever. Those Mormons might come back for it, when the news spreads!"

Barlow Woods was becoming a self-sufficient community, and the mill had been missed during the winter after the fire destroyed it. The town had developed rapidly. Enterprising young farmers were breaking the barren sod, planting and reaping crops that had not grown in northern Texas before. Buffalo grass had been replaced by golden fields of wheat, corn, alfalfa, and Mexican beans.

Scattered settlers were welding a community, a business, and social center for homesteaders from miles around. Josey's old cabin served as the schoolhouse during the week, and now it was ready to double as a church.

"Shack delivered the church pews from Nate Brannigan, too. In no time, we'll be needing a local carpenter, with all the lumber we're going to harvest," said Leo. "Maybe you could start building coffins again," he teased.

"And bury folks in our churchyard?" Ruby asked. "That would torment Sam Lester—we'll steal his collection plate and his bodies."

"That counterfeit Reverend Kincaid scares the faithful right out of his church; they can't wait to come over here. O'Brien has a different brand of religion than Sam—he doesn't take over the role of deity. And he doesn't reserve the preaching just for himself. No doubt Ruby Barlow will be sermonizing from the pulpit of her backyard Sunday school before she's thirty-four."

"The Greenville Ladies of the Methodist Ministry would have a heyday with that idea," Ruby said.

Pepper and Cowlick whinnied outside, signaling the return of Turk and the boys. Leo stepped onto the porch and took a gunny sack of spring onions from MJ. "Hey Turk," he said, "why are you wearing only one spur?"

"You get half the horse moving, the other half'll follow," replied the old cowboy. "Got something special, sweetheart," he told Ruby. "JJ shot you a wild pig. Liver and onions for your birthday supper."

It had been almost half a year since the fire, but MJ was still lost without Trespass. He dismounted and shoved his spectacles back on his nose, ready to water and brush the horses after the morning ride. Being with the animals seemed to comfort him, although he claimed he never wanted a pet again. "Don't worry," Leo consoled Ruby. "That dog was his first true love, but it won't be his last. Trespass taught him that love is worth the trouble."

As a result of his terror, and despite Leo's objections, JJ had taken to wearing his grandfather's Colt almost all the time. The gun seemed to reassure him, and after weeks of nightmares, his cheeky spirit was finally returning. He'd learned to draw and cock the weapon in a single motion, and he was proud to show off his split-second accuracy.

Apparently recovered, JJ's resentment still boiled under the surface. "Folks think Pa's yellow," he had said that morning when he passed the mill with MJ and Turk. "I would have shot those weasels after the fire. They deserved to die."

"Who exactly?" asked Turk. "Nobody hung around to take credit for the blaze."

"We all know it was Sam," said MJ. "There should be a bounty on that man's head, him and his henchmen. Are there really bounty hunters, Turk?"

The fount of knowledge for the Barlow brothers nodded. "All over Texas, there are hombres who are man-hunters. They make their living hunting down other men with prices on their heads. Lawmen and killers hire them—either way, they can get paid up to a thousand dollars for a murder."

"If it wasn't for Trespass, we'd both be dead. It's already murder, if you ask me," MJ said.

"I wonder if Pa would have gone after them if we'd burned up?" JJ scoffed. "Probably wouldn't have the courage. He'd sidestep our charred remains like a cow pie, spouting some forgiveness quote from Grandma Barlow."

"Now you listen up, Jage," Turk said. "You're thirteen years old and near growed. It's time you got some sense. There's fool courage and wise courage. Most of us don't live long enough to get the kind of courage Leo Barlow was raised on. We go blustering around thinking we're brave, when we have less sense than your horse."

JJ didn't say any more then, but when they passed the mill again on the way back to the ranch, he turned to Turk. "How did my real pa die? Tell it again, Turk."

"The way the story goes, Jack Smith overheard some insulting talk about yer ma. There was some whoop-te-doo in a saloon in Fort Worth, and Jack shot the blabbermouth, and winged the sheriff, a man called Gentleman Jake.

"Jack was making his escape when Gentleman Jake fired at him in an alley. There was enough blood to fill up a couple of men—the sheriff probably hit the horse, too. Both must have died outside of town somewhere, because they never found the bodies."

"Think he could have lived?"

"Not unless he's a ghost. Gotta have something left in your veins to keep this mortal upright."

"If my real pa was alive, he'd have gone after those murderers, even if it killed him," JJ said.

"If your real pa was alive, I'd wonder if he set the fire. Don't put any stock in Jack Smith, Jage. He was an outlaw."

"At least he defended his wife. I think a man should protect his family. That's not murder. It's like in war."

Turk shut his mouth, realizing he'd almost said too much.

JJ started up again. "I think Pa is rubbing off on Ma, them starting the Sunday school and all. Some men in Greenville were making fun of the idea. Seems downright cockeyed to me."

"Laws, Mr. High and Mighty," MJ retorted. "Ma and Pa raised a whole town from an arid prairie, overrun by grasshoppers. Reckon they deserve some respect. Totin' a gun isn't the only sign of grit, right, Turk?"

Lighting a cigar, the old man leaned back on his horse and relaxed into storytelling mode. "Heard about this cowboy called Bandanna, called after the green silk scarf he wore around his neck. Like all punchers, he used it for a dust mask in summer, an ear cover in winter, a dish dryer, and a sling. Prob'ly tied a calf's legs up with it during branding, or blindfolded a skittish horse. But he was more creative than most.

"One time, Bandanna was leaned over drinking from a creek, using his silk to strain out the mud, when a hustler came along and hightailed his horse. When he caught up to the varmint, he strung him up to a branch with the bandanna and skedaddled the horse, leaving him to blow in the wind 'til he was dead. Then he untied him and signaled with the bandanna for help. When the rescuers came, they found the robber all laid out for his desert wake, his bulged-out eyes discreetly covered by a green silk bandanna."

"Not much of a cowboy without a gun," JJ said. "I'm not even asking if this one's true—a bandanna killer?"

Turk clamped down on his stogie and said, "Just hope you're wearin' a silk scarf the day you run out of bullets."

It was time. According to Turk, JJ had answers to questions he'd never asked, and Ruby needed to set him straight. She didn't know what she was going to say. How do you destroy your son's history?

"Jage, I want you to ride with me to check the fence line this afternoon," she told him.

Following the swollen stream, they passed through the lush timbered basin onto the wide-open range. Spicy sage scented the late afternoon air, mockingbirds whistled, and woodpeckers tapped, but Ruby didn't notice her surroundings. Finally, she sighed and dropped her hands to the saddle horn.

The boy pulled up beside her. Without raising her voice, she said gently, "JJ, I want to tell you about your name. Can we walk?"

A breeze lifted his dark blond bangs, and he resettled his hat then dismounted and took his mother's reins to guide both horses.

"Your father was called Jack, Jack Smith actually." She started from the beginning. "I only knew him for one night. He was just passing through Greenville, and I was young and a little wild, like you, with a hankering to get out and see the world, make a new start. Anyway, this tall, black-haired cowboy flirted with me." She paused, remembering. "Oh, he was quite the sugar mouth, and he seemed so adventurous and bold..."

Ruby lifted the chestnut hair from the back of her neck, letting the cool wind blow on her neck. She unwrapped her black ribbon bracelet and tied her curls back in a ponytail, then arched the kinks out of her spine, twisting her shoulders back to her son.

"He had a beautiful red mare, almost the same color as Cowlick is. She was a hand taller than any other mount I've seen, sleek, well muscled, alert, with a pure white mane and tail. He'd raised her from a foal, and he loved her; he even talked to her, and he claimed she talked back. It took me two seconds to fall in love, first with Big Red, and then with Jack Smith."

JJ's eyes were wide, tearless, and unblinking, but his face was still soft and mobile with boyhood, and his mouth worked against trembling.

"I thought if he liked me enough, he'd take me with him," Ruby continued, "so I did what girls do when they want a man to like them. But he didn't like me enough. He was gone the next morning." Her voice trailed off for a moment before she went on. "So then, after a while, I had you."

She looked at him to see if he understood what she'd just told him, and when he wouldn't meet her gaze, she saw that he did.

"Did he ever know about me?" JJ asked. He couldn't quite hide the longing in his voice. Pine trees, dusky in the twilight sun, cast a shadow across the boy's face; frigid water bubbled in the stream, like the ice cold answer she had to give him.

"No, JJ. No, he didn't."

He plowed his toe into the damp brush edging the stream. A low bluff surrounded by limestone boulders overlooked them and shaded their path in the early evening chill.

"Can we go home, now?" JJ asked.

"There's more, JJ." Ruby stood and looked into the water. "The people in Greenville didn't have much use for a ruined woman like me. It got so folks crossed the street so their kids wouldn't be infected by my wicked ways—Turk was the only one in town that showed me any kindness at all, and I was losing him business at the Blue Belle.

"After all the catcalls and humiliation, and shame, I decided to run away after you were born. Grandma Dawson took care of you, and I went to Sam's Town to start over. What I didn't know yet was that if you want to change your results, you have to change your actions. I'd begun to think of myself as a fallen woman. Sam convinced me that was all I'd ever be, so I became a boarder at the Fat Chance Saloon. It seemed like a quick fix. But I hadn't started over; I'd just started again. Running away doesn't help when you take your old self with you."

The horses were getting restless, and they began to walk again.

"Then I met your pa." She glanced up quickly, and said, "Leo, I mean… anyway, he looked at me through his pure eyes, and he saw some goodness left in me. I'd thought it was gone forever. He helped me run away, but this time, I left my old self behind, and I truly did start over. And then he became your pa, truly your pa."

It was almost dark, and they turned back, cutting across a shallow place in the stream, stepping on boulders while the horses splashed through the current. Ruby hugged herself for warmth.

"So what about my name?" JJ asked.

"You're named Jeremy after my father—a name to live up to. And Jack after your father—'a name to live down' was what I thought. But you didn't have a true last name because I wasn't married. Leo made you a Barlow, but in the end, you'll have to make your name for yourself. You can be who you choose to be."

"Seems like I have three parents to take after," JJ muttered as he mounted his horse. "Not sure I like any of them." He rode off, headed away from the ranch.

Ruby's cheeks were bright red from the cold, and when she walked into the warm kitchen, Leo thought she was the prettiest woman he had ever seen. Then he noticed tears spilling from her blue eyes.

"I told him," she said. Sucking in too big a breath, her throat constricted, and the air escaped in a raspy moan, followed by jerky hiccups. She shuddered, and her shoulders quivered before her whole body convulsed in violent spasms. Sinking onto a chair, she held her head with shaky hands, her chest heaving with her sobs, the tears splashing on her cheeks. "I don't think he'll be able to forgive me," she cried. "I don't think I can forgive myself."

JJ spent the night with Cowlick in the barn, and the next morning, Leo found him up by the mill, shooting at cactus berries. "That's some shooting," said Leo, with enthusiasm he didn't often show toward JJ with a gun. He sat down on a log, characteristically stretching out his stiff knee and thumbing back his hat.

"Guess my real pa was the best gunslinger in Texas. Could of got it from him, I reckon." JJ still had the Colt gripped in his left hand, when he backed up into a bracket of prickly pear. "Dammit!" He swore with feeling and immediately shot at the berries on another bush before he tucked the pistol away and sank down in the dirt.

"Dammit." This time it came out softer. Pulling his knees in close to his chest, JJ dropped his head with a quiet sob. Barbed cactus thorns the length of darning needles stuck in his socks, and he clutched at them with abandon, heedless of the stabs to his fingers and hands.

"Let me help, son," said Leo. Squatting on his haunches in front of the boy, he plucked the barbed spines with caution. "Can't have you getting poison in your blood."

Twisting away from Leo, JJ stood up and almost spat the words. "My blood is full of poison, don't you see? A killer, a whore, and a coward—I don't know which of you I hate the most."

The jaw-crunching blow caught JJ unexpectedly. Hauled up by his shirt, he took another punch, this time to the gut, and fell on all fours, retching. Leo stood above him while he threw up in the dirt.

"I'm your father, if not by blood, certainly by choice, though I don't always get it right with you. You can think me a coward; Jack Smith was surely a killer; but you'll not speak of my wife in an insolent way. A man treats a woman, my woman, with respect. Carrying that gun has not made you a man. "

Leo recovered himself quickly and offered JJ a hand up, which the boy knocked away. "Suit yourself. You're welcome to come home when you've cleaned up your face, your clothes, and your language."

17

April 12, 1887

Hunger struck, and JJ went back to the house late for lunch, sheepishly hoping he could avoid his parents for a few hours. The easiest way back to normal would be to get Turk's tongue wagging about stampedes or jamborees from his long-lost youth and eating his way through the afternoon. Humble pie would be for supper after he apologized to Pa. Might as well face it on a full stomach.

The aroma of turnips, potatoes, and bacon filled the kitchen when JJ walked in. Pinching off dough for biscuits, Turk barely looked up. He seemed oblivious to the momentous family episode of the past day and a half, and the boy was grateful.

"There's soup. Help yourself," Turk said. "You're being talked about, you know."

Ladling the steaming chowder into a bowl, JJ prepared for a lecture on respecting his elders and kept quiet. He was surprised when Turk went a different direction and told him the local gossip.

"Seems that Sam Lester is out to get Snake. The fat man with the derby hightailed it for Abilene last fall, even before the fire.

Nothing upsets Sam like disloyalty, and he's been tracking the turncoat ever since. Now folks are saying you're the one chased him out of town. You scared a full-fledged outlaw, Jage!" Turk wiped his floury hands on his apron and saluted JJ with pride.

"Maybe there's something to me, after all, Turk," JJ answered. "Ought to go after him myself, earn a bounty. You think he killed Erly? Had to make a runner?"

"Not Erly. Snake was gone by then. Besides, I know who killed Erly." As ever, the cook got out his broom and swept his baking mess out the door, holding his tongue at the best part of the story.

"Who was it, Turk? Don't go all grownup on me. What did you hear? When did you find out?"

"I've known all along. And this is a secret I'll take to my grave." Flour drifted back into the kitchen on a breeze. "Better find something to do, or I'll have you scrubbing this floor." Turk made it clear he was through talking.

JJ pulled out the pistol and put it on the table before digging through a ragbag for his cleaning cloth. "Where's the gun oil, Turk?" he asked, rummaging in the cupboard. When the door swung open, he asked his brother, "You seen the gun oil anywhere?"

"Pa had it," MJ answered, snagging a biscuit.

"What would Pa be doing with it?"

"Don't know. Maybe he was cleaning the Last Resort?"

"Not likely," JJ said, just as Turk opened the other cupboard to display the greasy bottle.

"Put some rags on the table first, before you clean that gun," he instructed the boy, handing him the oil.

Turk's self-imposed silence was over, and he asked MJ when Ruby would be back from the mill. "She was right upset last night," he said. "Thought there was bad news about your grandma, she was taking on so."

JJ busied himself unloading the gun, soaking a rag with oil, taking himself out of the conversation. For a while, he had forgotten the shock of yesterday and the confusion of this morning. "You didn't have a true last name, because I wasn't married..." Remembering the words, he felt a wave of nausea engulf him; a sudden shiver shook his greasy hands, and he dropped the Colt.

Suddenly it was as if Turk had run into some invisible barrier; he stopped, raised his arms, and then his knees folded and he fell on his face. MJ screamed as the gun went off, but JJ could hear nothing but the roaring sound of his heart thumping like horse hooves in his ears. He looked down at Turk with horror and then at MJ. Together, they knelt and turned Turk over. He'd been shot high in the chest, and his wound was bleeding fast. MJ was fighting tears, trembling like a frightened filly.

JJ sank down beside the old man, the fear big in his eyes, with agony in his low cry.

"Turk? Gawd, oh Gawd, answer me, Turk! Please. Turk—?"

It was then JJ knew Turk was not going to move, was not going to answer him. He tried to swallow, the first sense of what had happened turning him sick inside.

At the sound of the door, JJ lifted his head and straightened his shoulders. "It was an accident, Pa. If you'll just let me explain," he said, his voice shaking.

"What have you done, Jage? Oh dear Lord, what have you done? This will kill your mother!"

It was a cruel, needless thing to add to the remorse and despair JJ already faced, and Leo was sorry for it the moment he said it. But he could not call it back.

Devastation overwhelmed JJ. Just yesterday, he'd been digging wild onions, laughing and joking with this man he'd loved like a grandfather, and now, he was standing over his body, responsible for his death. Yesterday, he'd known who he was, who he loved, who loved him. Today he was discarded, misunderstood. Why had they all abandoned him?

"Pa," JJ said, "I always thought you were fair. You let a man talk and judged him fair. Maybe it's because I'm not your real son, but you're not being fair."

"Forget about yourself, JJ! You just killed a man! Don't talk about being fair." Sounds of a creaking buckboard and horses snorting signaled Ruby's return. Leo looked down at Turk's body and the wretchedness of the situation washed over him. Dismissing JJ, he said, "MJ, cover Turk's face. I'll go tell your mother."

JJ stood there motionless, looking after Leo until he heard his mother's wails in the prairie wind. Then, with nothing remaining of his childhood, he turned and trudged miserably toward the barn.

Ruby drew a long breath; she was cried out. Swollen and puffy, her eyes looked empty now as she huddled in a quilt on the daybed. Leo propped his shoulder against the kitchen chair, easing the stiffness in his knee; then he lowered his head to his hands and thought back. This girl had become his life. She had put color into his world, been like music in his mind; he had walked the earth with a swing, with a secret laughter, because of her. He remembered the fire and the tumult she had awakened in him and recalled the way her lips first answered his own heavy impulses. It all seemed so long ago. Here they were now, quiet and solemn, desolate.

"I'm going after JJ," Leo said, as if to himself. Ruby glanced up, looking across the yellow, coal-oil lamplight at the lean face of her husband. He sat staring out the kitchen window, his coffee growing cold in front of him, unmindful of her, or of her watching him, his thoughts on the son he had because of her.

Time has been kind to his handsome face, she thought, *and to the form that goes with it.* Studying him now, Ruby saw his face, as it was that long-ago November night in the Fat Chance Saloon. As she did, her heart turned over, slow and sweet within her.

Gone was the soldier-straight posture. Now his shoulders were weighed down with responsibility and worry, the same pressure that had colored his hair gray. His body had widened and filled out with the thick muscle of years of labor, his youthful goodness had been deepened by experience. But his eyes were still as clear as the rain-washed prairie, gold mixed with fresh green. They glistened now.

"I'm coming, too, Leo. He's my boy... my blond-haired boy. But it's all changed." Ruby stood, resilience steadying her nerves, and put her cheek on top of Leo's head, her hands on his shoulders. He reached up and took her work-worn hands in his own.

"Things won't ever be the same. But we'll be happy again," he promised her.

"Can that be true?"

"Truer than..." Her eyes welled up, and he said, "Truer than true."

Leo found MJ sitting on the porch of the farmhouse. A bullbat twittered, and looking up, they saw the bird's blue-headed form launch itself from a far fencepost and labor awkwardly for altitude against the cool air of the evening.

"Can't mourn this loss, alone, son," said Leo. "Neither can your brother. We'll let him be tonight, but tomorrow, we'll go after him. I'll take Mama and ride south to Greenville to see if he went to Grandma Dawson's place. Without the buckboard, we can do it overnight. You plan on going west—you know where he goes better than I do. Take Pepper, food for a day, and your fishing pole. JJ's got too much sorrow to bear without kin. Hope he did go to Grandma's—Olive has strong shoulders to share his burden. She'll know what to say to Mama, too."

The moon shone in JJ's eyes, and the coyotes wouldn't let up yelping out in the thicket. He heard the deep bass of the longhorn bulls grunting to one another, wild pigs squealing far off in a thicket, an owl hooting forlornly, and the red vixens bickering. Willows made an eerie silhouette in the distance; the big dipper seemed close enough to drink from. It was too early for a triangle cactus, but there it was, white flowers gleaming in the dark.

"Will you look at that ... ?" JJ said to Cowlick. "An early bloomer. Wait'll I tell Turk." For a moment, he had forgotten—now who would he tell? "Some things are just Turk things," he told the horse. He wished Cowlick could talk back, deaden the raw sore in his heart.

What tall-tale would Turk conjure up right now to take his mind off his torment? That old man had a story for every situation, some almost true and some "truer than an outright lie." He had secrets, too. Had he killed Erly and left him behind the school after the branding fracas? JJ was eased to think Turk had loved them enough to avenge the torture. Now they'd never know; just like he'd said, he took that secret to his grave.

Rustling leaves tickled JJ's spine, and he remembered what Pa said about haunts: Leo wasn't afraid of them even though he believed. What was it he'd said? Uncle Josey's wife thought he stood beside her sometimes, even gave her strength to push the plow. Was Turk somewhere close by? Did he know it had been an accident? Oh, please, God, JJ prayed, tell him it was an accident.

Even with the torments of a man, he was just a growing boy. Tucking one blanket under his head for a pillow, and the other over his chest, JJ whispered his prayer one more time, and slept.

The next day, April 13, 1887, a man known as the Gunsmith swung his red mare down the street to the Brazos Hotel in Burleson. He'd just bought his best girl a fancy tooled saddle for her twenty-third birthday, and she held her head high, her back as strong as ever, her irregular gait familiar and comfortable to her rider. Big Red was the one female he'd never cheated on, the single constant in his life—

the only one who remembered the brokenhearted boy who rescued them both from her mother's demise.

Little children looked after the Gunsmith wide-eyed, impressed by his big hat, his pistol, and high-heeled boots, but the adult glances he received were cold and unfavorable, reminding him that he was a man people feared. Without a past and doubtful of a future, his present depended on skills he'd honed in another lifetime.

Jack Smith had been dead over thirteen years, and nobody ever thought of the man. The Gunsmith had the same steely eyes, but otherwise, Jack was buried deep in his new identity. Wavy, silver hair now flowed to his shoulders over his red cotton bandanna, and a salt-and-pepper scruff of beard camouflaged his handsome face. A shaggy, grayish mustache hid once perfect teeth, now stained a dingy tan by too many cigarettes and too much coffee. Still imposing, with a broad, solid back and sinewy muscles, he wore heavy calfskin chaps to protect his legs from thorns and briars, adding additional bulk to his lanky frame. Fringed, cuffed gloves shielded his hands when he rode the glossy red mare, and her tail and mane streaked white in the Texas wind.

The Gunsmith packed a sawed-off shotgun, loaded with buckshot. A .38 pistol was hidden inside his long gray duster, but his weapon of choice was the Colt .45 tucked in the waistband of his trousers, the butt pointed at his left hand. His split-second draw and deadly aim secured a reputation as a bounty hunter; custom-made boots of the finest leather attested to the high fees he commanded.

He ate alone at the Brazos and afterward returned to the hotel porch, where he slumped into a chair and put his feet on the rail, his face settled in melancholy. Presently, he made a cigarette and lit up. It was the old pattern again—waiting for trouble that could make him some money... and for what? A few hours at a poker table and the driving restlessness that pushed him into trouble again.

Across the street, an aging cowboy leaned against a wall with a bottle of cheap wine, the alcohol dulling his conscience and his loneliness. *That will be me,* Jack thought bitterly. I'll be having a drink and see myself in the bar mirror. I'll walk out, get on Big Red, and ride away, sick of myself and what I am, with little hope of what I'll meet over the next hill. Then I'll be officially dead, for the second time.

He was thinking this when a buckboard stopped in front of the hotel and Sam Lester stepped down from it and come toward him. Jack was not concerned that he'd be recognized by this weasely bully; he'd hardly been recognized as anyone unique, even in the days when he was Jack Smith. But he knew Sam immediately.

Twenty-three years later, the old traitor was still looking over his shoulder, expecting to be hung by Confederate soldiers for desertion. Flicking the stump of his thumb was an unconscious reminder of his old arrest and his offensive debt to the stuttering yellow-belly who shot down his captor. Haze and his renegades had needed a leader, and Sam eagerly filled the role, not realizing then that peabrains seldom grow in intelligence.

Sour whiskey oozed from Sam's pores, and Jack was glad to be outside where the fresh air dispersed the stench.

"You the man they call the Gunsmith?" Sam asked, pulling up a ladder-back chair. Pollen stuffed his nose, and he hacked then covered a nostril and blew his nose on the porch. His sallow complexion paled with the effort, accentuating the reddish scar on his left cheek.

Jack didn't respond in any way, repulsed by the nasty man. Sam continued, "I want to hire you to eliminate a competitor," he explained. "His name is Leo Barlow, and he won't give you any trouble."

"If he gives no trouble, why does he need to be eliminated, Mister...?"

"Lester. Call me Sam. You ever been to Sam's Town? That's me. Leo Barlow has been stealing from me for a dozen years, pilfering my profits. Calls himself an honest man 'cause he don't carry a gun, but he's a thief just the same—thousands of dollars he's stolen, one way or another. And I'm willing to pay you a thousand dollars when he's destroyed."

"A thousand dollars, Mr. Lester? I been to Sam's Town, and I know it's worth more than a thousand dollars. I might consider your offer if it's upped by five hundred dollars."

Pretending to choke on this expected counter, Sam said, "I'll offer you twelve hundred dollars in gold, sir." Then he produced a pouch with three additional $100 gold certificates contributed by Swede Dobson for the bounty. "A few folks hate Leo Barlow, for a variety of reasons. Fifteen hundred it is."

Jack took the paper money. "I'm obliged, Sam."

18

Later the Same Day

JJ reined his horse into a walk when he saw his brother. "Pa sent me to find you, Jage," MJ said.

JJ glanced at him, his eyes without humor. They didn't speak; both of them knew that this would be a battle of wills. It was late afternoon now; the sun heeled far over to the west, with a chill creeping into the air. Not once in the four miles to the river, where they arrived at dusk, did they speak.

Pepper wandered down to the bottomlands, and MJ picked out a campsite in the trees close to the river. JJ took Cowlick down to water her and staked out the horses below camp in a patch of coarse bunch grass. After lugging both their saddles back to camp, JJ began to collect wood; MJ went out in the opposite direction and did likewise. With a fire going, MJ unlashed his bedroll from behind his saddle. He had a small coffeepot, a sack of coffee, and a can of tomatoes. JJ quietly took the coffeepot, went down to the river and filled it, then came back and put it on the fire. It was full dark now.

"Jage." MJ pressed against his brother's stubborn pride, but he didn't answer, squatting down by the fire. The coffee water boiled, and JJ hauled the pot off the rocks and put in the coffee. MJ's clasp knife opened the can of tomatoes, and he stabbed one. "We can take turns," he said, offering the knife to JJ.

"We'll have to drink out of the pot," were JJ's first words of the evening. He strained the grounds through his teeth and ate a tomato.

The tension was wearing off now; MJ was quietly amused and a little angry, too. There was a ridiculous streak to the circumstance, but he had no intention of giving in to laughter first.

He watched his younger brother stare at the fire. There was a fleeting sadness in his face, and MJ studied it. "Jage," he started again but didn't get a response. "I expected more of you," he said.

"You shouldn't put so much stock in me," JJ told MJ. "I don't like the burden of living up to your expectations."

Quiet smothered the conflict, and both boys relaxed into a silent intimacy. During the small hypnosis that a blazing fire at night brings to everyone, MJ said, "You've got Mama and Pa in a dither, brother. It's been a bad time. Come on home."

"I can't, Josey," JJ said plaintively. "I've got things to figure out first."

JJ watched the stars, unable to sleep, thinking of the changes in his life. "Josey? Do you realize we're not even brothers?" he said into the dark.

"Sure we are, Jage," MJ answered, sleep heavy in his voice. When JJ woke up in the morning, Josey and Pepper were gone.

Two streams, both too low to paddle, flowed into the Brazos. Chaparral, juniper, and oak trees grew miraculously on the stony clay banks JJ and Cowlick followed that morning. He plinked at a bobcat and watched a beaver at work, stopping to boil some beef jerky into a broth, while the horse scavenged the grassy riverbed.

After lunch, they wandered the range without destination, stopping here and there for target practice.

Seeking out some shade, JJ reloaded the pistol and practiced his finger twirl, pulling the gun and tucking it back in his waistband to perfect the motion. Suddenly, a man stepped out from behind a clump of brush. Snake leveled the familiar Enfield rifle at JJ.

"You interfering showoff," Snake hissed. "A little kid that ain't even shaved, packin' hisself a big old gun."

Without warning and with blinding speed, JJ drew his Colt and fired. The lead slammed into the muzzle of the rifle, tearing it out of Snake's hands. With his .44 already tucked back in his trousers, JJ eyed the man calmly.

"Watch who you call 'kid,' mister."

"Look what we got, boys," said an accented voice. "Young Mr. Barlow here has caught us a yellow coyote." The filthy red blanket partially hid Bolte's Winchester, which hung from his saddle horn in a buckskin scabbard. It was slung butt forward, ready to shoot a bison, crease a mustang, or murder a man. "We been searchin' these parts since autumn for you, Snake," the Mexican bodyguard said. "Seems you ran out on Sam after you was embarrassed by this little cuss." He pointed at JJ and laughed.

"T-t-turn around, k-k-kid." The voice came from behind him. JJ turned slowly. Haze's pockmarked face had a deranged look of gratification on it.

"S-s-o we found S-s-snake." The stutter emphasized the sibilance of the man's name; Haze held the black coat open, flaunting his weapon; not at JJ, but at his old comrade in arms.

JJ had stumbled into a fight, and he wasn't sure who was the intended target; he didn't want to find out. Rolling to the ground, he threw himself at the closest man's legs. Off balance, Haze fell and his head slammed into the dirt, knocking him unconscious.

Snake's eyes darted from Bolte to the rifle at his feet. JJ could see him wondering if it would shoot after the blast to the muzzle from his own Colt. The men seemed to have forgotten he was there, and JJ made no move. Finally, just when it appeared Snake might give up, he leapt for his rifle. He was incredibly fast for his size, but JJ was faster. Without seeming to move, he had the Colt.44 in his left hand, spouting flame. His slug ripped into Snake's knee, right where the boy intended it to hit. Stumbling forward, the big man collapsed in the dirt.

Bolte had an evil laugh. "Two down, and the boy is still standing. You have the will, if not the wisdom, of your father. I respect that. Our fight is not with you today, kid."

"Don't call me kid," JJ said. "And stay off Barlow land."

Thoughts of home pricked at his mind. He couldn't stay out here forever, he realized. Frustrated by youth, disillusioned by weakness, and frightened by isolation, JJ picked up the trail back to Barlow Ranch, supposing he could get there before dark. They were a few miles from the fence line when Cowlick warned him of the storm. Her ears pricked, and she twitched restlessly, jogging a crooked course, while JJ looked for low ground and waited for the thunder. Lightning balls of electricity rolled over the prairie, and he had trouble controlling the petrified animal. Cold drops started before the thunder even stopped, and they hid out in a hollow littered with butterfly weed until the danger of lightning passed.

JJ thought he'd fall on his face before he got a fire started on the rain-pelted grass beside the stream. Too tired to make it to the pines where he'd have more shelter, he hobbled Cowlick under a tree and rigged his tarp as a lean-to for himself and the fire.

He pulled his boots off, propping them upside down on sticks in front of the fire and then warmed his half-frozen feet. The aspen branches clashed in the wind, and cold rain ran down his back, but he sat there exhausted.

After a minute, he dug out a can of beans and leaned forward toward the coals to warm them. Water poured down from the crease of his sodden black Stetson, turning the fire to wet gray ashes. With the dismal despair of a boy whose present misfortune is past calculation, JJ stood up to retrieve extra matches from his saddlebag and felt his sock feet sinking in the mud. His tarp and blankets were soaked now, and he sank to the earth close to tears.

Ahead, a vague shadow appeared in the night's blackness; the vaguest of shadows, at once defined by a whinny.

"Who's that?" JJ called out.

The horse whinnied again. The night wind got colder, and the rustling echoes from the nearby trees strengthened as the rain stopped. Squatted against the earth, JJ finally caught a silhouette of the horse against the pale-black sky but saw no rider. Rising, he clicked his tongue gently, stepping nearer the trees.

The horse moved toward Cowlick. "Steady—steady." JJ moved close to the horse and caught hold of the bridle, his palm touching a hide that held only faint warmth. And then he felt a hand.

Sweat cracked through his forehead, running down his face with the rain from his hat. Scratching a match on his belt, he held up the light to see a body, slumped in the saddle. In that moment, he recognized the derby hat and the waxen face that had belonged to Snake.

JJ whipped out the light and drew back, waiting. His heart pounded so wildly, it jarred his rain-soaked shirt. The rustling silence ran on. Sam's other men had long since ridden away. For it would be Sam's men—he knew that as certainly as he knew anything in his life. Sam Lester, the coward who sent this man after his mother because she'd stood up to him.

It was a long, long night. In the morning, he tied the two horses together, secured the body, and started for home. Presently, his head fell forward and did not straighten for several miles. Cowlick knew the way and kept her steady plodding as the boy slept. There was a coolness rising from the stream when JJ approached Barlow Road. His clothes were stiff, and he was hungry, and he could hardly wait to hand Snake over to Pa.

19

April 15, 1887

MJ brushed Pepper's mostly black hide and shifted his glance from the slow drift of high clouds to the distant bend of the Barlow road. Shortly, he pushed up his spectacles and stepped away from the horse. "Company, Pa."

Leo put down the awl and laid aside the waxed thread. Saddle mending could wait. He eased back from the worktable, hitching at the worn Levis.

"Looks to be alone," he told the squinting boy. A niggling premonition came to Leo. "Find your ma, and keep her inside," he said softly, face expressionless. "Let me handle this bird myself."

JJ had seen him, too. He hobbled Snake's horse away from the road, unwilling to be caught with a dead body until he'd talked to Pa. Shrouded by a clump of chinaberry trees, he waited, eyes narrowed. Presently, he heard it—the dust-clumping approach of a single horse. He drew back in the grove, catching a glimpse of silver hair when the cowboy passed by. Noiselessly, he guided his mount down to the stream, far behind the man.

Five minutes later, he reached the back road to Uncle Josey's house. A bright red mare was tethered to a tree, her rider somewhere out of sight. "Whoa, look at you," JJ said. "Cowlick, this is what you want to be when you grow up," he told his own horse as he dismounted.

Digging in his pocket for a sugar cube, he asked, "You skittish with strangers, girl?" His words were soft, flirtatious. "Aren't you the pretty lady...?" The horse tossed her white mane and looked at him from the corner of a china blue eye. "Here you go," he whispered. "I bet you're a sugar mouth... sure you are," he said as the horse nibbled the sweet granules from his hand. That's when he heard Leo's voice.

"Just keep a cool head, cowboy," Leo said in a familiar, soothing tone. "You could kill me, but what would that prove? That you're faster with a gun? I'll admit to that right now."

JJ was on the run now, coming from the opposite side of the barn. He could see the men standing in the backyard between the school and the house, Leo bareheaded, the cowboy towering over him in an uncreased Stetson, the crown domed to its full height.

"Pull a weapon, Barlow. For fifteen hundred dollars prize money, I like to think I won a contest." Without warning, the back door opened.

"My pa doesn't carry a gun." MJ stood with the Last Resort against his shoulder, the barrel aimed at the Gunsmith's heart. His youthful voice shook, but the shotgun was steady.

"Drop the gun, boy," the Gunsmith said quietly. "I'm empty-handed."

Surprised not to see a firearm, MJ was almost convinced then realized the monstrousness of what the man intended. He wanted a gunfight with his father. The thought of that terrible thing—the mean, small unfairness of shooting a decent man for no reason except money—brought blood rushing into MJ's desperate face. He suddenly had no fear of the cowboy.

"I'll not drop the gun until you leave our ranch," he said, with fury. "I'll shoot you in cold blood if I have to."

Leo's eyes darted frantically, and he spun toward MJ, showing fear for the first time. "Go back in the house, MJ," he pleaded, a strain in his voice. Then, with force, "Now! MJ—now!"

Unconsciously, the boy lowered the muzzle, his eyebrows drawn together, questioning his father with the wrinkling of his forehead.

Leo looked up at the sky and then back at the boy, slowly shaking his head. "It's too damp, son. That old Flintlock won't shoot after a rainstorm until it's been dried out."

Jack sniggered, noticing Ruby behind the boy. "Guess you married a sodbuster instead of a cowboy, Miss Blue Belle. See? I've remembered you." His left hand hovered near his gun while he examined her. "I've been lookin' for a pretty widow with a big ranch. Seems you'll soon be available."

JJ stepped out from behind the barn. "Leave my mother alone."

It came sharply to MJ then that the rules had changed. Sudden urgency rode him, hurrying him, pushing him. He leapt at his father, knocking him down, just as Jack's hand fell to his gun, lifted it deftly, cocking it in the same movement, and swung it toward JJ. A shot reverberated in the instant stillness.

Jack did not see the movement of the boy's left hand. Yet the orange flame burst the instant after JJ spoke. The .44 slug struck the bunched muscle of Jack's right shoulder with the force of a lightning bolt. Jack's gun arced up and settled, but JJ aimed lower and shot again. Leo saw Jack's body jar under the impact of the second bullet. It blasted him off his feet, and he landed on his left side. Through it all, the Gunsmith held onto his gun.

Jack saw a thousand pinwheel lights, then nothing but an echoing blackness.

The light returned slowly. Faces moved in brightly, shifted, grew dim, disappeared altogether. They came again, fled again, now clean and brilliant, now shadowed and blotted out, like stars among the broken clouds of a clearing night sky.

Shortly, one of the stars came near. Jack saw bright blue eyes and thick red curls moving in a whirling orbit, and he focused on the familiar face. "Jack...Jack...we need to turn you over."

Jack felt the bite of the bullets but lifted his left hip enough to tuck the .45 in his trousers as they rolled him to his back. He moved his head, tried to say something. The words would not come, but the blood did. The hollow bubble of it, building in his throat, caught at his breath.

"Ease back, Jack, you hear? I've got hold of you." He recognized her voice. She held him until the rack of coughing had spasmed and subsided and continued to hold him when it had. Jack moaned softly as Ruby lifted him in her arms. He smelled the clean scent of her hair and felt her fine straight body against him.

He heard a man's voice. "Ruby, he's hurt badly. We've got to get a doctor." Leo watched his wife's face, the man's identity finally becoming clear. "Fetch the wagon," he said slowly to MJ. "Break a bale of hay into it, and find some spare blankets. I'll take him into town."

"No, Leo. He's our responsibility now. Mine and JJ's."

She was lovely to look at, Jack thought, when he roused again. She knew herself. He remembered her sweet, youthful face, flushed with happiness. There was depth and experience in it now, and it made him feel old and tired.

JJ drove the wagon with skill. There was no doctor in Barlow Woods, so they were headed to Sam's Town, fifteen miles away. Ruby ripped her petticoat into strips and used them as compresses to staunch the blood pouring from his shoulder. Jack was in and out of consciousness, thrashing about with pain when he was awake, barely breathing when he passed out again.

"This is him?" JJ asked finally. "Does he look the same?"

"He's got a hardness, a bitterness now. Can't see a smile-line anywhere. It's like he's spent his whole life scowling."

"Does he look like me?" JJ wondered.

"He's tall. You might get this tall," Ruby said. "His hair used to be black. I knew his form, strong and muscled. You've got that." She'd taken off his hat and pushed back the heavy silver hair to mop the moisture sweating from his forehead. "He's suntanned, even under his beard."

Rousing, Jack grunted a deep moan and tried to moisten his lips. Ruby dribbled some cool water from the canteen into his mouth, and he eagerly sucked up the liquid.

"Try not to move, Jack. I'm holding bandages on your chest, and the bleeding's slowed down."

"Think I've lost it all?" He tried to joke, but it came out raspy, the pain strangling the words. His eyes focused on her face. "Still pretty," he whispered, and reached up weakly to touch her hair.

"I thought you were dead," Ruby told him.

"Almost was," he breathed, "kinda like now." Without warning, he strained to sit up. "Where's Red?" he asked anxiously, then sank back, breathless with the effort.

"Tethered to a tree on our ranch." JJ spoke for the first time, although he'd listened to every word. "She's too good for you…" he hesitated and then finished scornfully, "… Pa." Jack didn't seem to hear him, so the boy said, "I'm your son."

"Bad luck," Jack answered, almost to himself. Then he rallied. "What's your name, boy?" He looked at Ruby with sudden comprehension. "How do you know he's mine?"

"You were the only one, Jack. He's called JJ, after you."

"Your boy protected his family—he don't take after me none. Seems he's made a better name for himself."

The flinty, gray eyes were closed, and the man exhaled with deep, puffing sighs. "Didn't know Barlow was your husband," he breathed. He opened his eyes again, but this time, they were the color of goose down. He said softly, "I killed a man for you once," and then he was unconscious again.

"Hurry, JJ. There's so much blood. How can a man lose so much blood?"

They rode in silence for a long while, and then Ruby became aware of Jack looking at her.

"He's a good boy?" he asked.

"Oh, yes," Ruby answered, her eyes filling with tears.

"Let him keep the horse," he mumbled. "I want him to have Big Red." Then his eyes closed, and he fainted.

They rode in on Prescott Street and turned the corner at the French photography shop. Nothing seemed different to Ruby as they drove up Main Street past the church and the sheriff's office. Bolte stood outside the Empire Hotel as if he was a statue, only she knew he wasn't.

Loathing and resentment overwhelmed her as the wagon went past the Fat Chance Saloon. Sam Lester was holding court at his table, and she saw him look out the window at them.

"Doc Simpson is at the top of the street. Pull up there," she told her son. "And JJ—let me have the gun." When he started to protest, she said, "This town was the start of all our troubles. You've already defended us once today; I'm not having you tempted again."

JJ pulled the gun from his waistband, and she stowed it deep in her apron pocket. Even before the wagon stopped, a handful of men had gathered on the boardwalk. "This man has been shot," Ruby said. "Help him into the doctor's office."

"Ezra! Doc Simpson!" Calls and shouts notified the man of the emergency, and Jack was loaded on a stretcher.

"He's dangerous," JJ told them. "Keep a close watch on him. He tried to murder my pa." He helped carry the stretcher inside and then ran back down the street to the sheriff's office he'd seen.

Haze rushed into the street, his gun trained on her. Sam followed them leisurely, "You are not welcome here, Mrs. Barlow," he said in a dry, hating tone.

Ruby stood up in the wagon, her contempt spilling out. "What are you going to do about it Sam? Burn my mill? Hogtie my son? Kill our dog? Oh, or you could put a bounty on our heads, murder the whole Barlow family. And for what, Sam? For walking away from your sleazy business? For washing off your filthy ideas and cleaning up my spirit? Are you jealous, Sam? Jealous that you've had to buy protection, friends...that you've always had to buy love?" Ruby's rebuke attracted attention; people crowded the boardwalks on either side of the street. Listening from inside, Jack slowly became aware that he'd been left unguarded. He held his breath and cautiously pushed himself to a sitting position. The wounds knifed at him, and he waited, sitting upright until the pain subsided, then gently swung his feet to the floor and stood up. Again, he felt the searing in his side. He put a hand against the wall to steady himself and waited for his mind to adjust itself to the pain. It was bearable. His whole side was sore and hurt deep within him, but he could handle it for a few minutes. That was all he needed.

Jack heard Ruby say, "No more! I won't let you control my life another day!" and then an audible gasp from the group. He couldn't see Ruby draw the gun from her pocket, but he knew it was the moment he could slip out of the room unnoticed.

Sam had stepped into the middle of the dusty street, watching Ruby, watching the gun. He wouldn't dodge, she knew. Too much lay between them for that. That this was happening now was inevitable, the foundation of it lay with a long resentment she could no more help than she could help breathing. Ruby wasn't a coward, and after today, she feared nothing. She felt a cold, sure wrath that was beyond anger at the sight of Sam Lester; she knew she wanted to kill him, and she hugged the knowledge close, waiting.

"This is a pleasure, Sam," she said. Leaning against the seat, holding the gun in both hands, Ruby raised it and brought all the terrible force of her anger into the single concentration of her aim. The gun wavered, but she steadied it in one last effort.

At that moment, the raking, booming blast of a Colt.45 shattered the silence. Sam's knees folded, and he hit on his belly, and then lay there limp and unmoving.

Pushing through the crowd, JJ got to his mother just after the shot. She leaned out of the wagon and collapsed in his arms. "It's over, Mama," he said into her red hair. "It's over."

"He's dead," Doc Simpson pronounced, and it took a moment to realize he was talking about Jack. "Lost too much blood," he said, to no one in particular. Sam Lester's body was the main attraction

20

Big Red had been discovered by MJ and installed in the barn. Fresh sawdust already covered the bloodstains in the yard, and Leo was frying potatoes for hash when his wife and son got home. It took months to recover from the events of that horrible week in May, and, in some respects, the Barlows never recovered. Eventually, Sam's Town was renamed Prescott, after its founding father, and as more people moved to Barlow Woods, the rumors and legends were replaced. The outlaw attacks, the fire, Erly's murder, the Gunsmith, and Sam Lester were forgotten.

Forgotten until a day almost two years later. JJ was in the woods with MJ, trying to show a coonhound puppy what a raccoon looked like. The dog hadn't yet figured out his purpose in life, but he knew digging was part of it.

"Jage. The hound found something."

MJ was standing over a stack of rocks that was arranged purposefully. Under what seemed to be a shrine of sorts, there was a wooden box, carved with the name Leonard Barlow, as if by a child. Inside, there were boyish treasures: arrowheads, fool's gold, glass marbles, feathers, and a pencil sketch of the mill before it was rebuilt. There was a small Bible inscribed, "To my beloved wife, Elsie. Christmas Day, 1869." And there was a heavy revolver with a notched grip. Erly's Colt.45 Peacemaker.

"That son of a gun," murmured JJ.